HARLEQUIN

Blaze™

D0092563

$4.50 U.S. $5.25 CAN.

BODY CONTACT

Rebecca York

HARLEQUIN®
Makes any time special®

ISBN 0-373-79035-X

9 780373 790357

50450

AVAILABLE NOW:

#29 JUST WATCH ME...
Midnight Fantasies
Julie Elizabeth Leto

#30 A TOUCH OF SILK
The Bachelors of Bear Creek
Lori Wilde

#31 BODY CONTACT
Rebecca York

#32 NO STRINGS ATTACHED
www.girl-gear
Alison Kent

Maddy's nipples were hard

Her mouth was dry as she stared into the sea-green eyes of Jack Connors. He was tall, dark and dangerous. And she desperately needed his help.

Wetting her parched lips, she said, "I don't know you well enough to make love with you."

"Sorry, it's just become part of the job," Jack said evenly, his gaze leaving her face to travel appraisingly over her body, then come back to her eyes.

His gaze sent a shiver through Maddy that was part fear and part hot anticipation. She'd had wild fantasies about him in the past. "I'm in charge of this mission...."

"If you want me to go with you, you'll go to bed with me first." He made the statement a challenge, and she'd never backed away from a challenge. But she wanted him to feel something, some emotion.

"We've got to make it look as if we're lovers..." he said in an intimate tone.

Surely he was teasing her, or testing her? "Wh-what do you want me to do?" she said stiffly.

"Sweetheart, I want you to come into the bedroom with me...now."

Dear Reader,

When I first heard about Harlequin's new Blaze series I was intrigued and excited. Here was a line of sexy books that pushed the envelope in category romance.

My question was: could Blaze incorporate the kind of suspense plot I love to write for Harlequin Intrigue—with a lot more emphasis on the developing sexual relationship between the hero and heroine?

For me, the answer is yes. In *Body Contact,* I've had a wonderful time melding the two genres. I've fashioned a plot where danger and intrigue lurk around every corner, and the only way my hero, Jack Connors, and my heroine, Maddy Guthrie, can save their lives is by cultivating the hot sexual tension simmering between them. But each touch, each caress, each kiss turns up the heat—so that Jack and Maddy can barely focus on their mission through the haze of arousal fogging their brains.

Writing *Body Contact* has been a fun romp for me. I hope you enjoy it. And I hope you visit me at Harlequin Intrigue where I'm pushing the envelope with the relationships between my heroes and heroines. In fact, you'll meet my next Intrigue hero, Alex Shane, right here in *Body Contact*. His story, *From the Shadows,* will be out in June.

Happy reading!

Ruth Glick, writing as Rebecca York

P.S. Don't forget to check out tryblaze.com!

BODY CONTACT

Rebecca York

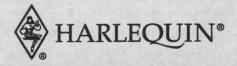

TORONTO • NEW YORK • LONDON
AMSTERDAM • PARIS • SYDNEY • HAMBURG
STOCKHOLM • ATHENS • TOKYO • MILAN • MADRID
PRAGUE • WARSAW • BUDAPEST • AUCKLAND

To Norman, with love

ISBN 0-373-79035-X

BODY CONTACT

Ruth Glick writing as Rebecca York

Copyright © 2002 by Ruth Glick.

1

MADDY GUTHRIE'S NIPPLES were hard, but her mouth was dry as she stared into the sea-green eyes of the man standing a few feet away. He was tall and dark and dangerous. A man she'd admired for his jungle cat reflexes, his steel-trap mind. His tough body, honed to the physical specifications of an Olympic athlete. Only Jack Connors was no athlete. He was an ex-CIA agent she often worked with on special projects. And he was here now because she desperately needed his help.

Wetting her parched lips, she said, "I don't know you well enough to make love with you."

"Sorry, it's just become part of the job," Jack Connors answered, his voice even, his piercing green gaze leaving her face to travel appraisingly over her body, then come back to her eyes.

That gaze sent a shiver of reaction over her skin, reaction that was part fear and part hot anticipation, if the truth be told.

Their working relationship hadn't stopped her from conjuring up fantasies about him. Wild, erotic fantasies. But she'd never dared imagine sharing them with anyone—least of all him.

Now she raised her chin. "Wait a minute. I'm the Winston Security Chief. I called you in on this assignment. That means I'm the one giving the orders."

He gave her a small shrug. "If you want me to go in with you on this mission, you'll go to bed with me first."

He made the statement a challenge, and she'd never backed away from a challenge, never wavered from a course of action, once she had determined it was the right thing to do.

She knew Jack had the same courage of his convictions. Which was why he must feel duty bound to give her a jolt of reality.

He stood before her, so calm and self-contained. His arms relaxed at his sides, his stance easy. She'd seen that pose before, when he was waiting for the other guy to make the first move. On previous occasions, she'd been standing next to him. Now they were facing each other—opponents instead of allies.

No, she corrected herself. Not opponents. They were still on the same side. Only the stakes had changed dramatically.

She raised her eyes, daring to probe his secrets. Did she detect a hint of emotion below his calm exterior? Something he didn't want her to see?

She *wanted* him to feel something, to let her know that this step was as awkward for him as it was for her.

He didn't give her that reassurance, so she thought about the reason she was here in this plush suite of rooms with him: A seventeen-year-old girl was in terrible trouble, and she, Maddy Guthrie, was the one responsible.

As if Jack were reading her mind, he said, "I told you to stop blaming yourself. Winston's daughter planned her escape carefully. She laced your soft drink with a potent sleeping pill. She'd already bought a bus ticket to New York. She had a suitcase stashed in the garage. From my point of view, it looks like somebody helped her. Someone on the Winston staff."

"Nobody would do that."

Jack shrugged. "I think you're wrong."

Maddy took a steadying breath. If there was someone

that misguided working here, then she had to find out who it was. But not now. Now the important thing was to get Dawn back.

"What matters," she said aloud, "is that Stan Winston trusted me to guard his daughter, and she slipped away when I was supposed to be on duty."

To herself, she silently added, *my first screwup in seven years.*

She'd worked security at Winston Industries since the summer she was a college senior and her father had asked her to help catch an upper-level manager who was selling crucial documents to a rival. She'd nailed the man photographing a cost analysis and escorted him at gunpoint to her father's office.

From that moment on, her career path had been set. She'd taken courses in criminal investigation, self-defense, covert operations. And she'd risen rapidly through the ranks of the security force. Now she ran the operation. But on this job she needed Jack Connors's help.

Jack had already done what she couldn't. Through some lucky breaks, his network of paid informants, and by calling in every favor that was owed him, he had found out where Dawn was. On Orchid Island in the Caribbean, held captive by Oliver Reynard, a man who had hated Stan Winston for years. As soon as the girl had set foot in Manhattan, she'd been scooped up by some of Reynard's men and whisked off to his island stronghold.

She'd been there for five days, five days during which God knows what might have happened to her. Maddy gave an involuntary shudder and saw Jack's expression change as he caught the slight movement of her shoulders.

Lifting her chin, she looked him square in the eye. When Jack had discovered where Dawn was being held, he'd told Maddy point-blank that the rescue operation was too risky for her to go alone. She'd dug in her heels, sure of her moral and emotional obligation. She was the one responsible, and she was the one who was going to make this come out right. As soon as she got some things straight.

"Okay, I know invading Orchid Island is dangerous. I know we've got to play carefully scripted parts. But why do we have to...to...go all the way now?" she asked, fighting a surge of panic, thinking she sounded like a teenager being pressured in the back seat of a car on some secluded lover's lane. Still, she couldn't stop herself from adding, "I mean, when we get there, nobody will know what you and your girlfriend are doing or not doing in the privacy of our room."

His well-shaped lips twisted into a sardonic smile. "I'm afraid you can't count on that. If Reynard is a fanatic about anything, it's security. So there's as likely to be a camera and recording equipment in our room as anywhere else."

She tried to swallow around the sudden thickness in her throat. "But making tapes of guests in their private rooms is...illegal...and immoral."

"Exactly. The perfect description of Orchid Island. If you add, treacherous, perilous and insidious, you get the whole picture. Once you go to a place like that, you surrender all semblance of privacy—and safety."

She conceded he knew what he was talking about. After leaving the CIA, he'd started his own security business. He had access to all kinds of covert information about the island that Reynard ruled like a medieval tyrant. Enough information for them to rescue Stan Winston's daughter, she hoped.

Jack was speaking again, his voice hard as glass. "The men who come to Orchid Island as Reynard's guests are there for two reasons. They want to do business with him. Or they want to relax in a no-holds-barred environment.

When they bring their women, they like to show them off to the rest of the guys. Dress them up for his cocktail parties in barely-there silks and expensive jewels. Outfit them in designer tops and shorts for daytime. Parade them around like expensive trophies. And we've got to fit the pattern Reynard is expecting. If he finds out we're on his turf to rescue Dawn, he'll have us killed as easily as he'd swat an insect."

The words chilled Maddy. Intellectually she'd understood the dangers. But until a few moments ago, she hadn't realized exactly how far Jack Connors was proposing to take their charade.

His eyes narrowed as he cut into her thoughts. "You called me in to help you get onto the island, and I can do it. But once we're there, your life will depend on following my lead. Or adhering to my explicit directions without question. So you'd better show me you can do that— under the most difficult circumstances you can imagine. Because if you can't, I'm going to have to find another partner who can."

Follow his directions. Under the most difficult circumstances she could imagine.

Did that mean he was really going to insist on the ultimate intimacy between them as a condition of getting her onto Reynard's turf? Or was he just testing her—seeing how far she was willing to go? Yes, maybe that was it. He was going to push her to the limit, then let her off the hook at the last minute. Because he couldn't be planning to take her to bed. Not with the cold calculation he brought to his job.

Well, if testing the limits was his game, she would play it.

"What do you want me to do?" she asked, thinking that there was still time to bail out.

"I want you to come into the bedroom."

He turned and walked through the door at his back as if there were no question in his mind that she would follow him. Pretending that her insides hadn't turned to jelly, she did as she was told, and found herself in a room that might have been transported from one of New York City's most opulent hotels. The Pierre or the Park Lane—places where she'd accompanied the Winston family. But this wasn't a hotel. It was a guest suite Stan Winston maintained on the top floor of the Winston Building in midtown Manhattan. She'd been here before, doing security checks. But never had she dreamed of using one of these bedrooms for her own intimate purposes.

The room was furnished with antique chests, Chippendale-style wingback chairs, a muted Oriental rug lying on the polished wood floor. But it was the king-sized four-poster bed that caught her eye as she followed Jack into the chamber and came to an abrupt halt five feet inside the door.

He moved in back of her, and she forced herself not to flinch when she heard him lock the door behind them.

He crossed to the high Victorian mantel, turning to face her, studying her with that unnerving green-eyed stare that was like a laser beam cutting all the way to her bones.

It was all she could do to keep herself from babbling then—from asking if he'd thought about who might have helped Dawn sneak away from the estate. If he knew how soon they could leave for Orchid Island. How they were going to get away once they found Dawn and freed her.

But she managed to keep all those questions locked in her throat. Maybe because she knew that if she tried, her voice would come out thick and shaky. Maybe because her training and her pride wouldn't allow her to show him her raw nerves.

So she stood there with her lips slightly parted and her hands at her sides.

He made her wait long, agonizing seconds before he murmured, "I think we'll start with a striptease. Take off your skirt and blouse and panty hose. Take them off for my pleasure; then fold them neatly, and lay them on the chair over there."

She knew this man. Had worked with him. Joked with him. Felt a deep connection between the two of them. But there was a line neither one of them had crossed—because both of them were sticklers for rules. And rule number one was—no dating the people you worked with. Involvement like that could confuse your objectivity, distract you from cool calculations. Make you take chances that could cost you your life.

She'd told herself he'd wanted to break that ironclad rule with her. She had certainly wanted to. And suddenly here they were together in this room, breaking every rule of morality and self-preservation she'd ever set for herself.

When she had dreamed of being with him, the scene in her mind had always started with an intimate candlelit dinner—at his apartment or hers. After dinner there would be good brandy. Mood music. They might dance slowly, intimately. Finally he would gather her to him and lower his mouth to hers for a kiss. She hadn't expected the kiss to be tender. But she'd expected passion. She had pictured him as a bold and skillful lover. A man who would give his partner pleasure as well as take it.

Now she wanted the reassurance of that kiss. Well, more than the kiss, actually. She wanted the traditional preludes to intimacy that she had imagined.

"Are you going to back out?" he asked, his tone mocking her.

That was enough to firm her jaw, to firm her resolve. If he thought she couldn't carry off this performance, he was dead wrong.

"No." Still, she fixed her gaze on the Renoir painting

over the mantelpiece—thinking it had to be a real Renoir, since Stan Winston would have insisted on the genuine article.

And she was the genuine article, too, she told herself as she reached for the buttons at the front of her blouse. She was a trained security operative who knew every nuance of her profession. She'd played roles before. Been in tight spots. And she'd always come out the winner.

Still, her fingers felt wrapped in layers of gauze as she slid the buttons open, thankful in some corner of her mind that she'd worn her peach-colored bra and panties, the ones that went so well with her blond hair and warm skin tones.

It seemed to take centuries to remove the blouse. Finally she had it off. Because she needed to clutch on to something, she crumpled the fine material in her hands, then turned and started toward the chair in the corner of the room.

"I told you to fold it neatly," he said, his voice hard, demanding obedience.

She blinked, looked at the tangled mess of fabric in her hands, then did as he asked, smoothing the soft silk with her fingertips, watching him from the corner of her eye, knowing he was following every tiny movement she made.

The skirt was easier. Only one button and a zipper. When she reached for the fastening, another sharp command stopped her hands.

"Turn around and face me. I don't want to look at your tush—although it's nice enough in its own way. I want to see your breasts jutting toward me when you reach in back of you to pull the zipper."

Her face heated as she turned, his vivid description echoing in her mind. He was right, groping behind her for the zipper thrust her breasts toward him as though she were begging for his touch.

She tried not to think about how she looked, tried to keep her mind blank, as she folded the skirt on top of the blouse, then kicked off her sling-back pumps and bent to roll down her panty hose. Keeping her eyes cast downward, she laid the stockings neatly on top of the other clothing.

Then, before he could give another harsh command, she turned back to face him. Still, in her lacy bra and panties, she felt too vulnerable and exposed to look him in the eye. She didn't need to see his gaze on her, taking in details. She felt it scorching her. And the tight points of her nipples were as embarrassing as her state of undress. God, this was turning her on. And she couldn't hide it from him.

She was almost naked, but he was still fully clothed in a crisp cotton dress shirt, a rep tie, beautifully tailored gray trousers, polished dark shoes. Only the navy blazer he'd worn earlier was missing.

"Come here," he ordered.

The ten feet of space between them had been a protective barrier. But she willed her legs to move as she took a tentative step toward him. Fixing her gaze on his broad chest, she crossed the room and came to stand a foot from him.

She had been able to stop herself from speaking earlier. Now words of protest tumbled from her lips. "This is wrong. We shouldn't be doing this. We don't have to go any further."

"Under ordinary circumstances, you would be correct."

"We don't know each other."

"We've worked together off and on for over two years."

"But there's so much about you that I don't know...."

"You can study a dossier on me tonight."

"I don't want a dossier. I want us to talk. I want this to be normal."

She knew the moment the words were out of her mouth that they gave away her fear, her uncertainty.

"Stop delaying the inevitable. I'm not going to take the chance of bringing you to Orchid Island without having...had you."

"Why not?" she asked, her voice barely above a whisper.

"Because our lives depend on how convincing we are. Our relationship can't come across as a journey of exploration. I'm going there to offer Reynard a drug trafficking deal he can't refuse. I pulled strings and spent a lot of Winston money getting an invitation to the house party he's giving in two days. He'll be watching us carefully, making sure I'm what I'm supposed to be: a filthy-rich crook who's brought his honey along. He and his pack of security men have to think that you and I have been lovers for months."

"But we could have just...become intimate. I mean, why do we have to make it look like we've been together for any length of time?"

"Our relationship has to be solid in every way—emotionally, sexually. You've got to seem important to me. Reynard has a reputation for hitting on women guests. He's also got a reputation for being...rough when he gets them in his bedroom."

She lifted her chin. "I can take care of myself with a man like that."

"But then you wouldn't be playing the role of my sweet little cookie. Which would mean you'd get us both killed. Maddy, I mean it. The penalty for messing up is death."

The words and the sharp tone of his voice made her chest go tight.

He gave her an appraising look. "If I've made the job sound too risky, you're still free to back out. I can find a replacement—a female operative who has the sexual experience to handle the assignment."

"No. I can do it," she answered automatically.

"Then let's get on with the audition. Undress me."

She squeezed her eyes closed. For a moment the temptation to call the whole thing off was almost overwhelming. Then she reminded herself that this was her mess. She was the one who had let Dawn Winston slip away. If there was one controlling factor in this whole episode, that was it.

"I don't want your eyes closed like a fifteenth-century virgin bride waiting for her husband to ravish her. I want you looking at me like you're enjoying what you're doing. Like you want to please me."

Her lids snapped open. She focused on his crisp white shirt, then the vertical line of his tie. Willing her hands to steadiness, she reached to the knot between the points of his collar, the slick fabric slipping under her fingers as she struggled to loosen it.

She undid the tie, leaving it dangling around his neck as she turned to the shirt buttons, her fingers as clumsy as they had been with her blouse. She could feel his warm skin through the fabric. Then she pushed the shirt open, her fingers skimming the thatch of dark hair that covered his chest. He didn't move, but she heard him draw in a sharp breath. For the first time she felt a glimmer of hope—hope that this performance wasn't as cold and calculating as he made it seem.

Feeling more bold, she continued her exploration. She had wondered about his chest. She'd known it would be broad, had wanted it spread with crisp hair. Now she winnowed her fingers through that thatch, pressing her fingertips to his warm skin. She could feel his heart beating. Fast. Fast and deep.

And that accelerated heartbeat added to her sense of confidence. He might have been standing here giving her orders, taunting her. But he wasn't indifferent to her. No, somewhere along the line he had become involved in this scene on a very personal level.

Her fingers found his flat nipples, circling them, and he made a sharp sound in his throat, a sound that emboldened her. She fought to keep a smile off her face as she undid the buttons at his cuffs, then pushed the shirt off his shoulders, pulled each arm through its sleeve.

"Do you want me to fold your shirt and tie neatly and put them with my clothing?" she asked silkily.

"Just get to the main event," he answered in a rough voice. "Take off the rest of my clothing so I can feel the length of your naked body pressed to mine."

Her nerves jumped again. But she wasn't going to stop now. Didn't want to stop. Couldn't stop.

Reaching toward his waist, she undid his belt buckle, then the clasp at the top of his slacks. Before she worked the zipper, she slid her hand down his fly, feeling how hard he was through the barrier of his slacks.

Again he reacted with a sound of pleasure that it seemed he was helpless to hold back.

She wanted to say his name, wanted to tell him that she knew this performance had gone beyond the boundaries of cold necessity.

But she kept the words locked in her throat.

She couldn't tell him what she felt. Or what she hoped for. But as she rocked her hand against his erection, she felt heat gather in her belly.

He made a sound of protest when she moved her hand away, but he had forgotten about giving her directions as she found the zipper tab, pulled it down. Skimming her hands down his flanks, she slipped his slacks and his briefs off together.

She had him naked in seconds, standing before her, his body lean and fit, his penis hard and thick and jutting toward her. He was large, potent, male.

He swore under his breath, gathered her to him, his head dipping so his mouth could capture hers. She opened for him, feeling his lips, his tongue, his teeth even as his hands went to the catch of her bra and snapped it open. He swept the garment off her, then caught her breasts in his hands, kneading, stroking, circling her nipples, making them throb with pleasure.

She had imagined this. Dreamed of it. The reality was far more heady than any fantasy. Her sex felt wet and swollen. Her brain felt ready to explode.

When he dragged her panties down, she kicked them away. He stared at her, his eyes traveling over her body, from the tight points of her nipples to the blond triangle of hair at the apex of her legs.

She was thankful then for the long hours she'd spent in the gym. Long hours that had tightened her muscles, flattened her stomach, brought her to the peak of physical conditioning.

"God, you're magnificent," he said, his voice so low it was almost a growl. "I knew your body would be like this. Feminine curves, with underlying strength. But I always wondered if you were a natural blond," he said thickly.

"You thought about making love with me?"

"Men think about making love with women," he said dismissively. "It's a natural reaction."

He was deliberately telling her not to make more of his words than their face value, when she wanted him to tell her his sexual fantasies about her had been as vivid as hers about him. But he didn't give her the chance to speak. His hand was between her legs, testing her, stroking her with sure, knowing fingers—bringing her a jolt of pleasure that made her cry out.

She tried to read the look in his eyes. Pure male satisfaction? Or something more personal. Before she could decide, he backed her toward the bed, came down on top of her. Raising up on his elbows, he stared down into her eyes, and she would have sworn the look that passed between them was the look of long separated lovers finally together in a blazing moment of reunion.

Then he plunged into her, going deep, stretching her to the limit of her capacity.

She took him, took all of him, her hips rising even as his pressed forward.

It was as if they had done this a hundred times, a thousand, moving to a remembered rhythm as his penis sank into her, then withdrew, each long stroke carrying her upward on a rising wave of pleasure.

There was no thought of closing her eyes now. She kept them focused on his face, on the rigid planes, the taut lines. Raising her hand, she stroked the dark stubble on his cheek, caressing him, tracing the upper curve of his lips.

He opened his mouth, took her finger between his lips, sucked it, then worried it between his even white teeth, while his hips moved in a rhythm that was driving her to the point of no return.

She felt him holding himself back, saw him watching her face, attending to the cues she gave him, listening to the sounds she made as his body plunged above her, in her.

And only when a hot, pulsing climax made her cry out, did he take his own satisfaction.

AFTERWARDS JACK DIDN'T STAY with her. He didn't hold her and kiss her because that would give too much away.

Instead, he climbed out of the bed, scooped his clothing off the floor, and headed for the nearest shower.

But he couldn't stop himself from turning and gazing at her lying on the bed. She was looking stunned and sated and besotted.

He knew he had to wipe that expression off her face, so he said, "That was an excellent performance, but there's still plenty of work to do before our flight to Orchid Island. You can use the shower in the bathroom off the lounge. Then get dressed so we can start going over research materials."

The devastated look that flashed across her features almost sent him climbing back into bed with her—to gather her close, to stroke his lips against her silky blond hair the way he'd wanted to do all along.

Instead, his fingers closed around the pair of slacks in his hands. "I've arranged to have dinner sent up. You'd better hurry and get dressed. You don't want to run into the waiter in your birthday suit."

Before he could say anything that would hurt her more deeply, he turned and bolted into the bathroom. Closing the door behind him, he stood with his back pressed against the hard wood panel, breathing hard, absorbing the enormity of what he'd just done. Then he tossed his clothing onto the dressing table and stalked to the shower.

Moments later, he was standing under the hot spray trying to wash away the wonderful smell of her skin that still clung to him.

From the first moment he'd seen her two years ago, he'd wanted her, wanted her with a passion that bordered on madness.

But he had never let her know that he felt anything beyond admiration for the way she did her job.

Her work was her life. That was the way her father, Spike Guthrie, had raised her. It had been an entirely satisfying life for her, until five days ago, when that stupid idiot, Dawn Winston, had drugged her and bolted from the safety of her father's home.

As soon as Maddy had called him in and explained what had happened, he'd told her that Dawn's disappearance wasn't her fault. The girl had planned everything with the utmost care. She'd counted on Maddy's friendship, then betrayed her trust. But the words had rolled right off her like spring rain off a rubber slicker. Seeing the panic and the misery on her face, he'd felt duty bound to give her a chance to set things right.

Then he'd started having second thoughts. He'd warned her of the dangers. But he wasn't sure she'd listened hard enough to that part. So just now, he'd tried to make the job so distasteful that she'd back out.

Instead she'd done every damned thing he'd asked. Including have sex with him.

No, he corrected himself. It might have started out as having sex. It had ended up as making love, because he had been helpless to do it any other way.

God, he had just fulfilled his most compelling private daydream—making love to Maddy Guthrie. And she'd been as warm and passionate and giving as he'd always hoped she'd be.

But his old friend, Spike Guthrie, wouldn't have seen it in those terms. Spike Guthrie would be coming after him now with a machete—if the tough-as-nails security chief had still been alive.

No, Spike would have hated him for this. And Maddy would hate him, too. Unless he kept this relationship where it had to be kept. Strictly impersonal. Because if he knew anything about Maddy Guthrie, she was her father's daughter. Tough on the outside. Vulnerable on the inside. Dedicated to her job at Winston Industries and to upholding the tradition her father had established.

Still, his mind started spinning a very appealing scenario. Maybe after this was over, he'd be free to have her where he wanted her, in his bed—on a regular basis.

He cut off *that* line of thinking before it could even get started. Mentally, he'd been down that road before. Sleeping with a colleague was unacceptable.

Shutting off the water, Jack stepped out of the shower and reached for a towel, already arranging his features into the set lines he knew he had to present to Maddy when he saw her next.

2

THE IDEA OF PUTTING ON the skirt and blouse that she'd taken off so provocatively a little while ago made Maddy's stomach knot, so she was thankful that the outfits Jack had picked for Orchid Island had already been sent up to the Winston guest suite.

Before getting into the shower, she picked something that was as buttoned up as she could find—a pair of beige slacks and an ivory silk blouse. She completed the outfit with low heels, then pulled back her hair and secured it at the neck with a mother-of-pearl clip.

Taking a deep breath, she stepped from the bathroom, but Jack was nowhere in sight. Fifteen minutes later, she was still waiting for him as she paced nervously across the room, her footsteps muffled by the rich Oriental carpet.

Surely it wasn't taking him this long to dress. So where was he? Was he trying to postpone their meeting as long as possible?

They'd made love for the first time less than an hour ago. Under circumstances that had started off like a male power trip.

Then...

Then everything had suddenly changed from stark and sterile to warm and wonderful. Until the end—that is. After her mind-blowing climax—when Jack had climbed out of bed and walked away from her as if the whole thing had really been just a training exercise.

The sound of the door opening made her jump. She wanted to clench her hands at her sides. Instead she moistened her lips, then turned.

Jack was standing at the other end of the room, his face a study in composure as he looked her up and down.

"I see you found the clothing I had sent over from Saks."

"Yes."

"That's the most conservative outfit in the lot," he commented, instantly picking up on the significance of her choice.

"It's comfortable," she answered mildly, noting that he looked entirely comfortable himself in the tailored slacks and white shirt he'd been wearing earlier.

Crisply, he said, "I'm sorry I've kept you waiting. I was gathering up the files we need. And ordering dinner. I hope steak, baked potato and salad are all right."

"Fine," she answered. Technically, as security chief, she should have been the one to do the ordering, although she'd completely forgotten about dinner. But it seemed Jack Connors had made himself perfectly at home in her domain. She flicked a glance at his face, then looked quickly away—thinking that he was probably an excellent poker player. She couldn't even catch a hint of what was behind those green eyes of his.

All she knew was that a good bout of sex left him hungry—judging by the meal he'd just described.

He crossed to the table and set down several folders.

"I've got a CIA dossier on Reynard. A map of the island. Background on some of his visitors. And a dossier on myself. You need to memorize that—so you can rattle off facts like when I graduated from Georgia Tech. We'll keep the facts as close to the truth as possible—to make it easier for us both to remember what our stories are supposed to be."

"Georgia Tech. That's where you went to school?"

"Yeah. On a scholarship. But you can read up on that after you go home tonight. And I need similar information on you. I can start with your personnel file, but I'll probably need more details."

"Like whether I get menstrual cramps?" she snapped.

"Yeah, like that. Do you?"

She wished she hadn't come back with the snappy retort. "Occasionally," she muttered.

"Since you brought up the subject, what about P.M.S.? Do your breasts get tender? Are they more sensitive then?"

She shot him a warning look. "That's none of your business."

"I beg to differ. Everything about you is my business. You've been my mistress for over a year. I need to know if you're bitchy before your period. Or if it juices you up—makes you more eager for sex."

"Both," she snapped.

"You seem tense," he observed dryly. "Would a glass of wine help relax you?"

She was tempted to walk over to the bar, pour herself a shot of bourbon and drink it neat. Hard liquor wasn't usually her style, but it seemed appropriate for the occasion. Still, she didn't let the temptation override her better judgment. She needed her wits about her tonight, so she managed a tight nod. "White wine would be fine."

"I believe there's a chilled bottle of Chardonnay in the refrigerator," he said, bringing it out. "The Jekel winery. 1996. A good year." Taking a corkscrew from the drawer, he began to expertly open the bottle.

She watched him for a moment before observing, "Perhaps I'd feel more comfortable if we were trading intimate information rather than having you do all the prying."

She stopped, casting around in her mind for the equivalent of the nosy questions he'd asked her. Sexual questions.

Prying wasn't usually her style. But she studied one of his broad shoulders as she asked, "Where did you have your first girl? In the back seat of a car? And oh yeah, how old were you?"

She had the momentary satisfaction of seeing the hand with the corkscrew falter. But that was the only sign that his composure had slipped. "That isn't necessarily information that I'd share with my mistress, unless I'm the kind of man who likes to brag about my sexual conquests."

"Are you?"

He pulled the cork from the bottle, took two long-stemmed glasses from the cabinet and began to pour the wine. "The persona I'm creating for Oliver Reynard probably would," he allowed as he handed her a glass, then picked up his own and took a small swallow before answering. "It was the summer I was fifteen. My father had an old army buddy, Ed Wyatt, whose family we were friendly with. Their daughter, Bethany, was seventeen, and I was attracted to her. But since she was two years older, I didn't think I had a chance. We were staying at the Wyatts' house for a long weekend, and the two sets of parents went out for the evening. I was in the den, feeling nervous about being alone with Bethany. So I was standing in front of the television turning the channels, trying to find some show that would take my mind off her. She came up behind me, reached around my waist, and put her hand on my cock."

He took another sip of wine, his eyes locked on Maddy's face. Her mouth was dry, but she didn't reach for her glass because, for the moment, she had lost the ability to move.

"I got instantly hard. I thought I was going to embarrass myself right there and then, but she knew what she was doing. She was obviously experienced, and she got both of us out of our clothes—and me into her in record time."

His eyes had taken on a faraway look. "I thought that first time was incredible. The second time she slowed things down a little—started showing me how to touch a woman and kiss her for maximum pleasure. The third time..." He shrugged. "That was when she gave me a lesson in oral sex."

Maddy couldn't help it. She felt dampness gather between her legs. She should be shocked, but it wasn't difficult to imagine the teenage Bethany seducing fifteen-year-old Jack. He was a stunningly masculine man. The girl must have taken his untapped sensuality as a challenge. And a gift—that her parents had unwittingly given her. She could imagine the fevered scene—the sexual energy of the teenage couple. And then there was the element of secrets shared. Naughty secrets. The teenagers pulling something over on their parents.

As if his thinking was paralleling hers, he said, "Our folks never suspected. Not even when I snuck down the hall the next night and into her bed." He laughed. "We had a few more mind-blowing visits back and forth that summer. Then she went away to college the next year and came home with a sophomore guy in tow. I was still in high school, and she wouldn't give me the time of day. That was a real blow to my ego. Especially since I knew exactly what she and the guy were doing in her bedroom at night."

With a jerky motion, Maddy picked up her glass and took a gulp.

"What about you?" Jack asked, his voice turning low and silky, his gaze probing her own secrets.

"What about what?"

"*Your* first time."

Unwanted memories flooded her. Her first time. She'd been sixteen. A bad age for making sexual decisions. She'd been dating Ben Hemsley and afraid that he was going to lose interest in her. He was a rich kid whose parents were friends with the Winston family. And she was the daughter of the hired help.

But he'd taken up with her, and she liked hanging around with him. Liked pretending that she fit in with his fast-lane lifestyle. So when he'd started putting pressure on her to go all the way, she'd agreed to let him do it to her. They'd met in the boathouse at his father's estate. And it had been a painful, thoroughly unromantic experience. Too fast. Too frightening. Too humiliating—at least for her. Ben had wallowed in the afterglow of his conquest. She'd felt cheap and used. And she'd vowed that no man would take advantage of her like that again. That degrading experience was one of the reasons why she was careful about her sexual partners, one of the reasons why she never let a man push her into anything she wasn't ready for.

Until tonight. Until Jack.

Well, that wasn't fair, she corrected herself. She might have needed a little push. But she'd certainly been ready.

She took another swallow of the wine, trying to blot out the long ago scene. It was something she seldom thought about. But Jack had brought it back.

And she couldn't exactly blame him, she silently admitted. She was the one who'd pushed him into his own revelation. And he was simply turning the tables.

He was still waiting for her to say something. Her hand clenched around the stem of the glass as she answered his question. "I don't think your mistress is willing to share that particular experience with you."

He was watching her with an unnerving intensity, and she wished she were more adept at hiding her emotions.

Unable to cope with his probing gaze, she poured herself more wine and downed half the contents of the glass.

"Careful," Jack said mildly. "You want to keep a clear head."

"For what?"

"Studying the material I brought. Perhaps we should start with some visual aids." He turned away from her, and she breathed out a little sigh, glad that he was giving her a moment of privacy.

Crossing to the table, he shuffled through the folders he'd brought and withdrew several glossy photographs which he handed to her.

They all showed the same man. Some were in color, some in black-and-white. Most had obviously been shot with a telephoto lens.

"Reynard, I take it," Maddy said.

"Yes."

She studied the crime lord. He was slim with neatly cut hair, lean cheeks and narrow lips. There was nothing remarkable about him—if you discounted the piercing eyes. They seemed to be staring at her, probing her deepest thought, though she was only looking at photographs.

He'd be a formidable opponent. She knew that much. Having his own island would make him arrogant—and ruthless.

Striving for detachment, she sorted through the pictures. Some had probably been taken twenty years ago and showed a man who looked like he was in his late twenties or early thirties. The more recent ones depicted someone in his early fifties—still vigorous and very sure of himself.

"Not many men can afford a private island with all the trimmings," she said. "How did he manage it?"

"He inherited wealth. His father, Bruce Reynard, saw the potential of electrical appliances when the industry was in its infancy. He started manufacturing stuff like vacuum cleaners, toasters, electric irons, radios. Things that made life easier and more pleasant for people who could afford them.

"He exploited the new rush toward consumerism. Oliver's vision of humanity was—is—darker. He saw the potential for corruption. Gambling. Drugs. Prostitution. His stock in trade is human frailty. And he made it pay off big—bigger than the happy little world of household conveniences.

"The FBI was after him—so he solved his problems by going offshore, where they can't touch him."

"But why would he go after Stan Winston's daughter? I mean, how does he even know Stan?"

"He and Winston go way back. Their fathers were business rivals. And it seems that Winston cut him out of some lucrative manufacturing deals when he was looking for legitimate ways to launder his dirty money. It's too bad Dawn got caught in the middle."

Maddy nodded. As she set the photographs down, Jack unfolded a large sheet of paper which he spread out for their inspection. It was a full-color aerial view of Orchid Island—taken either from a low-flying plane or a spy satellite.

She'd used similar photos to study the security of various Winston facilities, but the detail never ceased to amaze her. Looking at the legend, she saw the island was seven miles long and two miles wide. She could see surf foaming along the white sand that gave way at intervals to rocky shoreline. Near the eastern end of the irregular rectangle, a cone-shaped mountain rose from a dense swath of greenery.

Development was at the western end, which had been

cleared of its natural jungle covering and landscaped with lush tropical vegetation. Commanding a view of the widest beach was a sprawling building that looked like it took up several acres. Farther inland, scores of modest bungalows were lined along narrow roads.

Jack leaned over Maddy, his arm brushing hers, stirring a current of awareness through her as he began to point out the features of the island.

She slid him a sidewise glance. He looked cool and unruffled, while she was unable to control her reaction to him.

It took several seconds before she tuned back in to what he was saying as he pointed to a long, narrow building.

"This is the customs area. It's manned by extra guards, and they're likely to search our luggage. Reynard will have us taken into custody if he finds anything on his forbidden list."

"Does that mean we can't bring a transmitter? If we can't call for help, what are our plans for getting off the island? Do we have to steal a boat?"

"I've weighed the risks and the advantages. I think we can get away with communications equipment if we hide it in your makeup kit."

She swallowed. So she was the one who'd be caught red-handed if anything went wrong. All she said was, "Okay."

"And of course, there's no way we can send a long message. We'd be detected. It will have to be a spurt."

"I'm not going to pretend I know what a spurt is," she snapped.

"It's a compressed transmission, sent in a quick burst of characters. That way, the enemy can't get a fix on the radio's location."

She nodded. *The enemy,* she thought. *Yes, Reynard was the enemy all right.*

Jack was pointing toward a group of buildings set on paths that wound through landscaped grounds.

"Some of the guests stay in these villas. If things work out right, we'll be assigned to one."

"Better for a quick getaway?" she asked.

"That. And they're an indication of status. Only the highest-ranking guests get them. By the way," he went on, "I've picked names for us. I'm going to be Jack Craig. You'll be Maddy Griffin. Get used to it."

"I will." She paused. "But isn't he going to know they are false identities? Won't he do background research on us—the same way we're doing research on him. I mean, I can't believe he's not very careful about who comes to his private little country."

"He's very careful. But I've set it up so that we should check out. First, remember that Jack Craig would go to enormous lengths to hide his personal business from the world. But I've gotten some little tidbits salted into the databases he's likely to use for background checks. And I've arranged for a couple of key informants to back up the Jack Craig alias."

Maddy opened her mouth to ask for details when a knock sounded at the door.

Jack straightened and called out, "Come in."

A waiter in black slacks and a starched white coat wheeled in a cart with covered dishes.

"Would you like me to serve the meal, ma'am?" the man asked her.

Before she could answer, Jack spoke up. "We can do it ourselves. Thank you very much."

As soon as the man had left, he turned back to Maddy. "I'd like you to change for dinner."

"I'm comfortable like this."

"I want you to get comfortable with some of the other clothing you'll be wearing on the island, outfits drug lord

Jack Craig would have chosen to show off your charms.''
Crossing to the closet, he opened the door and began sliding hangers along the pole as he inspected evening wear. Finally he pulled out a turquoise, sleeveless chiffon knee-length gown with a plunging draped back. Matching sling-back pumps and a pair of ivory panty hose were in a heavy plastic bag attached to the hanger.

"I'd like to see you in this."

The tone of voice was the one he'd used earlier when he'd been ordering her to strip for him, and it set off a frisson along her nerve endings. Appalled at her reaction, she called up a touch of anger. Anger at his arrogance. And anger because she hated admitting he was right. Getting comfortable in this clothing was essential. So she snatched the gown away from him and headed for the bathroom down the hall.

"Lose the bra," he called after her.

Biting back an angry retort, she slammed the bathroom door behind her. After pulling off her blouse and slacks, she hesitated for a moment. Then she unhooked her bra and laid it on top of the discarded clothing.

Slipping into the dress, she closed the zipper and adjusted the bodice. The color was perfect for her, but the fabric clung to her breasts, clearly showing the outline of her nipples. She thought about disobeying orders and putting the bra back on. But that was out of the question, she decided as she turned and looked over her shoulder in the mirror. The back plunged so low that the band would surely show.

At least the skirt had a fair amount of softly draped fabric so that it swirled around her legs rather than hugging them.

Quickly she pulled on the panty hose and the sling-backs. They added three inches to her height—putting her on a more equal footing with Mr. Cool. If she didn't trip and fall on her face!

She rarely wore shoes this ridiculous. Practicing was definitely a good idea.

Turning again, she studied herself in the mirror. She hadn't bothered to put on any makeup after her shower, and suddenly it seemed as if she wasn't doing the dress justice. Determined to make an impression on the man awaiting her return, she yanked open a drawer and pulled out the makeup kit that she'd seen earlier.

It appeared the colors had been chosen for her. Quickly she brushed on two tones of eye shadow, then applied liner and mascara.

After smoothing on foundation and blusher, she started outlining her lips. When she'd filled in the outline with a lighter color, she stood back to inspect the effect. Like the high heels, the coating of war paint was far from her standard choice. But she'd attended enough formal affairs to know how to turn herself out to advantage. And she was pleased with the results. As a final touch, she undid the pin at the back of her neck and brushed out her hair so that it floated around her face.

"What took you so long?" Jack demanded when she sauntered back down the hall to the meeting room. Or as much of a saunter as she could manage with those heels.

"These things take time," she murmured.

He looked up, and she had the satisfaction of seeing his eyes flash with green fire before he recovered himself.

"Will this do?" she asked in a silky voice.

"Yes," he clipped out, uncovered one of the plates from the cart and slammed it onto the table. He managed to transfer the second one more gently.

In her absence he'd spread a white cloth, set out the napkins and cutlery, and poured water into long-stemmed glasses. She noted with a tinge of surprise that he'd gotten everything in the right places—a feat which her own father had never been able to manage. When Spike Guthrie had set a table, it had looked like the knives, spoons and forks had clattered down from the ceiling—either because he was protesting doing women's work or he really didn't know their proper placement. She'd never determined which.

So Jack Connors—or Jack Craig—was more civilized than he looked. Well, at least he knew the amenities of table service. She might have asked if he'd been a waiter at some time in his career. But she decided not to press her luck. So she simply pulled out her chair and sat down.

OLIVER REYNARD SWIRLED amber cognac in his glass, then took an appreciative sip. Leaning back in his favorite leather chair, he thumbed through the various lists that had been prepared by the heads of his departments. The executive chef. The head gardener. The recreation director. The ordnance officer.

He was having one of his magnifique parties in a few days, and no detail was too small to escape his notice.

The food, the assignment of the guest rooms, the number of uniformed guards and extra personnel in the public areas. The newly enhanced check-in procedures at the customs area.

He set down his glass on the marble-topped antique table, then picked up his gold pen and jotted a notation on one of the menus. "More tropical fruit at the opening reception."

Then he flipped to the list of housing assignments to see how his maintenance staff was coming with the video and sound recording equipment. He wanted it in perfect working order in every guest room. With double backup systems. Better safe than sorry. If one of his guests was planning to stab him in the back, he wanted to know about it quickly so the threat could be neutralized.

It paid to be thorough. His father had forgotten that little fact. And the omission had gotten him killed.

Oliver was determined that nothing of the sort would happen to him. He was planning to live out a long and satisfying life on this private island domain that he'd purchased twenty years ago with money he'd set aside from his inheritance.

Thinking about his father made his features contort.

The old man had been a legitimate businessman. In the outside world, he had earned a reputation for respectability.

But at home, and within his own company, he'd been a tyrant. Lording it over everyone under him. Making rules just for the fun of tripping people up.

Especially his only son.

But Oliver had turned the tables on his father very nicely. He'd dumped enough sugar into the fuel line of his private plane to make it crash off the Atlantic coast. Now he was the one in charge—making the rules. Making everyone who lived on Orchid Island or who came here as his guests conform to his policies.

His other goals were showing visitors from the mainland that they could have a better time here than anywhere else on earth, showing them how well he lived, and showing them that he was lord and master of this island.

He loved those aspects of the parties. The control. The aura of excitement. The undertone of sexuality that his male guests found so stimulating. Some of his most lucrative business deals had been made with men who were thinking with their cocks instead of their brains. He loved using sex to confuse the issues and manipulate powerful men.

And he loved inviting new people to his lair from time to time.

Like Jack Craig and a couple of others in the party. Craig was something of an anomaly, of course. He'd sent word through an acquaintance less than a week ago that he'd like to come down to the Island to discuss a very lucrative deal.

Oliver had given his okay to have Craig included. But he was still in the process of having the man investigated. And if he didn't check out, Craig and his companion wouldn't be coming home with the rest of the merrymakers.

He turned back to his lists, noting the security arrangements at the Dark Tower, where his very special guest was being held.

Stan Winston's daughter. Winston's most prized possession. Oliver had a long memory for wrongs done him in the past. And he'd been waiting for the chance to pay Winston back for screwing him out of several important manufacturing deals—deals that would have channeled a great deal of money into legitimate enterprises.

So when the opportunity to snatch the girl had come up, he'd leaped on it. But the party later in the week meant that he'd have to put any decisions about her on hold.

Maybe he'd even return her to Winston only slightly the worse for wear—if Winston came up with the right price. He was still thinking about what he wanted. Not money. Some terms that would humiliate the man, put him in Oliver Reynard's debt. But that was only one interesting possibility. It might be more satisfying to return her in a coffin, and demonstrate that he had absolute power over Winston's life.

THE STEAK WAS GOOD—broiled just the way Maddy liked it. The baked potatoes excellent, not steamed in foil but delicate and fluffy so that they mixed perfectly with the sour cream, chives and bacon bits that were provided as garnishes.

"Winston Industries knows how to cook," Jack commented as he cut off another piece of tender, juicy steak.

"Only the best for Stan Winston."

The comment came from the man himself. He was standing in the doorway, looking like an earthquake victim. His hair was uncombed. His clothes might have been slept in for the past month. And the lines in his face had deepened to furrowed channels.

"Mr. Winston," Maddy murmured. "Come join us. I'm sure the kitchen can send up something for you."

"Thanks, but I'm not hungry."

He pulled out a chair at the table and sat down.

Maddy nodded. Despite her invitation, it was impossible for her to talk to the man, to be in the same room with him without feeling guilty.

The dinner that had seemed so appealing a few minutes ago might as well have turned to library paste.

"Don't let me interrupt you," Winston said. "I was just wondering how your plans are going."

"We've been establishing the personas we're going to project for Reynard," Jack said. He had also put down his knife and fork. "And I've obtained detailed aerial photos of the island."

"Let me see them," Winston said eagerly.

The dinner forgotten, Maddy jumped up and brought the pictures, self-conscious in the revealing dress. But Stan barely glanced at her.

Jack stood too, coming over to point out the features he'd shown Maddy.

"Where do you think the bastard is holding Dawn?" Winston asked.

"Anything I tell you now can only be a guess," Jack

answered. "He could have her in the main house. Or somewhere else on the island."

The distraught father took the news badly. "This is all my fault," he whispered.

"No! How can you say that?" Maddy asked.

He turned his face toward her. "I know you're still blaming yourself—even after I told you that was nonsense. I've been working up the guts to explain what was really in that girl's head."

"You can't know her thoughts," Maddy protested.

"I can make an educated guess. What happened was that Dawn blames me for her mother's death last year. Jill and I had had a fight the night she died. And she was angry when she got into her sports car. That's why she was driving too fast and missed the turn on Thunder Road." He heaved a sigh. "Since then, Dawn has barely spoken to me. And I've been so afraid that something would happen to her, too, that I've kept her under virtual house arrest. That's why she planned her escape. To get away from me. Now both of us are paying the price—I mean you and me. We both think it's our fault. Only I'm the one responsible. Not you."

Maddy's heart ached for the man. "We'll get her back," she murmured.

"You have to," Winston said. "Or I won't be able to live with myself."

She moved into the background while Jack took over, emphasizing the research he'd done, and offering reasonable strategies for getting Dawn back. His speech was reassuring, even though Maddy knew that much of the presentation was designed to lift the man's spirits.

Jack kept up the encouraging monologue as they walked Stan Winston to the door.

The man was profuse in his thanks.

"You made him feel better," she said when the door had closed behind him.

"I'm praying we can deliver on those promises."

She nodded. She hadn't thought Jack Connors was the praying type. But then there was so little she knew about him.

She started to turn away. But she was so tired that when one of her stiltlike shoes caught in the rug, she stumbled.

Jack's arm shot out, catching her, and she tumbled into his arms. There was a shocked moment when her body registered the lean form and the hard muscles of him—when her breasts flattened against his chest—when her fatigue fell away, to be replaced by a sharp stab of sexual need.

She sucked in a breath, felt his large hand slide down her back. And she knew in that moment that the surge of sexual excitement wasn't one-sided. He was aroused. And as his hold shifted on her, a sudden tantalizing image swirled in her head. An image of what they had done together—and what they might do.

But the whole supercharged incident lasted only seconds. Before she could blink, he was setting her away from him, transferring her hand from his shoulder to the back of a chair.

"It's been a long day," he said gruffly as though the only thing that had happened was that she'd tripped and he'd caught her.

She nodded wordlessly. She'd thought he was indifferent to her. That their tumble on the bed had represented only a momentary burst of pleasure for him. Now she wondered if she'd been too quick to assess his reactions.

"Go home and get some sleep. We'll start again in the morning. And change out of those shoes before you kill yourself," he added.

She didn't have the energy to come back with a retort.

Or the courage to ask him what he was feeling. But at least she made an effort to straighten her shoulders as she marched back down the hall.

Jack wasn't in the room when she returned. She'd never thought of him as a coward. Now she wondered if he'd deliberately made himself scarce.

The speculation had a buoying effect as she rode down in the elevator. It was after ten, but there was no problem getting a ride home. Winston Industries maintained a fleet of private cars with drivers always on duty, and Maddy had no qualms about using their services tonight.

Twenty minutes later, she was saying hello to the door-man at her upper East side apartment building.

Just off Lexington Avenue, it was a small but exclusive residence for young executives. A luxury building by New York standards where rents had gone through the roof.

But she made a good enough salary to afford a two-bedroom unit—with one of the bedrooms outfitted as a home office.

Callie's meow of protest greeted her as she unlocked the door and stepped into her small foyer.

Coming down on her knees, she stroked the calico cat's silky fur.

"Sorry, sweetie," she apologized. "I know I've been gone a long time. And I'm going to be gone even longer," she added with a pang, thinking that the first thing she'd better do in the morning was call her friend Jan and ar-range for cat-sitting.

Tail up, Callie followed her onto the Berber carpet, then leaped into her lap, purring furiously as her mistress sat down on the corduroy sofa.

Maddy leaned back, closed her eyes and stroked the cat with long sweeps of her hand that started at her head and went all the way down her tail.

Shoes off, she swung her feet onto the old ship's hatch

that she'd found at a flea market, refinished, and bolted to metal legs so she could use it as a coffee table.

Smiling, she listened to the sound of her pet's contented purring. Dogs were affectionate because it was programmed into them. If your cat sat in your lap and purred, you knew it was because she loved you. Or because she expected you were going to feed her, she added with a laugh.

After a few moments, she shifted the animal off her lap, and padded into the kitchen to fill the food bowl.

Seconds later, Callie was chomping away, and Maddy was wandering toward the window to look out at the lights of the city.

She'd lived in New York all her life—except when she was away on assignment or during summers at the Winston estate. She loved the excitement of the city and loved the homey feel of her apartment. Usually she was content here. Tonight she felt restless.

She wandered across the room to the walnut bookshelves that spanned one wall and looked at the picture of herself and her father. It had been taken when she'd first joined the Winston security force—when she'd been infused with the passion to reach the top.

She couldn't hold back a snort. She had what she'd always wanted. Only now the luster had worn off the prize. It wasn't just the fiasco with Dawn. It was Jack, she silently acknowledged. This afternoon he'd made her realize how empty her life was, and she didn't like the realization.

When the buzzer on the intercom sounded, she jumped. Then her heart began to pound as she crossed the room.

Was he downstairs now? Had he forgotten to tell her something? Or did he simply want to see her?

"Hello," she said as she pressed the buzzer.

"Maddy."

Her disappointment was instant. It wasn't Jack; it was Ted Burnes, who worked for her at Winston Industries.

"Ted. What are you doing here?" she asked.

"I'd like to talk to you. Can I come up?"

She glanced at the clock. It was ten-thirty, an unusual time for a visit.

"It's important," he said.

"All right. I'll buzz you in."

Glad that she'd changed back to her work outfit before coming home, she scuffed her shoes back on and smoothed her hair in the mirror.

Seconds later, the chimes sounded, and she opened the door.

Ted surged across the threshold, then came to an abrupt stop as Callie dashed directly in front of him and bounded into the bedroom.

"What was that, the Cannonball Express?" he asked.

"My cat. She doesn't take to strangers. You won't see her again. I promise."

He nodded, then turned in a circle, inspecting her living room. "Very nice."

"Thank you. Uh—why did you stop by?"

As soon as she said the words, she knew she wasn't being very hospitable.

Ted shoved his hands into his pockets. He was a tall man—almost as tall as Jack. And he was muscular. But while Jack was dark, Ted was fair. With blond hair and what she thought of as Midwestern good looks. He'd tried to date her a time or two, but she'd made it clear that she didn't go out with employees.

Now, to her embarrassment, the recent episode with Jack leaped into her mind. Flustered, she turned toward the window so Ted couldn't see the flush that had crept into her cheeks.

"I guess you're tired. Maybe I shouldn't have come rushing over," he apologized.

"No, no. That's fine. I've just had a pretty trying day," she answered, forcing herself to turn back to him.

"I know. You brought in Jack Connors to help you get Dawn Winston back."

"How do you know that?" she inquired, making an effort to keep her voice even.

"People have seen him in the building. They put two and two together."

She nodded tightly.

"Maddy, I wish you weren't going with him."

Lord, another man trying to discourage her from doing her job. Quietly, she asked, "Why not?"

Ted looked down, then brought his gaze back to hers. "I've heard stuff about him."

"Like what?"

He sucked in a breath and let it out. "Like he's not the most reliable partner for the job."

"I think you'd better explain that."

Ted pressed his lips together. "Okay. You know he's ex-CIA. Do you know why he quit the agency?"

"He could make more money in the private sector, with his own company."

"That may be true. But his leaving was the direct result of an assignment in Albania. With a female partner. He lost her."

"You mean, she was killed?" Maddy asked tightly.

"Yeah. And it was his fault."

"How do you know?" she pressed.

Ted hesitated. "Confidential reports."

"Where did you get hold of something like that?"

"I can't tell you."

"Ted, you work for me!"

"But in this case, I can't reveal my source. You're just going to have to trust me on this."

"Okay."

"Okay what?"

"Okay, I acknowledge that someone wants to discredit Jack Connors. And if you can't tell me who it is, I can't make an evaluation of the information."

"I can't tell you," he repeated.

"Then I'll take it for what it's worth."

Ted folded his arms across his chest. "You're confident that Jack Connors can protect your back?"

"Yes," she answered, her voice ringing with conviction—because she couldn't drop out of this assignment, which meant her only choice was to trust Jack with her life.

Ted stood there, staring at her as though he thought she was making a serious mistake. Desperate to change the subject, she said, "Jack and I both think that Dawn might have had help escaping from the Winston compound."

"That makes sense," Ted answered, his voice tight. "Do you have any idea who might have aided her?"

"Actually, I've done some thinking about that myself," he answered quickly. "One of the maids in the household is new. I'm redoing her background check. And there's a gardener who was friendly with Dawn. I'm having him investigated, too."

"Thank you for getting on that."

"I thought you'd want the information."

"Yes," she murmured, shifting her weight from one foot to the other. "Why don't we continue this discussion in my office tomorrow?"

Ted didn't take the hint. "Who's going to be in charge of security while you're gone?" he asked suddenly.

"I'm not sure," she answered. Ted was one of her chief candidates, which he probably realized. But she wasn't going to discuss that now. And she wasn't going to make any decisions until she had time to review the recent work records of her senior staff.

Ted took a step back. "Well, I guess I'd better go." He looked up at her. "You won't…uh…tell Connors I spoke to you about…uh…Albania, will you?"

"Of course not," she answered, reaching to open the door.

Ted nodded tightly, then departed as quickly as he had come, leaving her with thoughts that were even more unsettled than they had been earlier in the evening.

3

OLIVER REYNARD SPENT part of the morning personally inspecting each of the villas and rooms in the guest wings. Then he toured the kitchen to make sure everything was ready.

After that he visited the guards on the target range—noting their proficiency with both machine guns and automatic pistols.

Now it was time for one last check on his visitor files.

Striding across the antique Oriental rug in his comfortable office, he stopped by the desk and ran his fingertips over the stack of folders on the wide mahogany desk.

The thicker ones held dossiers on the men who would be arriving on Orchid Island in a few hours. The thinner folders had information on the female guests.

The women hardly registered on his scale of potential threats—unless he wanted to worry about the ones who were daughters of mafia dons.

The males were his primary concern. All of them were rich. All were powerful and ruthless in their own right. And all thrilled to be visiting the home of the world's top crime boss. And all of them would murder him in his own bed if he gave them the chance.

He'd known some of them for years. Exchanged e-mails and teleconferences with others. The only ones he'd met face-to-face had come to Orchid Island. The island was an independent state. Subject to no laws but his own—which were modeled on the Napoleonic Code.

Guilty until proven innocent. And few men—or women—who crossed him got a chance to prove the latter.

Although he worked from home, he hadn't given up his U.S. operations. He'd only switched them to trusted operatives who were his legs—and his eyes and ears on the mainland. They'd brought him some of the information on his guests. The rest of it had been culled from the secret Internet databases that cost him a fortune in fees every month.

He reached for the folder on Jack Craig and opened it again. Oliver had never worked with him, but he was always interested in new moneymaking operations—particularly if they presented no risk to himself.

Like most others in his line of work, Craig had gone to considerable lengths to hide the details of his business operations from the world. But Oliver had discovered the interesting fact that Mr. Craig had recently moved into territory left vacant by the arrest of several key crime bosses.

So Jack Craig appeared to check out. And he had a couple of very well-respected mob kingpins who were willing to vouch for him. But there were some holes in his resume—some periods of time that weren't accounted for.

Stints in prison? Stretches when he had gone underground to avoid a murder rap? That was the rumor.

Which might or might not be true. If he'd been a federal prisoner, it had been under another name, although taking another identity in midcareer wasn't unusual for a man like Craig who wanted to hide some of the unfortunate incidents in his background.

Intrigued but still on his guard, he'd kept Craig on the guest list—partly for the challenge of sparring with the man. And partly because of the companion he was bringing. Maddy Griffin.

He opened her folder and looked at her picture—as he had done again and again over the past few days.

She was a looker. Blond and blue-eyed. Just the type he liked for a change of pace. She'd been with Craig over a year. Which meant that the man had some regard for her. Still, like most males, Craig would surely welcome some new diversions.

Oliver let himself slip into a little fantasy. He and Maddy Griffin alone in one of his private playrooms. He'd have to see if that could be arranged. Hopefully, with Craig's cooperation, since the man had said he was eager to do business—and lending out Maddy Griffin could be a powerful inducement to a meeting of the minds.

He lifted his head and caught sight of several gardeners pulling out begonias that had been there for a month and replacing them with kalanchoes, fresh from one of the greenhouses. A nice change of pace. He was glad he'd thought of it.

He smiled, satisfied that everything in his world was the way he wanted it. All ready for his guests. They were still in New York, but soon they'd be on his private jet where he'd start putting them in the mood for some serious partying. Then he'd give them a little jolt of anxiety in his customs area—followed by more of his generous hospitality. It was all carefully calculated to throw them a bit off balance. He smiled. Dieu, he loved manipulating people!

He was drawn back to the picture of Maddy Griffin, feeling the pleasurable response of his body as he looked down at her, wondering if she could possibly be as beautiful in person as she was in the photograph.

He looked at his watch again. They'd be in the waiting room at Kennedy Airport soon. With the others. He could catch the satellite feed from there and have a look at her.

"SHOW TIME."

Jack's voice cut through the tangle of thoughts chasing themselves through Maddy's brain as the sleek black limo pulled up at a small terminal at JFK International Airport. It was a restricted-access section of the airport that handled international flights for wealthy businessmen.

The uniformed driver cut the engine and trotted quickly around to open her door as if serving his passengers was his primary pleasure in life. He might look like a gung-ho chauffeur, but he was actually a trained security agent—Andrew Stanford. In fact, he was the man she was leaving in charge of security at Winston Industries while she was on Orchid Island.

"Thank you," she murmured as he set her matching designer luggage on the curb.

She could have assigned the top job to Ted Burnes. But she'd selected Andy instead. She wasn't sure exactly what prompted her to make that decision. Ted had always been perfectly competent in his job. But the late-night meeting with him two days ago had made her edgy. She kept telling herself that he was simply interested in protecting her. Yet she didn't like the seed of doubt he'd sowed in her mind about Jack. And she couldn't help wondering if his motives were tainted. Maybe he didn't like the idea of her working so intimately with another man, and had decided to undermine the relationship. That would certainly have been unprofessional on his part, and she'd have to delve into his motivation after she came home. But for now, she had too much else to worry about.

And she had given him a special assignment. He was in charge of checking out everyone who might have been in a position to help Dawn escape, and he knew he'd better have some answers for her when she came back.

She caught Jack eying her appraisingly. Probably he was wondering if she was ready.

Well, she was as ready as he was. Lifting her chin she gave him a smile that sparkled with false brilliance. "Oh, this is so exciting," she cooed for the benefit of the uniformed attendant who had begun piling the luggage onto a rolling cart. Probably he was a trained agent, too! Trained in surveillance and assassination.

When they reached the ticket counter, Jack pulled a money clip from the pocket of his custom tailored beige slacks and peeled off a twenty, which he handed to the man.

"Thank you!"

She watched the transaction from the corner of her eye as she took out a compact and dabbed powder onto her nose.

From his expensive haircut to his blue-and-white golf shirt and on down to his Italian leather loafers, Jack looked like exactly what he was pretending to be, a man with the money to indulge his every whim.

As his girlfriend, she was decked out in a lemon-yellow sundress cut too low in the back and front for a bra, but at least the matching jacket gave her some feeling of being covered up.

The chunky gold charm bracelets circling her left wrist were an annoyance, but she knew she had to put up with them—along with the four expensive rings that adorned her hands.

Jack had vetoed panty hose, so her legs were bare and her feet were simply slipped into two-hundred-dollar sandals.

In contrast, her face felt like an oil painting—with makeup that could have been applied with a putty knife—thanks to one of the special training sessions she'd attended in which she'd learned how to "make the most" of her features. At least that's what the beautician had called it. She'd called it a waste of time. But she'd known that the woman she was supposed to be playing would have spent twenty minutes in the morning in front of the mirror. So she'd gotten with the program.

Jack had stepped up to the counter and pulled out the voucher authorizing him and Maddy to take the Orchid Island charter flight.

"May I see your passports, please?" the attractive redhead behind the counter asked. Was she one of Reynard's operatives, too? Or was she just a civilian hired for her good looks?

Jack pulled out two small books with blue covers. It galled her that he was carrying her passport along with his own. But that was just another authentic touch, she told herself. And the real issue was whether the fake IDs passed muster.

As the woman inspected them, Maddy held her breath. When they were returned with a smile, she relaxed a fraction.

After their carry-on luggage was searched, they were ushered into a green-and-beige waiting room, where they joined six other couples. Maddy had been in many airport VIP suites with Stan Winston, but she'd never seen one quite so plush. There were comfortable couches instead of standard airport seats, thick carpeting, a wet bar and a linen-covered table with a breakfast buffet.

She'd also never seen so much heavy gold jewelry, diamonds, Italian leather, and designer watches. And that was just on the men.

Jack's one pinky ring and his Tommy Hilfiger shirt were small potatoes.

But it wasn't just the men's attire that hit her. She could sense a kind of simmering excitement in the room—part power trip and part sexual undertone. These guys were turned on.

Maddy cut Jack a quick look. Then, trying not to seem

overwhelmed, she glanced around, and realized that a number of the other women looked as nervous and shell-shocked as she felt.

She was an outgoing person, and she might have started a friendly conversation with one of the other female companions, but she noticed that they were all sticking pretty close to their guys.

Jack had somehow acquired a partial guest list, along with photographs. So she knew who a number of their fellow passengers were.

In the corner, the powerfully built, balding man with the heavy brows and the narrowed eyes was Don Fowler, a known drug dealer.

He regarded her and Jack, then leaned over to say something to his statuesque blond companion.

Another man she recognized was crime boss Jormo Kardofski. Tall and pale, he looked like he could have stepped out of a vampire movie.

Jack keyed right in to the level of excitement. "Hey babe, that looks like some spread. Let's check it out," he suggested expansively as he started toward the food table. He grabbed a plate and heaped it with eggs Benedict, bacon and fruit. She stuck with the fruit and a carton of yogurt.

Some of the couples were sitting at small tables. She and Jack took one, where he started putting away the breakfast, and she picked at her food.

It amazed her how happy he seemed when her stomach was in knots. Partly it was the unnatural atmosphere in the room. And partly it was a sudden surge of anxiety generated by Ted's warning. It had kept her awake in the small hours of the morning, ever since Ted's visit to her apartment. And she'd lain there in bed wondering whether she should simply confront Jack with the information.

That was the straightforward way to handle the suspicions. The way she *should* have handled it, she realized now.

Yet every time she'd thought about bringing it up, she'd felt her stomach knot.

On the upside, if he'd told her that Ted's information was false, that would have instantly relieved her anxiety. But what if he gave her the wrong answer? Or worse, if he told her Ted was talking nonsense—but she wasn't sure she believed him? Then what? When the two of them had no choice but to work intimately together on this assignment.

In the end, she decided that keeping quiet was her only option, even knowing that it was going to be a source of internal tension until it was resolved. Now it was too late to reevaluate her decision.

She'd been sitting with her head bent toward her plate. Looking up, she focused on a small blond woman staring at her. The woman was dressed in skintight hot-pink pedal pushers, high-heeled sandals and a lighter pink shirt studded with rhinestones. She was with a large, solid man whose face had been scarred by teenage acne, leaving the surface uneven and pitted. He stood with his arm possessively around her shoulder, his beefy hand adorned by a chunky diamond ring. The hand hung down so that his large fingers dangled across the top of her breast. It wasn't like he'd done it by accident, Maddy thought as she watched him possessively caress the swell of flesh.

The blonde saw Maddy observing them and flushed. Maddy quickly glanced away, not wanting to intrude on what should be a private moment. But she'd seen enough to wonder if public displays of lust were considered normal in this crowd.

Come to think of it, the blonde and her guy weren't the only two behaving in ways that Maddy considered inappropriate in a waiting room full of travelers.

Another couple was tucked into a corner exchanging little kisses and caresses. And a second man was standing in back of his girlfriend, his hips pressed to her bottom. She knew his name, too. Artie Proctor. He was heavily into the numbers racket, according to the background sheets she'd gotten from Jack.

Maddy lowered her eyes to her plate again—then felt a little jolt of sensation as Jack's foot slid against her ankle. He'd slipped his right foot out of his loafer, and was running his sock-clad toes against her. Apparently he'd noticed the overheated atmosphere in the room and had decided it was important to fit in.

The problem was, he hadn't touched her in days. She didn't mean touched in the strictly sexual sense, either. Since catching her when she'd tripped in her high-heeled shoes that first night, he had gone out of his way to avoid any physical contact. In fact, he'd acted like the awareness simmering between them didn't exist. And she'd done her best to seem as unfazed as he. But the sudden touch of his foot against her leg sent tingles of electricity skittering along her nerve endings.

His voice was as low and silky as his touch. "Reynard's island is my kind of place. We're going to have a great time. A little pleasure. A little business."

She swallowed, nodded, thinking that it wasn't so difficult to imitate the other women. Most of them seemed as off-balance as she.

Covertly, she studied them. They were all beautiful. Some were fashion-model slender. Others were built more like Playboy centerfolds—probably courtesy of breast implants and liposuction, she told herself.

But they seemed to have little choice about their behavior. She was sure they all knew that they either played along with these guys, or they could be replaced.

Her own choices were also limited. At least for now.

Because everything that happened over the next few days was governed by the one big decision she'd made.

She was going to Orchid Island to rescue Dawn Winston. No matter what. Up till now, she'd let her determination carry her along. Determination—and frantic work. Because every minute of the past few days had been filled with studying dossiers, plotting strategy, getting as comfortable as she could with her wardrobe, learning how to put on the makeup she was wearing, and ensuring that the security at Winston Industries ran smoothly while she was away.

All at once, the frantic activity had come to a halt, and she was sitting here in this luxury airport lounge playing the role she'd thought she was prepared for. Jack had warned her what it would be like. But she'd thought he was exaggerating to get her to back out. Too bad she hadn't taken him at his word.

"Excited, baby?" he asked, his toes moving higher, walking their way up the curve of her calf.

She licked her dry lips. "As excited as you."

His green eyes told her he knew she was lying.

She was rescued from his exploring toes by the woman at the check-in counter, her voice coming from a loudspeaker.

"Flight fifty-three-ten to Orchid Island is now ready for boarding. All passengers, have your boarding passes ready for the attendant."

Jack slipped his foot back into his shoe. The area was suddenly full of activity as people stood, grabbed their carry-on luggage, and moved toward the exit door.

With a mixture of relief and trepidation, Maddy picked up the small, specially designed case that held enough makeup for a Broadway chorus line. That was another reason her face was so overdone. She looked like a woman who never traveled without the contents of a cosmetics counter. But actually there was more than lipstick, foundation and eye shadow in the bag. Hidden in the padded bottom and sides was the transmitter they would need to summon their transportation after they'd located Dawn.

The thought of Dawn sent a sudden pang spearing through her. It had been over a week now since they'd had any information about Stan Winston's daughter, so they had to be prepared for anything.

Jack must have sensed her sudden shiver, because he draped an arm around her shoulder.

"I've told you, honey, flying's safer than walking across the street."

"I know you're right," she managed. "I just can't help get a little uptight every time I think about takeoff and landing. Those are the most dangerous times, aren't they?" she asked in a slightly quavery voice.

"Don't worry your pretty head about that. We'll get you a nice glass of wine as soon as we're settled."

They walked down the jetway and into the midsize plane. Maddy sucked in her breath as the decor registered. The interior looked more like a nightclub than an airplane. The sumptuous seats were upholstered in orange-and-purple fabric and arranged in rows facing each other, with small tables bolted to the floor between the rows.

There was no assigned seating. Couples were free to occupy any part of the cabin they wanted. Several had already made themselves comfortable. As in the waiting room, they were all staking out their own territory—with each twosome a little island unto themselves.

Apparently nobody in this group was the outgoing type. Or they didn't trust each other even to make small talk.

Jack led her toward the back, probably because that gave him the best opportunity to observe the others, she figured as she slid her carry-on under the seat opposite her and settled into a chair like a luxury lounger. There was even, she discovered, a little footrest that swung out of the superstructure.

As the plane taxied onto the runway, Maddy found herself fighting a surge of panic.

"All right?" Jack murmured, pressing his hand over hers.

She turned her head, raised her gaze to his, seeing determination mingled with regret in his eyes.

So he still didn't think she was the right woman for the job! Well, she would show him what she was made of. Deliberately she relaxed in her seat, pretending she was getting ready for the most delectable experience of her life.

As soon as they had reached their cruising altitude, a couple of flight attendants wearing skimpy little skirts, low-cut blouses and mesh stockings came around to take drink orders.

Maddy asked for white wine.

Jack ordered an island punch, to get himself in the mood for fun, he told her loudly.

She took small sips of her drink, feeling the cool liquid slide down her throat. She was no wine expert, but this stuff tasted like top quality.

Fifteen minutes later, she was more relaxed. So relaxed in fact, that she couldn't stop herself from contemplating a little devilment. If Jack could tease her in the waiting room, she could do the same thing here. Giving him a sly smile, she slipped her hand onto his thigh and began to caress the fine fabric of his slacks. Obviously he hadn't been expecting the move, because she felt his muscles tense. The response gave her a jolt of satisfaction. She'd show him how well she could fit in here.

She was distracted when she saw the beefy guy with the pockmarked face lean over and whisper something to the blonde in the pink outfit.

His companion flushed and gave a quick shake of her head. But he spoke again, his face going hard. The woman paled at his aggressive expression. Unbuckling her seat belt, she made her way quickly down the aisle, keeping her gaze on the floor as she ran the gauntlet of curious eyes.

Probably everyone in the plane had seen the exchange. And they were all wondering what was going on.

Maddy expected the woman to approach one of the attendants who was at the back filling drink orders. Instead, she slipped into the rest room that was directly opposite where she and Jack were sitting. Although she closed the door firmly behind her, she didn't slide the lock into place.

Moments later, the guy got up and followed her, stepping through the door she'd just entered and locking it with a click.

Maddy stared at the closed door, then flushed as she heard a deep masculine laugh coming from inside the rest room. A very satisfied laugh—that ended in a groan.

Jack leaned back in his seat as he regarded the closed door. "I guess he's decided to become a member of the mile high club," he muttered.

Maddy rolled her eyes, then stiffened a moment later as she heard a grunting sound from behind the closed door. Other noises followed, noises she could unfortunately interpret quite accurately, and she felt her face flame.

She was embarrassed for the woman in there. And embarrassed for herself—at being forced to endure the intimate sounds coming from behind the door. Once, she'd been in a hotel where the couple next door were having a very vigorous bout of sex. At least that time, they hadn't necessarily known that someone in the next room could hear them. Now, there was an airplane full of people very aware of what was going on behind the closed bathroom door.

When she felt Jack's hand cover hers, she kept her eyes averted. But she turned her palm up and knit her fingers with his, gripping hard, as if he could rescue her from the helpless chagrin she shouldn't be feeling.

Lord, what kind of people had she gotten mixed up with on this trip?

Stupid question. She'd gotten mixed up with a plane-load of gangsters who didn't subscribe to the normal rules of society, and all of them eager to get to Orchid Island, where there were no rules—except those made by Oliver Reynard.

She slid Jack a glance and saw by the tenseness of his body and the slight flush of his cheeks that he wasn't having quite the same reaction as she. The jerk was turned on!

Men!

The door opened, and she kept her eyes cast downward as the guy sauntered out with a smug grin on his face and headed back to his seat. It was five minutes before the woman followed, her head down and her hands pressed to her sides. Maddy knew she was dying inside at having everyone on the plane knowing what she'd been doing.

She shot Jack a scathing look.

He gave a little shrug.

"We are turning down the cabin lights so that you can enjoy some of our fine selection of movies on your individual television screens," one of the attendants announced. "But if you prefer to read, the controls for the reading lights are on the arms of your chairs."

Maddy didn't think she could concentrate on the written word. Jack must have agreed. Leaning forward, he reached for an arm that pulled a small television set in front of them—positioned so that the screen could not be viewed from the aisle.

"Let's see what's on," he suggested. Without waiting for an answer, he pulled out the wired remote control cradled in the seat arm, then handed her a set of earphones, which she put on. When the menu appeared, Maddy stared at the titles, none of which she recognized.

Jack found a show, and she stared at the image that flicked to life on the screen. A man and woman were in a stark, modern bedroom, done in shades of gray and mauve. But the focus was on the couple standing in the middle of the thick carpet. She was wearing a filmy gown that did nothing to hide the dark crests of her nipples or the triangle of hair at the juncture of her legs. He was naked and seen from the back, all powerful muscles, tight buttocks, tanned skin.

As Maddy watched, he stepped toward the woman, took her in his arms, the camera angle shifting so the viewer could see him kissing her mouth, her neck, her shoulder. Then, with purposeful hands, he slipped down the straps of her gown, trapping her arms as he exposed her breasts.

It was all done artfully, erotically. Her breasts were perfect, not too large or too small. He lifted their weight in his hands, squeezed and kneaded, then circled her nipples, wringing a moan of pleasure from her—and a strangled sound from Maddy.

She didn't dare look at Jack, or anybody else who might catch the stunned expression on her face. Instead she kept her eyes glued to the screen.

The woman was obviously turned on by the attention because her nipples puckered. Her hand moved restlessly up and down the man's back, finding his buttocks and kneading with her fingers.

That questing hand sent a skitter of sensation along Maddy's nerve endings. And when the man bent to suck one of the woman's distended nipples into his mouth, Maddy felt the reaction in her own breasts. In her sex.

Beside her, Jack had gone very still, his gaze riveted to the screen, his lips slightly parted.

She could hear his quick intake of breath. And her own.

There had been love scenes in movies that had turned her on. But none of them had been like this. Not this vivid or erotic.

It took almost no effort to put herself and Jack in the places of the man and woman making love on the small screen—because that was what she'd longed for since that first and only time.

She closed her eyes for a moment, scrambling for a sense of calm. But calm was beyond her. Maybe it was simply the permissive atmosphere all around her. Or perhaps it was easier to let the erotic images of the movie carry her along rather than to let her mind dwell on this planeload of ruffians and their women—or on what awaited her at Orchid Island.

Her eyes blinked open again to see that the actor on the screen had removed the woman's gown. And when his body turned slightly, Maddy saw that he was fully aroused, his penis standing out from his body, hard and firm.

The movie love scenes she'd seen before had all been simulated sex. She'd known that the Hollywood actors weren't really doing it. This was completely beyond her experience—a movie where the man was definitely not faking his arousal. Her first porn flick.

All she could do was goggle as she watched the woman take his erection in her hand, her fingers moving and caressing in ways that wrung a gasp from his lips.

Drops of liquid formed on the tip, and she caught them, massaging them into his distended flesh.

Then she knelt in front of him, took him into her mouth

while her hands played with her own breasts, fondling them the way he had done, plucking at her nipples while she pleasured him.

It was unbearably crude. And unbearably stimulating.

What was going to happen now? Was the woman going to bring him to climax like that? Or were they going to have intercourse?

She never got a chance to find out, because the screen went blank, and she was left sucking in air, left with a throbbing sensation between her legs.

"I think we've had enough television," Jack growled, pulling off his earphones.

She gave a tight nod as she removed her own earphones. More than enough, actually.

She looked down at Jack's hand. The fingers were curled slightly as they rested on the arm of his chair. And she could imagine reaching for his hand and moving it six inches to the right and downward to her thigh.

She told herself to stop it. But she couldn't shut out the imagined sensation of his fingers pressed to her flesh. To her thigh and then over four more inches, to the juncture of her legs, to the part of her that pulsed and throbbed and radiated heat.

She squeezed her eyes shut again, angry with herself. Angry that she was behaving like a...a woman who was ruled by her passions, not her brain. Lord, she was no better than that couple who had slipped into the bathroom.

She sat there—thinking that if she could just focus on something else, the need to feel Jack's touch would go away. But it was impossible to turn off the sensations. Not when Jack was so close. Not when that hand of his would feel so good against her pulsing flesh.

Stop it. Just stop it!

"What?" Jack questioned, his voice husky.

"I didn't say anything."

"Didn't you?"

She turned her head so that she was facing him. Her lips parted, but she couldn't force any more words out. For a long moment, they stared at each other as though they'd just been caught doing something they shouldn't.

Then she decided she had nothing to lose by revealing at least part of what she was feeling. "I'm having a little problem coping with that film."

"Yeah. I should have turned it off faster."

"Why didn't you?"

He laughed. "It was...um...interesting."

She blew out a stream of air, as if that might clear her head. "Yes. I've never seen anything quite like it."

"You lead a sheltered life."

"Maybe." Needing to break the intensity of the moment, she looked around the dimly lit cabin. Several other couples were watching TV, and from the looks on their faces, she was pretty sure they were watching the same or a similar show.

"You could try and get some sleep," Jack murmured. "Rest your head on my shoulder."

Could she manage that, she wondered. Gingerly she lowered her head to the wide, firm surface, feeling strangely comforted by the contact. When his hand came up to stroke through her hair, she closed her eyes.

He made her feel calmer, safer. But she knew it was only the illusion of safety. And, at any rate, she was too keyed up to sleep. Keyed up from the film, and keyed up from the knowledge that they were drawing closer to Orchid Island. And since they didn't have to detour around Cuba, the way a U.S. carrier would, the flight would be less than two hours.

Some time later, the attendants turned on dim lights and served a sumptuous lunch of lemon pepper chicken, wild rice, and baby green beans. After the trays were cleared away, Maddy felt the plane begin its descent.

She watched out the window as they approached the island, an irregular rectangle of green, like an uncut jewel laid on turquoise velvet.

It was beautiful, yet the beauty of the place only accentuated the feeling of danger.

Enter at your own risk, she thought as they skimmed along the last stretch of open space before the runway. Leaning back in her seat, she worked at finding the sense of calm that she could invariably muster up when she was in the middle of an assignment.

She'd always done it before. But this was different. Her nerves were screeching, and she couldn't make them settle.

She tensed as she felt the plane come to a halt on a stretch of tarmac in front of a low, white building.

There was a sense of anticipation in the cabin now. A suppressed excitement.

Some of the men were talking to their women, touching them. Others were craning their heads out the windows, intent on getting a preview of their destination.

The door opened, flooding the previously sealed interior with instant heat and rich scents—tropical flowers and an underlying layer of rotting vegetation.

The air was almost too thick to breathe, or perhaps it was only the tight feeling in her chest that was giving her problems.

Minutes later, they stepped into white-hot sunlight and descended a flight of stairs.

But it wasn't the heat that had Maddy's skin breaking out with a thin layer of perspiration. It was the gun emplacements manned by uniformed guards at the corners of the low metal buildings facing them.

4

As THEY CROSSED fifty yards of oven-hot tarmac, Jack was cataloguing details and impressions. The heat. The guards. The people around him.

But most of all he was aware of the woman at his side. He knew her nerves were stretched taut. Unfortunately, he had something to do with that. He should have turned off that porno movie on the plane as soon as he'd seen what it was. But something had stayed his hand. He'd wanted to catch Maddy's reaction. Wanted to find out if she was operating on sexual overdrive, the way he was.

He'd gotten his answer—in spades. And it had given him a rush to know she was as hot and needy as he was. Then he'd silently conceded that his mind had gotten pretty off track from what he was supposed to be doing.

But then he'd known the danger all along. Known that working with Maddy was going to be a considerable distraction. That was one of the reasons he'd tried to get her to stay home. None of his arguments had been persuasive. He'd been left with a feeling of failure mixed with anticipation, and with the knowledge that he was responsible for her safety, which meant that he had to keep his head screwed on straight.

His hand clenched around the strap of his carry-on bag. Deliberately he switched his attention to the guards who manned the gun emplacements at the corners of the building's roof. An interesting show of force from a man who was welcoming a group of friends to a house party.

Well, probably not friends. He doubted if Oliver Reynard had any bosom buddies. But the gunners did make a statement about security on the island.

He was amused to note the varying reactions of the people around him as they closed the distance between themselves and the over-equipped guards. The men stood up straighter. Most of the women—including Maddy—moved closer to their guys, as if hard male bodies could protect them from machine-gun bullets.

One of Reynard's private army was standing at the entrance to the building where they were headed. Jack had studied their insignia, and he knew that the guy was a lieutenant. Kind of a high rank to be playing doorman, which meant that he was there for more than ceremonial purposes. He was taking a good look at the deplaning passengers—and he'd be asked for his opinion later.

As the first of the guests drew near, the man clicked his heels. A nice touch, Jack thought. Kind of like a storm trooper.

The lieutenant opened a heavy metal door that said Passport Control/Customs and held it deferentially as the passengers filed past.

Jack looked around at Passport Control and Customs. What he saw was a stark, low-ceilinged room with a bare cement floor and corrugated metal walls that might have been constructed and maintained in any third-world country.

Quite a different setting from the luxury of the waiting room in New York. Lord, what had Dawn Winston thought when she passed through this grim space?

Probably that it was an anteroom to hell. If she'd been in any shape to observe her surroundings, which she might not have been. According to his information, she'd been drugged when she'd arrived on the island.

For him, it was reminiscent of a prison intake area. Or

the perfect shooting gallery. With Reynard's guests as the targets. If the guy wanted to wipe out a whole planeload of passengers in one swift barrage, he had the perfect venue. For a sick moment, Jack couldn't let go of that image. Reynard had invited these gangsters here to eliminate the competition.

Maybe the notion had invaded Maddy's mind, too, because he felt her press her shoulder against his.

He schooled his features into a cocky smile. "We'll get to the good part soon. Our host just wants to make a point."

"Which is?"

"That he means business—when he wants to."

"Um," she answered, raising her gaze to look at one of the video cameras recording the whole scene.

He studied the fine sheen of perspiration on her cheeks. "You're probably hot," he murmured. "Why don't you take off your jacket and get comfortable."

"Yes. Right."

As she took the jacket off and folded it over her arm, a disembodied voice issued from a loudspeaker. "Have your passports ready. You may line up double file with your companions, facing the counter at the end of the room."

The passengers dutifully shuffled two by two into line like animals headed for the Ark. Letting others go ahead of them, Jack made sure that he and Maddy ended up in about the middle of the group where he could observe the procedure before it was their turn. He watched with interest as Don Fowler and his honey were asked a series of questions by a uniformed official. Then their carry-on luggage was opened and examined. Finally, they were ushered toward a duo of guards—one male and one female who went over their bodies with hand-held metal detectors. As the machines beeped, Fowler was relieved of his cell phone and pager.

Did the jerk really think he was going to carry communications equipment into this place, Jack wondered as he saw the drug lord ask for his property back.

"I'm sorry, sir," the attendant answered. "If you wish to make a call to the mainland, we have excellent facilities that can be placed at your disposal."

I'll bet, Jack thought. Excellent and monitored.

Finally, Fowler gave up the argument and hustled his woman through a door beyond the customs barrier.

The jerk who'd pulled the stunt in the rest room and his girlfriend were next. As Jack watched Mr. Sexy's body language, he could tell the guy was nervous. It turned out there was a good reason. They passed the question and answer session, but when it came time for the metal detector, the guards found something a little more significant than a cell phone or a pager. The lunkhead was wearing an ankle holster, with a small-caliber pistol that apparently hadn't been detected back in New York. Perhaps that had been on purpose, Jack mused. Maybe Reynard wanted to assert his authority on his own turf.

And the inspector didn't simply take it away. He pushed a button that activated an alarm. As a deep, clanging noise filled the room, more armed guards materialized from a door at the side of the enclosure.

Again Mr. Sexy and his honey became the center of attention, although this time the guy wasn't swaggering. A burly guard took him by the arm and hustled him swiftly out of the area. His honey was marched off behind him. She tried to resist, but the guards kept her moving, and the last thing Jack şaw was her pink-clad shoulders begin to shake with reaction.

Too bad for her, Jack thought. She'd hooked up with the wrong scumball.

The small drama took less than a minute and left the group standing in the customs area in stunned silence.

"Next," the uniformed official called out.

Jormo Kardofski and his lady stepped smartly up to the barrier. They were both acting like they had nothing in the world to worry about. Indeed, Jormo was absolutely clean. Not even one of those computerized date books. Maybe he'd been here before. Or maybe he was smart enough to know that electronic devices and weapons were not duty-free items on Orchid Island.

Jack and Maddy were next, and he strove to project the same sense of nonchalance that Kardofski had exhibited. He'd known enough to leave his toys back in New York, even if it did make him feel naked going unarmed into this hostile environment. But that didn't mean they were home free. The real worry was Maddy's makeup case with its hidden transmitter.

He saw her fingers tighten on the handle. But she kept her expression carefully neutral as she turned the box over to the guards.

Jack reminded himself to breathe as the man snapped the latch and lifted the lid, but the contents had the intended effect. After a quick check through the tubes of lipstick and bottles of foundation, the man turned it back to her.

Well, a major hurdle crossed, Jack thought as he and Maddy submitted themselves to the body inspection.

Even though he knew there should be no problems, Jack fought to stay cool as the man's hands moved up and down his body.

"You're free to go in," the guard informed him. "Enjoy your stay with us."

"Thank you."

He reached for Maddy's hand, and they strolled toward

a door at the far side of the room where the other cleared passengers had exited.

As he pushed it open and stepped through, he had the sensation of walking from a station on the way to hell into a portal to heaven. Or at least as closely as a tropical paradise could duplicate heaven. The door led directly from the customs area to a covered flagstone patio bordered by manicured planters edged with lava rock. A delicate green carpet crawled across the earth and onto the rocks. Rising from the ground cover were arrangements of small palms and pink and red bougainvillea that climbed wooden posts and wound gracefully through vertical supports overhead.

In one corner of the patio, a small combo clad in red-and-yellow costumes was playing soft island music. Opposite them, a buffet table took up one whole side of the area, heaped with a spread that put the one at JFK to shame.

Jack heard Maddy let out a rush of breath as if she were finally free to relax. Of course she wasn't.

That was probably what Reynard wanted everyone to think when they took in the contrast between the customs area and this outpost from Bali Ha'i. They'd passed the test—and now they were being rewarded.

But he was sure they were probably still being videotaped. And he'd better remind Maddy of that fact. As he gave her an expansive grin, he said, "A lot of potential for home movies here."

"Yes," she murmured, and he gave her points for not trying to spot the cameras.

"Happy?" he asked, aware that the question carried several meanings. Anybody listening would assume it was Jack Craig making small talk with his lady while they waited for the party to begin. But Jack Connors was also asking Maddy Guthrie how she was feeling now about having come on this mission.

"Deliriously happy," she answered without missing a beat.

"Glad to hear it." He casually stroked a finger up her arm, feeling gooseflesh bloom under his touch.

She might look cool, he thought. But she was strung tight as a Nashville banjo. Which she should be. Because they were about to put their charade to the ultimate test.

A waiter wearing black pants, a white shirt and a red sash offered them planter's punch, and they each accepted a tall glass. Maddy took a large swallow. Jack sipped at his while he waited for something memorable to happen.

He didn't have long to wait. The last of the passengers were nibbling shrimp and tiny crab cakes or sipping their drinks when the combo stopped in the middle of "Yellow Bird" and played a little flourish.

As the band members glanced toward their right, Jack followed their gaze. When he saw a sleek black panther glide onto the patio, he thrust Maddy protectively behind him.

Then he relaxed a fraction as he realized that the large cat wore a rhinestone-studded collar to which a stout leather leash was attached. A man followed along behind the animal, holding the other end of the lead firmly in his right hand.

It was Reynard, Jack knew from the photographs he'd studied.

The Master of Orchid Island. The man who could do anything here he wanted. With anybody.

Dawn. Or himself and Maddy.

And if he decided to bring a jungle cat to a social gathering—so be it. The cat appeared to have learned some manners, but if the animal sprang at anyone, Reynard would simply be dragged along behind it.

Or more likely, he'd let go, Jack thought as he shifted his position slightly, still keeping Maddy close, but trying not to act as if he thought their lives were being threatened.

Would the guards shoot if the beast started mauling guests? Or would that just be part of the entertainment?

Aware that he'd very effectively garnered everyone's attention, Reynard stepped onto the patio, his eyes sweeping over the crowd. His gaze noted Jack and Maddy, moved on, then came back to them.

Apparently they were of special interest.

Jack would have liked to take that as a good sign, but he couldn't muster any real enthusiasm for the assumption.

As Reynard studied them, he returned the interest, sure that Maddy was taking the same opportunity.

Somehow mere photographs hadn't caught the essence of the man, the subtle atmosphere of evil and depravity that wafted around him like a cloud of poison gas.

Jack pulled back from the fanciful notion and tried to be objective. For example, the pictures had conveyed an aura of power that had made him look larger than he really was. In fact, the man was only slightly over medium height, trim and lithe, with dark hair just beginning to gray at the temples, a healthy-looking tan and deep-set gray eyes that seemed to miss nothing. He was dressed in navy trousers and a brilliant white shirt open at the neck. In the V of his collar, several heavy gold chains nestled in crisp salt-and-pepper hair. A smile flickered at the corners of his well-shaped mouth as he observed the reactions of his guests to the pet he'd chosen to bring along to the party.

"I assure you, Sabina is a very well-trained kitty. She only mauls guests who try to bring weapons or other contraband into my island paradise."

Silence greeted the pronouncement.

He gave a small laugh that grated along Jack's nerve endings. "Please, that's supposed to be a joke. Mr. Sandstrom and his lady have not been punished for breaking my rules. The only penalty is expulsion. They will be returning to the U.S. as soon as my jet refuels; and since they'll have the whole cabin to themselves, they can have sex right in their seats." He laughed, letting everyone know he was fully aware of the incident on the plane. Then he stretched out his arm. "If we haven't already met, I am Oliver Reynard, and I welcome you to my home."

Jack was relieved when he hooked the end of the leash over a metal post and snapped a ring into place, securing the animal. Sabina lay down on a straw mat and began to lick her paw. But when Reynard wandered over to the buffet table, forked up a wad of roast beef and tossed it to her, she caught it in midair, her curved claws shooting out as she speared the morsel and conveyed it to her mouth.

The crowd flicked their attention back to the cat's owner as he began speaking again. "I want you all to have a wonderful time while you are my guests," he continued. "In your rooms you'll find a leather-bound loose-leaf book describing some of the attractions here and the hours of operation. The Greek outdoor pool. The Roman indoor baths. The ladies' spa. The gym. The golf course. The shooting range. You can read up on them later. Right now, I want you to unwind. I watched your arrival on video. And I understand why you might be reluctant to introduce yourselves. You are business rivals of sorts." He turned his palms up. "But there are no business rivals here. We're all friends. So I'll break the ice." He pointed to the couple on his right. "Arnold Ving and his charming lady, Cynthia." Then he went on to name the others. "Don Fowler and Rosalie. Jormo Kardofski and Buffy."

None of the women appeared to have last names because in Reynard's world equality of the sexes hadn't yet
been invented. Jack had known that, of course. But hearing it in person was chilling.

He and Maddy were the last to be named, so that Reynard was standing next to them when he finished the in-
troductions and bade his guests mingle.

"I was so looking forward to meeting you and discussing business," he said to Jack. "But I had no idea
your lady was so lovely. Let me extend a special welcome
to you, my dear." He reached for her hand, and there was
no way Maddy could refuse the contact.

He held her hand for several seconds too long, then
stroked a beautifully manicured thumb over her knuckles
before releasing her.

"Maddy. Is that short for Madeleine?"

"No. My parents were just plain folks, with just plain
tastes," she answered.

"So where did you and Jack meet?"

She gave the answer they'd rehearsed. "Las Vegas."

"Were you a showgirl?"

"Oh my, no. I'm not that talented. I was a lounge host-
ess."

"I'm sure you're very talented," Reynard answered,
continuing to eye her with a sexually predatory look that
sent a zing of alarm knifing through Jack. She might not
be the most beautiful woman in the room, but she had a
feminine quality that apparently attracted Reynard.

The man's eyes flicked back to Jack. "It would be de-
lightful to get together for some fun and games—just the
three of us," he murmured.

Jack was pretty sure he wasn't suggesting a private session of "Name that Tune."

Hoping the sudden knot of ice in the pit of his stomach
didn't show on his face, he stepped closer to Maddy and

slipped an arm possessively around her shoulder. "My lady and I have a very special relationship. I don't share her with anyone else."

Reynard smiled, but the smile didn't meet his eyes. "It's always a challenge to encounter a man who stands on his principles."

"Um," Jack answered, deliberately running his hand up and down Maddy's bare arm, feeling the fine hairs ripple. Not from his touch, he surmised. From Reynard's obvious interest.

Just great! It was clear the man had taken a fancy to her.

Reynard kept his pale eyes on her for several more seconds, then gestured to the rest of the patio. "Well, I should personally greet my other guests. My welcoming cocktail party is at seven o'clock. Don't be late."

"We won't. And I deeply appreciate your having asked us here," Jack added, the words almost sticking in his throat. Then he murmured, "We had to get up early to catch your flight. Would it be possible to relax in our room for the afternoon?"

"Certainly. Your checked luggage has already been sent to your villa." He flicked a hand toward one of the uniformed attendants stationed around the room, and the man trotted over.

"Sir?"

"Henri, show Mr. Craig and his companion to their quarters."

"Yes, sir."

As their host strolled toward Fowler and his woman, Maddy let out a little breath. Jack slid his hand down and caught her fingers in his.

"I've been looking forward to getting you alone," he whispered as Henri took their carry-on luggage.

She gave him a grateful nod, and they followed Henri

out of the patio area and into a landscaped garden that would have taken his breath away if he'd had any to spare.

How many men did it take to maintain the island's grounds, he wondered as he spotted several gardeners in green overalls. One was plucking yellowed vegetation from plants. Another was raking up leaves that had fallen on the ground. And a third was planting masses of small pink flowers.

He looked up as they passed, his interest more than casual. Well, that was logical, since some of the gardeners were probably from the security force—dressed in workmen's uniforms.

The path, made of flat limestone rocks cemented together, wound across a golf-course-quality lawn bordered by a riot of flowers, then into the cool shade of a manicured tropical forest where parrots watched them from perches scattered through the foliage.

"Leg or breast man?" one of the parrots squawked.

Jack laughed, glad the bird's off-color comment had broken some of the tension.

"Bedroom eyes," another chimed in.

"Naughty birds!" Maddy said, the comment imitated by one of the feathered commentators.

"I guess he's got them trained the way he wants them," Jack answered. *Like the rest of his minions,* he silently added.

There were side paths with signs pointing to various structures whose pastel stucco walls and red tile roofs were vaguely visible beyond the foliage. "Hibiscus Cottage. Jasmine Cottage. Plumbago Cottage."

Henri took a path toward "Agapanthus Cottage."

Lily of the Nile, Jack thought as he caught sight of the lavender flowers on their tall stalks—planted in beds along the front of a large one-story Spanish-style house.

"Here you are, sir," Henri said, bending to unlock the door, then handing the key to Jack.

Maddy was quiet as the attendant showed them around the sumptuous interior—pointing out the well-stocked bar and the VCR in the large living room, the lighting controls at the built-in bedside tables, the king-sized marble bathroom with its separate glass-enclosed shower and huge soaking tub.

Did the VCR come with a supply of tapes like the one from the plane, Jack wondered, unable to snuff out a stab of arousal as he remembered the scene he and Maddy had watched together.

His attention snapped back to Henri who was flipping through the Orchid Island brag book, showing off the glossy photographs.

He closed the leather cover and swept his hand around the room. "Is everything satisfactory, sir?"

"Perfectly." Reaching into his pocket, Jack brought out his wallet and extracted a twenty-dollar bill, but it was quickly waved away.

"No need to tip here, sir. Mr. Reynard takes excellent care of the staff. Is there anything else I can get you? If there's anything you need, don't hesitate to call. My pager number is 53."

"Will do," Jack answered heartily as he watched Henri head toward the door.

THE RECEPTION WAS STILL in full swing when Oliver excused himself, pleased with the way his guests were loosening up. Two stunning women had been flagrantly offered to him, and he might have accepted the offers, if he wasn't lusting after Maddy Griffin.

Taking hold of Sabina's leash, he led her back to the small zoo he'd had stocked with interesting animals from around the world—all in facsimiles of their natural habitats.

After turning his pet over to the zoologist who ran the place, he headed back to his private quarters, thinking about how well everything had gone at the reception. In his mind's eye, he pictured the setting and the people, then narrowed his focus to Jack Craig. The man was a tough customer. And he seemed to have developed a strong attachment to his sweet little companion.

Still, there must be a way to persuade him to share, because one thing Oliver knew: he was going to have Maddy Griffin before she left the island.

So what were Craig's weaknesses? He went back to the folders on his desk, finding nothing he'd overlooked. Well, there was more he could discover on the man. He just had to keep asking questions of the right people. He debated booting his computer and getting in touch with some of his contacts on the mainland.

No, there would be time enough for that later. It might be more interesting to see how they were enjoying their first few minutes of privacy on the island.

He walked down a short hall and into a darkened room that looked much like the control room of a television studio.

There was a duplicate room in the security building, where his men were randomly monitoring the activities in the guest quarters, as well as in selected public areas of the complex. All of the feeds were being recorded on videotape. And all of the screens could be controlled independently at this location and the security monitoring station.

In addition, there were microphones he could switch on independently, in case the video monitors went down—which had happened on occasions.

Some of the screens on the opposite wall were blank.

Others showed views of rooms in the guest cottages and visitor's wing of the main house. Jack Craig and Maddy Griffin had been assigned to Agapanthus Villa, one of the most luxurious. Sitting down at the console, he flicked several switches and brought in a view of the living room—where he found the occupants standing, facing each other.

Leaning back, he watched the scene with interest. Too bad Maddy was facing away from the camera.

THE MOMENT SHE HEARD the front door close behind the man who had shown them to the villa, Maddy turned toward Jack, opened her mouth to speak. He wasn't sure what she was going to say. But the look of distress in her blue eyes told him that he couldn't risk any hidden microphones picking up her comments. Or any hidden cameras catching him clamping a hand over her lips.

So before she could get any words out, he grabbed her and pulled her into his arms, his mouth coming down over hers.

The kiss was a calculated strategy to keep her from giving away any information to security guards who might be listening, but he wasn't prepared for the bolt of sensation that shot through him.

Before this morning, he hadn't touched her in days, and as soon as they'd stepped into the sexually charged atmosphere of the airport waiting room, he'd known he'd made a mistake. The admission had taken on clarity as they'd viewed the erotic video. Not exactly porn. It was more suave than that. At least until the woman had gone down on her knees and started giving the guy head.

That had been too damn much for him. Way too much, under the circumstances.

The movie had primed his pump. But not as much as the feel and the taste of Maddy. Greedy for more, he gathered her in, reveling in the sensation of rubbing his mouth back and forth against hers, sipping, stroking, then taking her lower lip between his teeth and nibbling.

It was gratifying to discover that she was as caught up in the kiss as he. He heard a little sound well from deep in her throat, a sound that incited him to riot.

The kiss went from smoldering to flash point in the space of heartbeats. He angled his head, his mouth hungry and demanding, his hands sliding down her back to cup her bottom and pull her middle against his aching erection.

He felt her small hands anchor themselves against his shoulders so that she could press her body more tightly to his.

It seemed that wasn't enough. For either one of them. When he felt her grind her hips against him, he went from civilized man to primitive male. A male hell-bent on claiming his mate.

Vivid pictures flashed in his mind. And they weren't from any movie. He saw himself tearing off Maddy's clothing, throwing her down on the bed, plunging into her hot, eager depths.

Then he thought of those same images caught on videotape—and he went very still.

"Jack?"

"We can't. Not here. Not now."

Her answer was a moan of frustration that almost cut through his objections. Almost.

With a tremendous effort, he wrenched his mouth away from hers, took her by the shoulders and set her heated body several feet away from his.

She looked up at him—dazed and confused and aroused, the tight points of her nipples clearly visible through the thin fabric of her sundress.

He stared at those tantalizing little knots of flesh. Wanting to touch. Wanting to taste. He felt almost as dazed as she looked, but he knew he had to keep his wits about him. After dragging in several ragged breaths, he managed to say, "Remember what I told you about Orchid Island, sweetheart? This place is wired for sound and pictures. For security reasons, of course. But I'm not taking a chance on making love to you in front of a hidden camera."

His eyes stayed locked with hers until he was sure she had taken his meaning. This wasn't about making love. It was about discussing their mission.

They might want to assume they were alone. But if they did, they were both fools. Dead fools.

"A camera in our room?" she gasped, looking around with a panicked expression on her face. "I know what you said. But I can't believe we don't have privacy here...."

"Yeah, well, hold on a few minutes before I give you any action, baby."

He began to prowl the bedroom, like an angry man who isn't used to having his pleasure interrupted.

His eyes scanned the shelves, the books, the knick-knacks, even the mirror on the ceiling above the bed. He had considerable training in unearthing spy equipment, and he found what he was looking for in less than ten minutes. A wicker basket high up on one of the shelves with an open weave large enough to hide the lens of a video camera.

MADDY CLASPED HER HANDS in front of her to keep them from trembling as she watched Jack pull the camera down, then hold his face a few inches from the lens.

Deliberately spacing his words, he said, "Mr. Reynard, I understand your need for security, and I appreciate your desire to keep tabs on your guests. But I will not tolerate recording equipment in my personal space.''

That said, he opened the French doors, took the camera outside and smashed it on the limestone patio. Then he repeated the procedure with the camera's twin, which he unearthed in the living room inside a planter.

She squeezed her hands together tighter, hating the sick shaky feeling that trembled inside her, hating her own unprofessional behavior. She was familiar with covert operations. She had trained for this mission. But she knew now that she'd just been kidding herself.

The airplane and the customs area had been bad enough. But it had been Reynard who had struck terror in her heart—terror as he'd looked at her with those pale, predatory eyes. And Jack had been the only thing standing between her and the man's lust.

She had been about to blurt out her fear and horror— until Jack had taken her into his arms and prevented her from speaking. He'd also reminded her of the stakes they were playing for—their lives and Dawn's.

When he'd kissed her, she'd tried to cast everything from her mind but the taste of his mouth, the feel of his body against hers. She'd used blind, mindless sex to try and wipe away the image of Reynard.

She wasn't proud of that. And the present tightness in her chest did nothing to make her feel more competent as a covert agent with a vital mission to fulfil.

She shuddered as Jack came back into the room, his gaze appraising as it swept over her.

That knowing look made her straighten her shoulders.

"Well, I've taken care of two of the cameras," he said with an easy shrug. "There could be more. There could be microphones I haven't spotted."

She gave him a tight nod, telling him she understood

there was no way they could talk about their assignment in these surroundings.

"At least there won't be video equipment aimed at the bed when I screw you," he said, then added in the same casual tone, "although I do admit that the thought of being watched has dampened my ardor for the moment. I have my faults, but exhibitionism isn't one of them."

The tossed-off comment made her mouth go dry.

"Um," was all she could manage as she struggled to come to grips with reality—their present reality.

She was still a bundle of nerves. He'd morphed into Mr. Cool the way he had that first night back at Winston headquarters. Still, she knew she hadn't been imagining the hot encounter a few minutes ago. He'd wanted her every bit as badly as she'd wanted him. But that was probably just an exercise in letting off steam. And he was the one who'd come to his senses and gone in search of hidden video cameras.

Now he was telling her that he might not have taken care of the problem. That they might still be under surveillance.

He let her absorb that before asking, "Want to go out and do a little exploring?"

Out of the cottage. Where they might be able to talk.

"That sounds like fun," she answered gamely.

"Good girl. Why don't you slip into something more comfortable first?"

"Okay," she agreed, then realized that taking off her clothes in this room might be treating someone to a peep show. A guard. Or Reynard.

Reynard!

Swallowing a sudden sick feeling, she rummaged in the suitcase that had been set out on a stand in the dressing area. Grabbing a pair of white slacks and a turquoise

T-shirt decorated with bright tropical fish, she disappeared into the bathroom.

Please, Lord, not in here too, she prayed as she glanced from the toilet to the tub and then to the shower. With her bottom lip between her teeth, she pulled off the sundress, wishing she'd been able to wear a bra underneath.

In one smooth motion she tossed the dress onto the counter while she pulled the T-shirt over her head. The slacks followed in record time. Then she zipped out of the bathroom and grabbed a bra.

Jack had come back into the room, and gave her a warning look. "Nervous?"

"Well, the idea of putting on a free show doesn't set too well," she allowed.

"Yeah. It's kind of different for me. I can just think of this place as the guys' locker room." As he spoke, he reached for the hem of his shirt and pulled it over his head. Her eyes were drawn to the magnificent expanse of his chest, and for a moment she couldn't stop herself from remembering the feel of his hair-roughened skin and hard muscles pressed to her softness.

Maybe he was remembering that, too, because he went very still, his gaze focusing on the front of the T-shirt where she suspected that her nipples were clearly visible through the sea of fish swimming across her front. But she didn't look down to find out.

For a long moment, neither of them moved, then he seemed to give himself a mental shake and turned to his own suitcase.

"Let's go see if we can find the beach. Maybe there's a hidden cove where we can enjoy each other's company in private."

He ushered her out the French doors and across the patio to another path that led through the foliage. In the distance, she could see more villas, but the path stayed away from all of them. Apparently Reynard believed in giving his guests privacy—except from himself.

She wanted to ask Jack if he thought the cameras were to satisfy some kinky sexual appetite of their host. Or if they were for security reasons. Probably both, she decided.

She wanted to ask a lot more questions, but since Jack only made small talk, she followed his lead, and she soon realized why.

Jack nodded toward the greenery on one side of the path, and she caught a flash of movement.

With a little frisson, she realized they weren't alone. Two men in camouflage outfits were keeping pace with them, outfits that made them all but invisible in the dense foliage.

5

MADDY SUCKED IN A ragged breath, then let it out slowly.

Was there no place where they could find some privacy, no place where they could talk about the assignment that had brought them to Orchid Island, and about the unfortunate complication of Oliver Reynard's interest in her?

Jack shot the men an annoyed look.

It was all she could to keep from clinging to him. Instead she made her touch casual as they rounded a curve, and she saw blue sky ahead of them.

She could hear the crashing of surf, smell the tang of sea air, feel the wind coming off the water. The path ended on a ridge that sloped down to one of the most beautiful white sand beaches she'd ever seen. Together they stood for a moment staring out at the breaking waves.

"Want to go down there?" Jack asked.

"Not in three-hundred-dollar shoes, I guess," she answered, thinking that they'd lost the chance for a private conversation.

"Yeah, well, let's go spend some of Reynard's money. Why don't you go to his spa and primp up for that party tonight?"

"Oh, right," she answered, following his change of subject. During their preparation sessions they'd discussed various strategies and had decided that one place Maddy might pick up valuable information was the beauty salon. "Do you think I can get an appointment?"

Jack gave her a little grin. "Sure. They're there to serve

you." Turning to face the closest guard, he said, "Can you direct us to the ladies' spa?"

Surprise spread across the man's broad, brown face. But he stepped out of the shadows and answered with a polite, "Yes, sir."

As he came closer to them, Maddy saw that, like Henri, he was wearing a name tag. It said Evans.

She also noted that he had the strap of an Uzi slung casually over his shoulder.

Jack didn't look fazed by the weaponry. Probably the character he was playing had his own private security force of armed thugs back home. "Then lead the way. But take us past the path to our villa first, so my sweetie will be able to find her way back."

The man led them past the villa and back to the main garden area, which they crossed on a diagonal, then took another short walkway that led to a building that looked like an Egyptian temple.

"Right here, sir."

Jack inclined his head toward Maddy. "Then I'll expect you back in a couple of hours. All dolled up for me."

"Yes," she answered with what she hoped sounded like eager anticipation. "I'll see you later."

Jack turned and left her alone. Very alone, she thought with an inward shudder. If Reynard knew she was here… She ruthlessly cut off the thought.

Near the entrance to the building were several gardeners, apparently busy plucking more leaves from the manicured lawn. Probably they were positioned to pick up tidbits of conversation, too, Maddy thought. She also thought that the island was making her paranoid. Which was probably a good thing—because she understood the risks now. In New York she hadn't quite wrapped her head around the level of danger. Now she was very aware that any slipup could be fatal.

With an inward sigh, she pulled open one of the spa's heavy glass doors. Inside, the hard marble surfaces were softened by sweeping draperies, magnificent vases of cut flowers and deep, cushioned furniture. Reynard might not treat women as equals, but apparently he knew how to cater to them when it suited him.

Carrying out the Egyptian theme, a receptionist dressed in a short tunic came forward as soon as Maddy stepped inside. Like the guard who had showed them here, she was an islander, with coffee-colored skin and large brown eyes. "Can I help you?"

"Yes, my name is Maddy Griffin. I'd like my nails redone. And my hair sculpted into something special for tonight."

A woman who had been sitting in a chair near the desk jumped up. "It would be a pleasure to serve you. Right this way. Can I get you something? Iced tea? Coffee?"

"Iced coffee would be wonderful."

The drink came almost immediately on a tray with cream, skim milk and sugar syrup.

"We can do your nails first."

Maddy followed the attendant to a table and found she was seated next to one of the other women from the plane, who was having her nails polished.

She looked up, surprise registering on her classic features. Then her lips turned up in a smile that seemed a bit forced. "Hi, I'm Rosalie. We were introduced, but I'm so bad at names."

"Maddy," she said as her manicurist took one hand and began to remove perfectly good polish.

"It's good to get away from the guys for a while," Rosalie commented.

Maddy nodded.

"I'm never so relaxed as when I'm being fussed over," she murmured.

Maddy agreed in the same languid tone, although if there was anything she hated, it was being fussed over.

Rosalie lowered her voice conspiratorially. "I noticed you sitting back there by the rest room on the plane. What did you think about the couple going in there?"

Before Maddy could reply, her new friend answered for her. "It was disgusting, don't you think?"

Well, she could certainly agree on that. "Very," she answered as the manicurist dipped her hands into a bowl of viscous liquid.

"Could you hear anything through the door?"

"No," Maddy lied.

The woman's voice dropped even lower. "It turned Don on. What about your guy?"

"Yes," Maddy admitted.

"Don waited until we got to our room." She gave a little laugh. "It was quick. Hardly even mussed my hair. But that's Don's specialty. The quick in and out."

Maddy made a little choking sound. She didn't explain that Jack had spent the time right after their arrival finding and smashing video cameras.

"Just let me put a quick-dry layer on your nails," the manicurist interrupted softly. "Then you can go have that nap you mentioned."

"Yes. Thank you," Rosalie said. When the woman was finished, she held up her bright red nails to admire the polish.

Maddy tried not to sigh with relief as Rosalie departed. Looking around, she saw that she was the only remaining guest in that part of the spa. As she leaned back in her chair, she regarded the delicate woman with thick, jet-black hair who had begun to work on her cuticles. The woman's name tag identified her as Juanita.

"Have you worked here long?" she asked.

"Not too long. I lived off the island when I was little."

"Where?"

"Oh, here and there."

So Juanita didn't want to talk about her background, Maddy thought as she switched topics and asked, "Um...how do you like your job?"

"It's what I know. I like to make women's hands look pretty." She finished with Maddy's cuticles and gestured toward a tray of bottles. "Which one you like best?"

"That one," she answered, pointing to a soft pink. As the manicurist began to stroke the color on a nail, she asked, "Do the same women come back to visit the island?"

"Sometimes yes, sometimes no." She looked down, applying more polish to Maddy's nails.

When she and Jack had talked about the spa, she'd assumed she could ask some questions. Her recent experiences had made her cautious.

"I bet all the women are young."

"Of course."

"Any teenagers?"

Juanita shrugged. "I'm not sure."

"I have a young friend who came here not too long ago. Donna," she said, giving a name that was close to Dawn's. "She's got light brown hair and big green eyes. And she has three holes pierced in each of her ears. Did you meet her?"

The manicurist looked up, then quickly down again. "I didn't see her," she said carefully. Too carefully.

Maddy stared at Juanita's hand. It was shaking slightly, so that she had to stop applying polish for several seconds.

The woman raised her eyes, studying Maddy intently. Then she went back to work.

"We never talk about other guests," she murmured. "You understand?"

"Yes," Maddy answered. Her next comments were about the beautiful landscaping and the luxurious rooms.

Was she reading too much into the woman's reaction? Or had she seen Dawn? She couldn't be sure. But she had the feeling Juanita knew something. And she realized suddenly that the woman had specifically asked to work on her after hearing her name.

She gave none of her thoughts away as she held up her nails admiringly. "Thank you," she said.

"You come back to the spa while you're here. We are happy to serve you."

"Yes. Thanks," she answered, thinking that the woman's tone of voice was almost an order.

Juanita turned her over to a beautician who styled her hair into a romantic upsweep. Congratulating herself that nobody had come in to arrest her while she sat under the hair dryer, she headed back to the villa.

And she got a little jolt of pleasure as she walked back into the villa and watched Jack's eyes light up.

"Well, you're looking dazzling," he murmured.

The compliment made her glow, until she remembered he wasn't speaking entirely for her benefit.

"Why thank you, sir," she answered, repressing the impulse to glance around the room, looking for microphones.

He was studying her carefully, and she realized her face betrayed some of the disquiet she'd felt here earlier.

"So what's Reynard's spa like?" he asked.

"Nice, and there are some…unexpected touches," she answered, wanting to tell him about Juanita and their conversation. But that was out of the question until she knew they could speak privately.

He stared at her, as if he were hoping to get the information from direct brain-to-brain transmission.

She lifted one shoulder, then said, "We had to get up so early. Maybe I should relax before the party tonight."

He sighed. "Yeah, okay."

Before her own frustration could reach boiling point, she turned and left the room.

Her first few hours on the island were so disturbing that she thought relaxing would be impossible. But after she'd carefully propped her head to keep from mussing her hairdo, she closed her eyes and drifted away from the world.

He should wake her, Jack thought, as he stood staring down at Maddy. She needed to start getting ready. Instead he found himself standing beside the king-size bed staring down at her, watching the gentle rise and fall of her breasts.

Ten more minutes, she could use ten more minutes' sleep, he decided as he wedged his hands into his pockets to keep from reaching for her.

It was an interesting exercise, because he knew it was going to happen sooner or later. One taste of Maddy Guthrie had only whetted his appetite for her. And he needed more. Craved more. He should have kept his hands off of her in the airport lounge and then in the plane. But he'd succumbed to the temptation, and now he was paying the price in frustration.

With an inward curse, he forced his mind to switch gears. She'd found something out this afternoon at the spa. Something that disturbed her. Or gotten her wondering. And he wanted to know what the hell it was. But he couldn't ask. He couldn't even write a damn note because he didn't know if he'd gotten all the cameras.

He'd prowled around after she'd left, looking for more bugs. But he hadn't found anything obvious. Still, he had to assume there were a couple of mikes active in this place.

He'd told her this assignment was going to be difficult, and he'd thought he was prepared. Now he felt as if a crushing weight was pressing down on his shoulders.

He sighed, and Maddy stirred. Her eyes blinked open, and in that first unguarded moment of transition from sleep to waking, she gave him a smile that made his heart turn over.

Then he watched as memory flooded back. Memory of where they were and what they had to do.

"Rested?" he murmured, stepping closer to her—his hand moving toward her like a magnet to steel.

"Um-hum."

She looked like she expected him to climb in bed with her. Which wasn't on the program until later.

Later. God, what was he going to do when their charade dictated that they crawl under the covers together?

Turning abruptly from the bed, he went to the closet where her evening dresses were hanging. They were all indecent. Either too tight or too low. Too clingy or too transparent.

When he'd selected them, he'd told Maddy she would have to fit in. Now he was thinking that he'd probably still been trying to get her to stay home. And, failing that, to punish her for putting herself in danger.

Well, he hadn't known just how much danger. Now he cursed inwardly again. That slimy bastard, Reynard, had a special interest in her. And the clothing was going to put her on display for him.

With a sigh, he picked a slinky midnight-blue number that he knew she was going to hate. Yet the thought of seeing her in it made his already overheated blood boil. He rationalized the choice by telling himself there wasn't anything more modest.

MADDY STOOD in front of the mirror trying not to tug at the hem of the dress. The damn thing left half her thighs showing. But if she tried to pull it down, that would only display her cleavage to better advantage.

Trying to relax her mouth, she gave her hair and makeup one more inspection. And her jewels. A necklace, earrings and a matching bracelet. Real diamonds—provided by Stan Winston—which she hoped were going to make it home with her.

Satisfied, she marched out of the bathroom in the two-inch heels that went with the dress. At least they weren't as bad as the pair she'd worn that first night. She'd told Jack she couldn't manage anything that high, not and move with any degree of speed.

The expression of lust on Jack's face when she stepped into the bedroom was almost worth it—almost. She wanted to sail past him out the door, but she knew that would be out of character for the woman she was supposed to be. So she waited while he shrugged into his tuxedo jacket, then checked his bow tie in the mirror.

Lord, he was devastating in formal attire. All the more so because the dark jacket and pants hid the lean muscular body she knew was beneath the clothing.

"Ready to go have some fun?" he asked.

She managed not to grimace as she answered, "Yes."

She'd wondered how they were going to find the party site. But as soon as they stepped out of the cottage, she found rows of small lights along the path—blinking in sequence and pointing them in the right direction. Like that airplane emergency lighting that was supposed to guide you to the exit in case of disaster. Only now they were heading *for* the disaster, not away.

As they emerged from under the trees, there was no doubt where they were going—toward a white wedding cake of a house that blazed into the darkness from a hundred windows.

Apparently the idea of energy conservation hadn't reached Orchid Island. Or more likely, Reynard didn't care how much money he spent on luxuries.

She confirmed the opinion as she encountered the air-conditioning which wafted into the tropical night through the open double doors. Along with the cool air came music—a big band sound played by what must be a full-size orchestra.

As Maddy and Jack strolled through the door, she automatically scanned the guests. The men were all wearing the latest fashion in tuxedos. The women were in gowns that left good portions of their skin showing. One number seemed to be all net, except for slightly more opaque patches covering crotch and nipples. If the women's clothing was light on fabric, their accessories made up for it. The gold and gems on display could have stocked a good-size jewelry store.

Through the crowd, she caught sight of the panther, its chain secured to a sturdy post at the side of the room. It was sitting up, watching the people as though contemplating its next meal.

Switching her gaze away from the animal, she saw Don Fowler watching her and Jack with narrowed eyes. Then he bent to Rosalie and said something, and they both laughed.

The little exchange made Maddy pause. Like Reynard, Fowler had apparently taken special note of her and Jack. Actually, he'd done it before. Back in the airport departure lounge. Did the mobster and his lady know something? Something incriminating?

Her mind spun back to the conversation in the beauty salon. It had seemed friendly enough—women talk. Nothing consequential. At least she hoped not.

Beside her she noted that Jack had caught the byplay, too. Not from his expression, which gave nothing away, but she was learning to read him, and his body language cued her in.

A tinkling sound several feet away drew her attention. Buffy, Jormo Kardofski's girlfriend had shaken her arm, sending half a dozen gold bracelets clinking together.

Maddy saw then that their host was talking to the couple. The woman was stunning, Maddy thought. Why couldn't Reynard hit on her? But it was obvious that the master of the house had only polite interest in Kardofski's girlfriend.

In fact, he must have been on the lookout for Maddy and Jack, because it took only moments before he headed straight toward them.

She instinctively drew closer to her man, and he slung his arm around her shoulder in a gesture that was both protective and possessive.

"I'd ask how you're settling in," Reynard said smoothly. "But I've already been informed about the incidents with my equipment. You smashed a couple of twenty-thousand-dollar cameras."

Jack shrugged. "They shouldn't have been in my living room and bedroom. The fact that you know so quickly tells me that they were turned on."

Now it was Reynard's turn to shrug. "I have the right to stay informed about my guests' activities."

"Not their *private* activities. Not *my* private activities."

Tension crackled between the two men. Then Reynard smiled. "I suppose if you're clever enough to discover my enhancements to your quarters, then you have the right to turn the system off. But a simple request would have been just as effective."

"I have a quick temper."

"So I gather. I hope we won't have any further reason to incite you."

"I hope not."

It was Reynard who had offered a halfhearted apology, Maddy noted. Jack hadn't actually backed down.

She was starting to relax a little, when Reynard turned his attention to her again.

"You look lovely this evening, my dear."

"Thank you," she managed.

"Diamonds become you."

"Jack is very generous," she answered.

"I'd like to invite you to my private suite later tonight."

She was about to object, when Reynard continued. "To accompany Jack, of course. He and I have some business to discuss."

She glanced at Jack, waiting to take her cue from him.

"As you know, I'm eager to discuss a mutually advantageous arrangement between the two of us," he answered Reynard. "What time tonight?"

"Around ten."

"I'll be there."

"Both of you, I hope," their host said firmly.

"Um-hum."

The man smiled again, a smile of triumph, Maddy decided.

"Until later. I mustn't neglect my other guests."

"Of course not," Jack agreed.

Maddy breathed a small sigh of relief when he'd gone off to speak to Fowler and Rosalie.

"I could use a drink," Jack said, his voice casual yet carrying a taut underlayer.

They strolled to the bar, where Maddy got a wine cooler and Jack opted for a bottle of Red Stripe beer.

After several swallows he looked more in control. "We should eat a little something," he told her.

She nodded, thinking that it would be difficult to choke food down, but that he was right. They needed fuel, and they needed to create a carefully cultivated impression before they got to the real business of the evening.

Jack put the bottle of beer down on a table and helped himself to crab cakes. When an attendant took the drink away, he secured another—then another—never consuming more than a few swallows from any bottle. Yet if you didn't know he was discarding most of the beer, you might think he was on his way to getting sloshed. Which was exactly the impression he was trying to create.

It was more difficult to pull off the same act with the wine coolers, because they were served in transparent glasses, rather than dark glass bottles. But Maddy did manage to get rid of one drink before ordering another and chugging half of it in a few gulps—grateful that it wasn't too strong.

Before leaving New York, they had rehearsed their upcoming moves. Reynard might be holding Dawn somewhere in the house. And if he was, they were going to figure out where.

While they chatted with the other guests, their speech slightly slurred, they stayed close together, with Jack's arm firmly around her waist, as though he couldn't stand the idea of letting go of her.

There were two components to the image they were presenting. "Sloshed," and "Hot and bothered." So that when they slipped out of the room, it would look like they were indiscreet enough to be searching for a place where they could make love—rather than looking for a place where Reynard might have hidden a reluctant young female guest.

Maddy wasn't having any trouble with either the tipsy

or the aroused image. It was partly the tension of dealing
with Reynard. She didn't want to think about him—so
she focused on looking and sounding out of control. The
wine helped. But the major factor was her reaction to
Jack. He turned her on, and knowing she'd been given
permission to cultivate those hot feelings sent flames sear-
ing through her. Every time she moved, she felt Jack's
hip rub against hers. And when he shifted his arm so that
it slid along the side of her breast, she made a purring
sound that she imagined was audible to anyone within ten
feet.

His head turned and he looked down at her, his eyes
burning into hers.

"Let's get out of here, baby," he said in a husky drawl.

"Yes."

They swayed together, slipped toward the door. As they
reached it, she half turned and saw that Fowler was watching them intently. Still interested, apparently.

"Fowler is watching," she whispered to Jack.

"Probably jealous of me," he murmured, leading her
down a wide hallway paved with large terra-cotta tiles.
She knew that several other guests had noted their departure. Undoubtedly tongues were wagging.

Pretending she was the kind of woman who went along
with anything her man proposed, she wove down the corridor with Jack, past sitting rooms, an enormous dining
room with a carved mahogany table and chairs, and a
billiard room.

They turned a corner into another wing, and Maddy
thought for a moment that Jack might turn her loose. But
he kept her close to his side as they climbed a short flight
of steps.

At the top, he pressed her against the wall, thrust his
hips against her, and she knew without doubt that he was
aroused.

"Do you think there are any of those damn cameras around here?" he asked.

"I hope not," she muttered.

Jack bent to slide his lips along her cheek, sending a trail of heat over her skin, and she couldn't hold back a small, pleading sound.

He lurched back a few inches, his hot gaze sweeping her face before he twined his hand with hers. "Come on. I need to get horizontal."

She hadn't considered that the threat of surveillance cameras added to the realism of their search. But they turned out to be an excellent excuse for moving through the house. Each time they stepped into a room, Jack would look around, then mutter that he was worried about being watched.

They rounded another bend in the hallway, then stopped short as they came face-to-face with iron bars.

She and Jack exchanged looks. "Maybe that's the private side of the house," he mused, his hand stroking up and down her arm, sending little prickles of heat along her nerve endings as he contemplated the barrier.

The private side? Or the prison side, Maddy wondered.

"We can't go in there," she said for the benefit of any hidden microphones.

"Want to bet? When I want to get in your pants, baby, no little gate is going to stop me."

The crude statement should have made her cringe. Somehow the words only fueled the need simmering through her. He didn't really mean it, but she was beyond caring at the moment.

He inspected the lock, then took a small nail file out of his pocket and began to work on it. When it snapped open, he made a low sound of triumph.

They slipped through the gate. On the other side, Jack reached for her, brought his mouth down on hers.

The kiss might be designed to demonstrate Jack's reckless need to anyone watching, but it had a supercharging effect on Maddy. It was rough and deep, and it momentarily swept everything else out of her mind.

Her head was spinning as he linked his hand with hers and hurried down the hallway, seemingly hell-bent on finding a bed.

They stopped at the doorway to a comfortable sitting area—where a wall rack housed a dozen machine guns.

Maddy made a small sound. Jack ignored her, then pulled her away and toward the next room.

It contained office equipment: a computer, fax, printer, copy machine, all top of the line as far as Maddy could see. And filing cabinets.

She and Jack glanced at each other. The cabinets were tempting. But if anywhere in the house was likely to be under surveillance, it was this office. Rifling through the files would be taking too big a chance.

Jack gave a tight nod, and they moved on.

They had just stepped into a larger bedroom when a sound grabbed her attention—several pairs of feet moving rapidly in their direction.

"Party's over," Jack muttered, his eyes boring into hers. "And I'm afraid we're going to have to take some drastic measures."

She stared back, fear leaping into her throat. She wanted to ask what they were going to do now, but she couldn't squeeze the words past her constricted windpipe.

He answered the unspoken question by pulling her against himself as he slid the straps of her dress down her arms.

"No!" she managed to say.

But he ignored her protest, exposing her breasts as he lowered his head, taking one nipple into his mouth. It immediately beaded for him, immediately set a charge of sensation through her body and downward toward her core.

It registered somewhere in her mind that the circumstances hardly mattered. When this man made love to her, she was helpless to stop herself from responding.

There was nothing she could do besides moan her pleasure. She moaned again as his free hand found her other nipple, his thumb and finger applying pressure, doubling the heat of her response.

Every thought had been burned from her mind. Nothing existed beyond the pleasure that Jack was giving her. It had been days since he'd made love to her. Days since she'd felt this alive.

She wanted him to hurry. She wanted him to throw her on the bed and pull her skirt up so that he could plunge into her.

"Jack, please." Her hand slid between them, finding the firm, hot shaft behind the fly of his formal trousers. She pressed, stroked, gloried in the instant response that she drew from his body—in the sound of need that escaped from his throat.

Then the spell was shattered by a voice from the doorway. "Hold it right there."

Her hand jumped away from Jack's erection. Her eyes blinked open, colliding with those of a man dressed like the guard who had shadowed them through the foliage that afternoon. He wore the identical fatigues. Carried an identical machine gun. And standing beside him was another guy who could have been his twin.

She was mortified at being caught like this, and the mortification increased a thousandfold as Jack stiffened, then straightened and allowed the guards a quick, calculated glimpse of her breasts before pulling the bodice of her dress back into place.

There was a moment of stunned silence. Then the closest guard roared, "This is a restricted area. What the hell is going on?"

6

JACK TURNED, thrusting Maddy protectively behind him as he stared down the muzzle of the machine gun that was now leveled on them.

He'd expected to get their asses hauled out of here. He hadn't expected to get them shot.

'I think it's obvious what's going on," he said in as steady a voice as he could manage. "My lady and I were looking for a place where we could have some quality time together."

"This area is restricted," the guard repeated. Jack glanced at his name tag. It said Sparrow. The guy looked more like a turkey, but he kept the observation to himself.

Jack shrugged. "I didn't see any signs."

"You saw a gate."

"It was unlocked."

Sparrow stared at him, still with his gun leveled. Probably the guy thought he was lying. But there might not be any way to prove it, since the lock was open now. "You were in the office complex."

"What office complex?" Jack asked innocently.

"I have you on tape, inspecting the office equipment," he said, confirming Maddy's assumption that the room was bugged.

Jack laughed. "I don't give a damn about your office equipment. We were looking for a bed, not a copy machine."

"You can tell Mr. Reynard about it."

"I'd love the chance to do just that!" Jack snapped, matching Sparrow for belligerence.

"Well, no time like the present." A familiar voice entered the conversation. "You can lower your weapons, men. We wouldn't want anyone to get hurt here."

Jack felt Maddy suck in a little breath as Reynard strode around the corner and into the room.

He slipped his arm around her, holding her securely against his side.

Reynard eyed the two of them with interest. "Misbehaving again?" he asked.

Jack raised one shoulder. "Just following my natural inclinations. When we got to our villa, I was all set to enjoy some play time with my fiancée."

Reynard cocked an eyebrow. "Fiancée?"

"We have a very close relationship. Which is why we came here. Your cameras were kind of a turnoff. This evening I figured we'd slip off where we wouldn't be disturbed."

"You and I have a business meeting scheduled at ten."

"No problem. Pleasure before business."

"Perhaps we'll make it business before pleasure," Reynard countered. "Since we're all together, why don't we get started."

Jack had planned to show up for the meeting without Maddy. Now he had no choice but to usher her along as Reynard led the way farther into the gated complex.

The two guards walked behind them, but with their guns slung from straps over their shoulders.

They arrived at another gate, which the master of the house opened with a key.

Maddy glanced at Jack as they walked through. They followed Reynard down another corridor to what appeared to be a wide entrance hall. In fact there was a door that looked as if it opened to the outside. Opposite was a sitting room with plush couches, an elaborate parquet floor topped by an Oriental rug and a huge wall filled with electronics equipment.

"Sit down," Reynard said, gesturing to one of the couches.

It was more of a command than an invitation. Jack reached for Maddy's hand as he took her down to the couch with him.

Reynard chose a seat next to an end table with a built-in control panel. When he pressed a series of buttons, a picture sprang to life on the 45-inch television set opposite them. It showed an empty bedroom.

But Jack knew it wouldn't be empty for long. He watched himself and Maddy step into the picture, watched himself raise his head for a moment, then gather Maddy in his arms in a jerky motion and begin making love to her.

He tried to view the image on the screen objectively. Did the man in the center of the picture realize he was about to be discovered? Was that why he'd started making love to his partner?

At least he looked like he was enjoying himself, he decided. Despite the circumstances, Jack felt his body tightening as he watched the couple on the screen.

Beside him Maddy made a small sound as the scene heated up. Luckily, his body hid most of the activity, but it was clear what he was doing. And clear where she'd lodged her hand. Then at the end, there was that one startling view of creamy, coral-tipped breasts before he pulled her dress back into place.

The scene with the guards followed, but Reynard snapped off the video.

MADDY COULD ONLY SIT THERE in shock. Never in all her life had she been caught in such a compromising position.

On tape, no less. And by the slimeball holding the VCR remote control.

"A very interesting tape, don't you think?" Reynard asked. He was addressing Jack, yet she knew he was probing her reaction as well.

She was mortified. And she assumed the woman she was supposed to be would be mortified, too. Wordlessly, she studied the tips of her shoes.

"If you like that sort of thing," Jack answered Reynard's question.

"You don't like to watch yourself in intimate activities? It can be very stimulating. But then, I think you know that."

Jack cleared his throat but said nothing.

"I'll have this tape delivered to your villa. A souvenir of Orchid Island."

"You're too kind," Jack answered.

Reynard crossed to the bar and brought out a Red Stripe beer, which he handed to Jack. Then he expertly mixed Maddy a wine cooler.

Jack kept one hand on her arm as he set his beer on a coaster on the glass-topped coffee table. She knew he could feel fine tremors rippling over her skin and wished she could make them go away.

But she didn't know what to expect now. Would Reynard accuse them of spying? Or was he going to make some suggestion that would turn her stomach.

Jack's hand slid reassuringly up and down her arm, and she wanted to sink her head to his shoulder. Instead, she played with the condensation on the outside of her glass, feeling Reynard's eyes on her and Jack.

"If you'd wanted a tour of the house, you had only to ask," their host said affably.

She tried to evaluate the statement and knew Jack was

doing the same thing. She was pretty sure Reynard was probing for information.

"We didn't want a tour. We wanted to be alone," Jack clipped out.

"You'll have to wait until later," Reynard said, his eyes sweeping over her in a way that made her skin crawl. "And I'm sure she's worth the wait. But right now, why don't you tell me how we can help each other out."

At Jack's lifted eyebrow, he added, "Business-wise, of course."

Jack took a pull on his beer, then set the bottle down. "I have several tons of coke coming to the U.S. every year from South America. Sometimes DEA patrols make it impossible to get my cargo to the mainland. It would be a great advantage to me if I had a drop-off point not too far from the U.S. where I could land cargo—or simply anchor a ship for a few days until it's safe to head for Florida. I was hoping you could provide such a place."

"I might be able to do that," Reynard answered, "but I'd want a cut, of course."

"How much?"

"Twenty percent of the street value. In advance."

Jack took another swallow of his beer. "That's a pretty steep price. Plus if you expect the cash up front, then you're asking me to spend money I haven't earned yet."

"I assume you can afford it."

"I can afford it. The question is, do I want to take that kind of financial risk."

"There's another man who's come to me with a similar proposition. If you don't like my terms, I can always strike a deal with him."

Jack sat up straighter. "Who?"

"Another one of my guests. Don Fowler."

Jack's eyes narrowed. "Is that why the bastard has been

eying me? He knew that you were going to talk to me—and I didn't know about him.''

"He came to me first. I felt I had to inform him he had a rival.''

"Did he tell you we left the party?'' Maddy asked. "Is that how you knew where to look for us?''

Reynard's attention switched instantly to her. "An astute observation, my dear. You have brains as well as beauty.''

She gave a little shake of her shoulders. "It wasn't all that difficult to figure out.''

"Your little indiscretion would have come to my attention soon enough.''

She struggled not to react as he continued to scrutinize her before turning his attention back to Jack.

"Of course, I give preferential treatment to men who do me favors,'' he said.

The words hung in the air.

"What sort of favors?'' Jack asked.

"I'm sure you know what I'd like from you.''

Jack tightened his hold around her, the gesture conveying a warning as well as protection. "Perhaps we should break off negotiations.''

Reynolds looked taken aback. "Are you withdrawing your proposal?''

"No. But I think we've reached an impasse—at least for now. Perhaps we should resume the discussion again tomorrow.''

"That's up to you.''

Jack stood, bringing Maddy with him. "You and I have some unfinished business,'' he murmured to her, then nodded to Reynard. "Thank you for the hospitality. I'll see you tomorrow.''

She held on to his arm, walking quickly to keep up with him. She had felt numb during the meeting, but the numbness lifted abruptly as they stepped out the door and the heat and humidity of the tropical night slapped her in the face.

The air was clammy, making it suddenly hard to breathe—although she knew the reaction wasn't simply from any physical sensations. It was partly from the knowledge that Reynard wanted her and was willing to go to extreme lengths to get her.

And partly from the way Jack had behaved in the meeting. He'd been cold and calculating. And now that they were away from Reynard and she could think again, she couldn't help remembering what Ted Burnes had told her. He'd told her Jack was unreliable. That he was responsible for the death of a female partner.

Somewhere in the darkness, a wild animal shrieked. At least she hoped it was an animal and not some hapless employee or guest on whom Reynard was taking out his anger.

Because despite his calm demeanor, she'd recognized the anger simmering under the surface.

OLIVER POURED HIMSELF a double measure of cognac. Bringing the glass to the sofa, he rewound the tape, this time farther back—to when Jack and Maddy had first entered the private areas of the house.

The cheeky bastard, he thought as he watched Jack lead his companion down the hall, poking his nose into places where it didn't belong.

Was he on a fact-finding expedition?

Or was he telling the truth? That he was simply looking for a good place to dally with his little sweetie.

The last time he'd viewed the tape, Oliver had focused on Maddy. This time he watched Jack, watched the way he strode into the bedroom as if he owned it.

You could almost make yourself believe that he had

been telling the truth—that the only thing on his mind was making love.

To his fiancée! He snorted.

He watched them together. She slipped her hand between them, found his penis. Urged him on. And he was all too happy to oblige. Another few moments and he would have had her on the bed.

Oliver licked his lips as the view of Maddy's breasts—swollen with arousal—filled the screen.

Then he watched the denouement when the guards had put an end to the fun and games.

It was obvious that the man and woman on the video-tape were both hot and bothered. But that proved nothing, really.

Oliver stroked his chin. He wasn't a man who took chances. Whether or not Jack Craig and Maddy Griffin looked like they were simply searching for a bedroom, he'd better assume the worst—that they were up to something more.

Were they spies, sent by some rival in the States bent on horning in on his business operations? Were they assassins? Or could this have something to do with his unwilling visitor—Dawn Winston?

Whatever they were up to, he'd better assign extra surveillance to them. Starting right now. Striding to the telephone, he made a call to security.

ALONG THE PATH, leaves rustled, and Maddy felt as if a thousand eyes were staring at her from out of the darkness.

The impulse to flee grabbed her by the throat. To flee from this place. From Reynard. From Jack.

But there was no escape. She was here because she'd made it very clear that Jack Connors wasn't coming to Orchid Island without her. And all she could do was keep walking beside him as he led her rapidly toward their villa.

They reached the front door, and Jack pulled his key from his pocket. The seconds before he had the door open were agony. Then relief washed over her as she stepped inside. But the feeling of safety was only momentary.

She was locked in with Jack.

Sucking in a breath, she let it out with deliberate control.

Stop it, she ordered herself.

You can trust him. He's the only person on this whole island that you *can* trust.

Hadn't he found the hidden cameras in here? Hadn't he kept her out of Reynard's clutches?

But there could be other cameras. Or microphones. And if there were, Reynard was surely tuned in.

She had just kicked off her shoes when, against her will, the mortifying images she'd seen on the screen a little while ago flashed into her mind, and she had to hold back a moan of protest.

She wanted to scream at Jack—to ask him what the hell he'd been thinking when he'd exposed her breasts that way. But she knew exactly what he'd been doing—distracting the guards, giving them something to focus on besides the fact that they were trespassing.

Her eyes flicked to him. He was prowling around the living room, probably looking for spy equipment. When he stalked into the bedroom, she followed, watching as he walked to their suitcases.

They'd left their clothing piled inside. And now the clothing was gone.

Jack opened drawers, and she saw that the items had been put away—and probably thoroughly searched. Luckily she hadn't hidden anything important in the folds of her T-shirts.

It was all she could do to stop herself from rushing over to her makeup case and checking the transmitter.

"Well," Jack said, his voice low and sardonic. "I see the maid's been very efficient."

"Yes," she managed to answer. "How nice."

He turned and gave her a look that made her go very still. "You know baby, what we need is to unwind."

Casually he shrugged out of his jacket and hung it in the closet. Then he began to undo his shirt studs.

She swallowed, her gaze flicking to the bed and back to his face. Nothing had changed as far as she knew. This room might still be the star attraction on Orchid Island Television.

His expression remained impassive as he hung up the shirt, then kicked off his shoes, pulled off his socks, and unzipped his trousers.

Dry-mouthed, she watched him put those away.

Naked except for his briefs, he stepped toward her— tall and muscular and overwhelmingly masculine.

And aroused. That too. Because he couldn't hide the fact—not in a pair of knit briefs.

When he took her hand, she stiffened. But instead of leading her to the bed, he urged her toward the bathroom, giving her no choice but to follow him.

He turned on the shower, and the room suddenly filled with the roar of water. Not just from the overhead spray but from four jets in the walls of the tiled enclosure.

She felt as if she were observing from somewhere far away as he stepped toward her, his intentions very clear. Unzipping the dress, he pulled it over her head and flung it onto the counter. Then he skimmed down her panty hose and panties in one quick motion, leaving her naked.

Turning away, he stripped off his own briefs and adjusted the hot water that was already filling the room with steam.

As he stepped into the shower, he brought her with him, brought her under the sprays that hit her body from several directions, instantly turning her skin hot and slick.

But it wasn't only the heat of the water that enveloped her. It was the heat of the man as he pressed her body to his while a groan welled deep in his throat.

For several seconds he simply held her under the pounding water. Then he lowered his mouth to her ear.

"We can talk in here. The running water should mask the conversation—screw up the microphones. We *have* to talk."

Lord, he was thoroughly, sexually aroused. Yet he was doing his best to ignore the demands of his body.

And if he could do it, so could she, she told herself sternly. "Yes." Then, "Are there microphones in here?"

He made a low, frustrated sound. "Probably. If we're lucky, it's a camera-free zone."

She squeezed her eyes closed, trying to shut out the image of someone watching them now. The seconds of exposure in front of the guards had been bad enough. But here she was in the shower—every inch of her skin on view.

The thought made her press closer to Jack, which was a mistake—at least on the physical level.

Yet she was powerless to ease away. And she had gone beyond questioning his judgment, or his methods. Still, the sob she'd managed to hold back until now welled up—spilled out. Just one small sob before she wrested control of herself again. "I didn't know," was all she could whisper at the moment.

"Yeah, well, neither did I. I thought I was prepared." The observation ended with a curse. "Maddy, I'm sorry." He turned his head, sliding his lips along her cheek, then finding the sensitive place just above her right ear.

For a moment her mind went blank. Then she whispered, "For what?"

"For getting you into this." He stopped, and she felt his jaw tighten. "For flashing those guys a look at your breasts."

She hadn't expected him to apologize—for anything. And his words touched her at some deep level that she barely understood. She had been afraid of him—angry. Now she pressed her forehead against his shoulder, wanting to bury herself in his hard flesh. "I know why you did it," she answered in a barely audible voice. "And about the other part…you didn't get me into anything. I insisted on coming with you because it was the right thing to do. It's still the right thing."

"No."

"You think I'm not up to the job?"

His hand stroked down the length of her bare back, then traveled lower to cup her bottom. Heat shot through her then, heat she couldn't deny, even when she knew there were things they had to say.

"I think you've been doing magnificently," he told her in a thick voice. "Nobody could have done it better. It's just damn bad luck that Reynard has a fixation on you."

She nodded against his wet skin, struggled to speak when her nerves were dancing and tingling. "The beauty salon…I couldn't tell you about it before. But Rosalie was there. I thought she was acting strange. I guess I know why now."

His hand continued to play across her back, sending currents of heat through her. "Did you find out anything else?"

Lord, he was still trying to concentrate on business when both of them were so turned on that the spray was changing to steam as it hit their bodies.

"One of the manicurists asked to work on me after she

heard my name. I was afraid to say anything to her directly. But I had a roundabout conversation with her. I think maybe she's seen Dawn, but she was afraid to talk about it. Probably she knows the place is bugged.''

"Yeah.''

She raised her head, stroked her lips across his cheek, entranced by the electrifying, abrasive quality of his beard. He'd shaved only a few hours ago, yet she could clearly feel the stubble against the sensitive skin of her lips.

For several moments neither of them spoke. Then she remembered something else she had wanted to discuss.

"And I was thinking about Fowler. It wasn't just tonight when he noticed us coming in. It was at the airport, too.''

"Yeah.''

"Do you think Reynard's lying to us about him?''

"Why would he?''

"I don't know,'' she admitted, unable to keep herself from sliding her hand down his hard flank.

She felt him react to her touch, knew that if they stayed this way for many more seconds, coherent discussion would fall by the wayside.

"What do we do?'' she managed, trying to focus on the problem that had brought them here in the first place.

His voice was husky as he answered, "Keep looking. Follow the plan we outlined before we left New York. Find a place where we can exchange information. Somewhere else besides this damn shower. Because this is...''

The sentence trailed off as she felt his body moving against hers, felt him stroke his erection against her belly.

She struggled to hold on to the last shreds of coherence. But they evaporated when she felt Jack's hands on her buttocks. He must have reached behind her and lathered his hands with soap because they had turned slick, running over her wet skin with a total absence of resistance that was like fire streaking over dry grass. Touching her the way the woman in the movie they'd seen on the plane had touched the man.

"Oh God," was all she could manage to murmur as slick, wet heat pooled between her legs. And when he shifted her body so that those soap-slick hands could lift and fondle her breasts, she answered him with a sob of need.

She had wanted him again almost as soon as he had climbed out of bed that evening back at Winston headquarters. Though desire had receded to the background, it had never entirely left her. Today and tonight had only added fuel to the fire.

And now need pulsed like a throbbing jungle rhythm through her bloodstream, through her brain, through every cell of her body.

He began to play with her taut nipples then, the soap and touch of his fingers combining to bring her close to the edge.

He used a light, circling motion that drove her wild, alternating the rhythm with flicks of his thumbnails across the very tips, so that she thought she might start the water around her boiling.

Panting, she found the soap dish, slicked her own hands, then boldly found his jutting cock, starting with a teasing stroke that drew a quick indrawn breath from him. The breath turned into a moan as she closed her fingers around him, squeezing and sliding up and down his length with the same maddeningly slick touch that he was using to drive her beyond insanity.

Looking down, she admired her handiwork. He had been hard when she'd started. Now his penis was red with engorgement, the skin like velvet over tempered steel, radiating life and heat.

"Jesus!" he gasped. Then in a strangled voice, he commanded, "Don't. I want to come inside you, not in your hand."

The hand fell away, because she wanted that, too. Wanted it with a desperation that bordered on madness.

He stepped out of her reach, and she cried out from loss. But he was only washing the soap off his hands, letting the water wash the front of his body.

She imitated his action, ridding herself of the soap, watching his hot gaze follow the water cascading downward toward her sex.

She had hardly noticed the configuration of the shower. But when he lifted her up onto a triangular ledge in one corner, she realized that the interior had been designed for sport as well as cleanliness.

"Brace your feet," he instructed, and she did, against small wedges positioned perfectly to hold her legs open for him—hold them open so that his scorching gaze could find her swollen sex. She had never felt so exposed, so helpless, or so utterly needy.

"Please," was all she could say. "Please, don't make me wait."

Water beat down on them like an added caress as the hot, hard rod she had teased and stroked plunged into her.

She cried out at the joining of their flesh, cried out again as his fingers found her clitoris, stoking her need as he moved within her in a fast, hard rhythm.

The intensity was too great for the joining to last more than seconds. He drove her to a sharp, overwhelming climax that was like an electric shock jolting her body. And while the waves of pleasure still lapped through her body, he followed her over the edge.

He collapsed against her, his head drifting to her shoulder, and she reached to stroke her fingers through his wet hair, turned her head so that she could skim her lips along his cheek, drinking in water and man taste.

JACK EASED HIS BODY out of Maddy's, feeling the loss of contact keenly and immediately. If he were free to do anything he wanted, he would start up all over again. No—not just start up. He would have begun arousing her once more while their bodies were still joined.

He squeezed his eyes closed, because thinking about that had him hardening again. Lord, if he were inside her now, building her pleasure again, he'd be able to feel the small clenching of muscles, the glorious contractions of her sex around him that he knew would result from touching and caressing her.

She was so responsive. So damn hot. So giving.

And he wanted her every bit as much as he had a few minutes ago.

He'd known how the session in the shower was going to end up. Known that there would be no way either one of them could resist the hot, slick pressure of body to body.

Yet he hadn't been lying to her. The shower was one of the few places on this whole damn island where they could safely hold a conversation about anything important.

Of course, there was also the jungle. He'd been tempted to step off the path and pull her into the underbrush. But he'd known that was too risky. Not with the animal sounds all around them—and the foliage rustling. For all he knew Reynard let that damn panther loose at night to prowl the grounds.

Maybe he even thought it was amusing to find an occasional mauled guest in the morning. That would certainly fit the man's warped sense of humor.

So he'd gotten Maddy back to their villa as quickly as

possible. And into the shower. With two distinct purposes in mind.

As he stroked his hands over her shoulders, he found he could no longer kid himself. Making love with her had meant something. Not just sex. Something more personal. Something he couldn't afford to examine too closely—at least while the two of them were on Orchid Island.

He sucked in a small breath and felt her catch the subtle change in him.

"What?" she whispered.

He didn't tell her he was calculating their odds of getting out of this place alive. And they were not as good as he'd assumed when they'd planned this rescue mission.

"We should get some sleep," he murmured, shutting off the water, then reaching outside the shower for a large, fluffy towel.

He helped her down from the ledge where she was still sitting, then leaned her against himself as he began to dry her body, trying not to react to the intimate contact.

He worked the towel over her hair, appreciating the silky texture. She felt boneless, relaxed, her eyes heavy-lidded.

Draping the towel around her shoulders, he whispered, "Wait here."

Outside the shower, he grabbed another towel and did a quick job of drying himself. Then he stepped into the bedroom, crossed to the dresser, and opened the drawer where he'd seen her sleepwear.

He found a little wisp of a gown with spaghetti straps and delicate lace at the top edge of the bodice.

Bringing it back to the bathroom, he slipped it over her head, helped her get her arms free of the gossamer fabric.

If there was a camera in the bedroom, at least the bastards wouldn't see her naked, he thought as he lifted her into his arms and carried her toward the bed. He didn't care about them seeing him. It was just Reynard and his guards, after all.

Pulling back the covers, he settled her in the wide bed, then went back and closed the bathroom door almost all the way, leaving only a narrow shaft of light knifing into the room.

When he slipped in beside her, she rolled toward him. With a small sound, she wrapped her arms around him, and he gathered her to him, holding her in the darkness, vowing to get her out of this mess if it was within his power to do it.

7

MADDY COULDN'T HOLD BACK a small stab of disappointment when she woke alone in the big bed.

As she lay there curled on her side, she remembered falling asleep in Jack's arms. And before that—the incredible session in the shower.

Heat rushed through her body when she remembered their wild, uninhibited lovemaking. Not just wild and sexy. Caring. Because if there was one thing she'd discovered about Jack Connors, it was that he cared as much about his partner's pleasure as his own.

His absence now told her that he'd pulled back from her again. Or maybe he'd just awakened early and hadn't wanted to disturb her.

Yeah, right.

She could hear him out in the living room, talking on the phone. She hadn't heard it ring, so he must have been the one to make the call—or he'd turned off the bell in the bedroom. Checking, she found that wasn't the case.

So who could he have called? Nobody on the mainland, certainly, because she was sure that wasn't permitted. The only person she could think of was Reynard. And that had her nerves jangling again.

Sighing, she pressed her hand to her forehead. Last night, after their talk with Reynard, she'd started worrying about whether she could trust Jack. Then, in the shower, he'd wiped away her doubts.

One phone call, and she was on edge again.

Damn! It had been a colossal mistake not to talk to him about Ted's accusation before they left New York. Now she needed to get his side of the story. But she wasn't going to drag him back into the shower to do it. Which meant they had to find another place that was safe for personal and business discussions.

But where the heck was that?

With a grimace, she swung her legs over the side of the bed and headed for the bathroom. Inside the door, she stopped short, her gaze focusing on the shower as vivid images played through her mind.

Going very still, she tried to get a grip on herself. After the first time they'd made love, Jack had acted like it had never happened. And probably she'd let him know she was hurt. Well, this morning, she wasn't going to make that mistake.

Of course, things hadn't ended quite so abruptly last night. But she could come up with a reason for his behavior. A reason that certainly hadn't entered her head last night when she'd rolled toward him in the bed and snuggled into his arms. If he thought somebody was watching the bedroom proceedings on a video camera, than he would have turned in a performance for the cameraman.

A white terry robe was hanging on the back of the door. She took it down, pulled it over her gown and tied the belt before heading toward the living room.

Jack was just replacing the receiver in the cradle.

"That was Reynard," he said, without waiting for her to ask, his voice matter-of-fact. "He wants to talk business with me again this morning."

"He called you?" she asked carefully, mindful that the walls had ears.

"He sent over a note with breakfast." Jack swept his arm toward the cart that stood beside the door. "We have

coffee. It's excellent by the way. Kona, I believe. Tropical
fruit, a quiche lorraine and a selection of Danish pastry—
also quite good. I recommend the cherry. If we want anything else, there's a buffet on the patio outside where we
had the cocktail party last night. You know, I love this
place," he added enthusiastically.

"It's certainly luxurious."

Jack was watching her, and she kept her face carefully
neutral as she crossed the room and poured herself a cup
of coffee from the carafe, then added cream and sugar.

After selecting a blueberry Danish, she sat down at the
table by the sliding glass door.

"Do you mind finding something else to do this morning?" he asked. "I know business bores you. And you
had to sit around listening to us last night."

"You're right." She patted her head. "Actually, I need
to go to the beauty salon. You did a fine job of messing
up my hair last night—and I simply can't face the world
looking like this."

JACK STUDIED MADDY as she took a swallow of her coffee, then bit into the Danish and chewed appreciatively.

"This is really good," she murmured. "I should indulge myself more often."

He considered her words, found himself looking for
hidden meanings. She was showing more enthusiasm for
the breakfast bun than she was for him. In fact she was
acting like what had happened between them last night
was no big deal.

The way he'd acted after that first frantic session back
at Winston Industries.

He supposed he should be grateful that she wasn't making any claims on him. But the reaction was unsettling.
He found himself wanting to stride across the few feet of
space that separated them, pull her to her feet and fold

her into his arms. For the pleasure of feeling her body pressed to his. And the reassurance that he could get a reaction out of her.

He had to stop his tongue from stroking across his lower lip as he thought about the delicious taste of her. The wet, hot joining of her mouth with his.

Hell, the wet, hot joining of more than mouth-to-mouth.

Against his will, memories of last night flooded through him like a riptide. For several seconds, he couldn't move as he was caught again in the lovemaking—in the incredible look of arousal on her face, in the incredible feel of his cock sliding in and out of her. Then he blinked, turned away before he could do or say something he would regret. Before she could see that he was turned on.

Pretending he needed more coffee, he sloshed some into his cup and took a gulp, burning his mouth.

Without turning, he said, "Then I'll meet you back here around lunchtime. Perhaps you could join some of the other ladies at the Greek pool complex?"

"Perhaps. Or I might get a facial and a massage," she answered languidly.

"Yes. This is your vacation, too. You do whatever you like."

"Um."

Again he fought the urge to yank her to her feet—to crush his mouth down onto hers and force a reaction from her.

But he stayed where he was.

Since when had he needed reassurance with a woman?

Since Maddy, apparently. He made a small, choking sound.

"What?"

"Nothing!" Turning, he strode toward the door. The hot tropical air slapped him in the face as he stepped outside.

Grimly, he began striding up the path they'd taken the night before. Then he caught his breath, slowed his pace as he remembered where he was and what he was here for.

MADDY WATCHED the tense set of Jack's shoulders as he disappeared from view.

It flitted through her mind that playing hard to get was a little difficult to manage, when the man you were teasing had made wild, passionate love to you the night before.

But she was pretty sure she'd pulled it off. And the knowledge brought a smile flickering over her lips.

He'd been thinking about last night. So had she. They'd both been aroused. But that was the advantage of being a woman, it was easier to hide your physical reaction. If your nipples got hard, you could always blame it on the air-conditioning.

She leaned comfortably back, enjoyed another bite of her Danish. It was good. Hardly her usual breakfast in New York. But just the thing this morning.

As she chewed, however, the smile died on her lips, and the pastry turned to clay in her mouth. It was all she could do to swallow as a wave of guilt assaulted her.

She was pleased with handling Jack this morning!

But she'd forgotten about a couple of important things. She still didn't know how far she could trust the man. And she'd come here to rescue Dawn Winston, who was here on the island—at the mercy of a cruel, vicious man— because Maddy Guthrie hadn't done her job.

She balled her hand into a fist, pressed it against her mouth. Lord, she'd never been more off-balance. Never less able to do her job. Jack Connors had turned her brain to mush, the bastard.

Standing, she strode toward the bedroom and began pulling clothing from drawers, silently admitting that she couldn't blame Jack. The only person she could blame was herself.

It wasn't until she was standing beside the dresser naked that she remembered that someone could be spying on her.

With a grimace she started to grab her clothing and dash into the bathroom. But it was already too late for that. Resolutely, she stepped into a clean pair of panties, then a bra.

Two minutes later, after pulling on a sequined T-shirt and black shorts, she shoved her feet into sandals and started out the door toward the spa.

JACK ROUNDED A BEND in the path and saw the white mansion sprawled in the sunlight like an enormous wedding cake.

He walked rapidly past some of the inevitable gardeners and up to the French doors where he and Maddy had entered the night before.

As he approached, a uniformed guard snapped to attention.

"Mr. Reynard has asked you to come around to the front door," the guard informed him.

"Where we left last night?"

"Exactly."

Jack thanked the man, then took the path around the building. Sunlight flooded through the high windows of the entrance hall as he stepped inside, to be greeted by yet another employee—this time a formally dressed butler.

"I hope you won't mind waiting for just a moment, sir," the man said, directing him into a small sitting room.

He had just turned to take a seat when he saw Don Fowler step out of one of the larger rooms.

He and Reynard shook hands. He could tell that Fowler

hadn't seen him as he strode out the front door, his step springy.

Son of a bitch! So Reynard had booked more than one appointment this morning.

The butler approached him and spoke. Reynard looked up, spotted Jack and smiled.

"Come in. Come in. I'm so glad you could make it."

Jack kept his expression untroubled as he followed the other man into the television room where they'd had their interview the evening before.

"Sit down. Can I get you something? Coffee? A Bloody Mary?"

"Well, I don't drink anything alcoholic so early in the morning." As he accepted a cup of coffee, he didn't add that he'd already consumed enough of the stuff to keep him on a caffeine high for hours.

Leaning back, he said, "I see you've already had a morning appointment."

"Well, I do have to keep my options open."

Jack took a sip of the coffee he didn't want.

"I'm sure I can offer you a better deal than Fowler."

"Perhaps. But that might depend on your definition. I have plenty of money, so I don't always make my business decisions strictly on a profit motive basis."

"You can never have too much money," Jack answered, keeping his voice neutral.

"To be blunt, you have something I want. And getting it could be a major factor in our working relationship."

Jack didn't speak, didn't move a muscle.

"Maddy, your lady, is very charming. Very desirable. You know I have a sexual interest in her."

Jack set down his coffee cup with a thunk on the glass-topped table. "She belongs to me."

"I'm not asking you to leave her here. I'm asking to enjoy her favors while she's on the island."

"I don't lend her out."

"Not when a simple favor to a friend can mean millions of dollars in your pocket?"

Jack pretended to consider that. Then he said in a deliberately mild voice. "I have a little trouble with the thought of another man touching her."

"I was prepared for you to say that. And I admit that touching her has quite a bit of appeal. But what about another alternative? One we might share—so to speak."

Jack raised a questioning eyebrow.

"Have you ever thought about how…stimulating…it would be watching another woman make love to her?"

Jack swallowed, considered several answers and discarded them. He knew damn well that watching two women make love was a top-five male fantasy. He'd entertained the fantasy himself when he'd been a teenager.

Reynard smiled, continued. "We could have a nice private session. Wouldn't it be exciting to see her with a really beautiful woman—a woman who enjoys her own sex as much as she enjoys men. There's nothing more captivating than watching two beautiful females together, giving each other pleasure." His voice turned husky. "I mean seeing one of them take the other's nipple in her mouth, swirl her tongue around that aching tip while she rolls its mate between her thumb and finger. Then she slides her lips down her partner's body, finds her hot core and brings her off with her lips and tongue." The man's eyes were bright, his face slightly flushed, and it was obvious he was enjoying the vivid description. "And there's always the educational factor, of course. You can learn so much from watching them stimulate each other. Who but a woman knows better what gives another of her sex pleasure?" He made an expansive gesture with his hand. "If Maddy's a novice with female partners, she doesn't have to do any of the work. She can just lie back and enjoy having an expert bring her to a deep, rocking climax."

Jack pressed his hand flat against the sofa cushion. It was a struggle not to leap across the space that separated him from Reynard and smash his fist into the man's smug face. The idea of Maddy with another woman made his stomach knot. But he managed to stay where he was—barely.

"What happens afterwards?" he asked, hearing the dangerous edge in his own voice. He hoped Reynard would mistake it for excitement.

"Well, I assure you, you'll be hard as a lead pipe by the end of it. You can work off your head of steam with Maddy. And I can enjoy the other lady. I have someone perfect in mind. Her name is Calista. Her mother was from Jamaica and her father was from the mainland. He had some Native American blood. The combination was very fortuitous. Calista is stunning; she's got a wonderful body, and she enjoys having fun."

"You've provided her services to other guests, I take it?"

"Of course. Usually, it's the guest who elects to screw her afterwards. And I enjoy *his* lady." He spread his hands. "But if you feel more comfortable sticking with your own partner, I understand entirely." He crossed his leg, clasped his hand around his knee. Probably his pants were binding him at the moment.

"I sense that you're a man of strong sexual appetites," Reynard went on. "But being brought up in the land of puritanism, you might have felt constrained to follow conventional patterns in the past. That's not necessary on Orchid Island. Really, I cultivate a very uninhibited atmosphere here, both for myself and my guests. I can provide anything you want. I mean *anything*. If you'd like a stunningly beautiful girl to join you and Maddy in bed this afternoon, you have only to ask. And if you feel that Maddy has been a bad girl, and you'd like to experiment with some interesting forms of punishment, then I've got a facility you'll want to see.''

''What kind of facility?''

''A very realistic dungeon. Would you like a tour? Some of my guests go there first thing on arrival.''

''Yes, yes I would like to see it,'' Jack answered, ruthlessly ignoring the feeling of pressure building in his chest. He was stalling for time, of course. Because sooner or later he was going to have to give Reynard an answer to his earlier proposal. But perhaps he could make it look like he was so excited by all the tantalizing prospects that had been laid on the table that he was having trouble deciding which to pick.

Reynard inclined his head, studying Jack for a moment before standing. ''Perhaps I've hit on one of your secret desires. Let's go have a look at my playrooms. If you want to bring Maddy down there, you can use the equipment yourself. Or you might want to watch someone else working her over. A man or a woman. Your choice.'' He paused. ''Or you might like to practice on some other woman—or a man.''

''I'm not interested in men,'' Jack snapped, fighting another wave of revulsion.

But Reynard must have caught the flash of something ugly in his eyes.

''I didn't mean to offend,'' his host said quickly. ''I'm only trying to explore every option. Orchid Island is a place where anything you can imagine can become reality.''

''Yeah.'' Jack pushed himself to his feet, struggling to keep an expectant look on his face as he followed Reynard out the door and down the hall. He was thinking about how to slip his mind into neutral gear so he could endure the tour without throwing up.

JUANITA HAD TOLD HER to come back, Maddy thought as she stepped into the spa. But getting her nails redone so soon might look suspicious.

The hairdressers were busy with other guests, so she asked about the other services available, hoping the woman did more than nails.

She'd mentioned to Jack that she might get a facial. Now she thought, why not? It would keep her here for a while. So she'd entered the dressing room and exchanged her shorts and top for a light pink robe. Then she'd let the receptionist show her to a cubicle that overlooked a lushly planted patio.

As she settled into a padded chair that reminded her of the dentist's office, she decided that she didn't have to stick with questioning Juanita. She could try to get information out of any of the women here—if she kept the questions indirect, the way she had yesterday.

That goal proved elusive, however, when she tried to start a conversation with Sarita, the attendant giving her the facial. Either Sarita spoke minimal English, or someone had warned her not to talk to Jack Craig's woman.

She hoped it was the former explanation. Because the implications were chilling if she was being talked about at the spa. It meant that she'd drawn attention to herself yesterday. And that wasn't good.

All at once she felt trapped. The feeling intensified as Sarita said, "You must close eyes now. You no want this in your eyes."

It would look really weird if she backed out now, so she obeyed and felt small cups being placed over her closed lids. Then the woman began smoothing some kind of heavy goop over her face.

"You wait twenty minutes," Sarita said when she had finished.

Maddy gave a small nod, but she felt frighteningly vulnerable. If someone wanted to hurt her, this would be the perfect opportunity.

She forced herself to lie there in the recliner, eyes closed, trying to control her breathing and her tension. Finally, she heard the woman's footsteps recede, and she let out a little sigh, then considered that Sarita might be standing in the doorway, still watching her.

Her hands clamped over the armrests, until she deliberately eased the pressure and knit her fingers in her lap.

Twenty minutes, she told herself. Only twenty minutes. Deliberately she went through one of the relaxation exercises that she used when she had the time. But it was hard to concentrate with the skin of her face tingling and her nerves stretched taut.

She couldn't rid herself of the feeling that someone was watching her. When light footsteps sounded again, her whole body stiffened, and she prepared to leap out of the reclining chair.

"It's all right. Stay still," a low voice ordered. "I'm just coming to check you."

She sensed a presence bending over her. Then a hand closed over hers and she felt something being thrust into her fingers. A folded piece of paper.

"Hide it," the voice whispered.

She tried to speak, but she could only make an inarticulate sound as she thrust the hand with the note into her pocket, hoping that if there was a camera in the room, the body bending over hers had hidden the note from view.

In a silent rush of movement that stirred currents in the air, the person was gone. Eyes squeezed closed, she fingered the note in her pocket. Every cell of her body burned to know what it said, but there was no way to do it now. All she could do was lie there and feel the minutes drag by.

She jumped when she heard Sarita's voice again.

"Let's take that mask off you."

"Um."

"It feels tight, no?"

"Um."

The woman gently peeled the hardened stuff off her skin. When the cups came off her eyes, she blinked. Somehow it was a surprise to see that the room looked exactly the same.

"Your face feels good?"

"Yes." She took the mirror and inspected her features. As far as she could see, she didn't look much different. Well, maybe her skin was firmer. And it did feel fresh and clean. But it wasn't a treatment she'd pay for back home with her own hard-earned cash.

Of course, there weren't *any* beauty treatments that she paid for—beyond a basic haircut every few weeks.

"What else can we do for you?"

She glanced at her watch. "Well, I'd like to stay. But I think my guy is waiting for me back at the villa."

The beautician opened her mouth, then closed it again with one of those looks that said, "The customer is always right."

"Maybe later."

She hurried into the dressing room, then thought of the cameras again. So she slipped into a toilet stall. But she was still nervous about opening the note. So while she was unwinding a length of toilet paper, she managed to bend over and block the view of her other hand as she got it out of the dressing gown pocket.

When she pulled up her panties again, she transferred the note to the elastic band. Finally, as she faced the row of lockers, she slipped on her shorts and covered the note.

As she quickly stepped out of the locker room, she caught sight of Juanita staring at her. The woman met her eyes for a second, then turned quickly away, leaving Maddy no wiser than she'd been before. She didn't even know if Juanita was the one who had given her the paper. All she knew was that she had to read the message as soon as she could—then somehow tell Jack what it said.

Intent on that mission, she headed for the entrance. Just as she was about to escape into the sunlight, she caught sight of herself in one of the mirrors—and groaned. Her face might be glowing with mud-induced health, but her hair was still a mess from last night in the shower. She'd totally forgotten about her reason for coming here in the first place. What's more, she knew that the woman she was supposed to be would never leave the spa with her hair looking like it had been commandeered for a parrot's nest.

So she took a breath, then turned and made her way to the front desk, smiling.

"Sorry. I was so focused on getting back to my guy that I forgot all about my hair. Are the hairdressers free? Could one of them do a wash, dry and comb out for me? Something simple that won't take too long. 'Cause Jack and I have plans."

"Certainly. We'll be with you in just a few minutes."

"Of course. No problem," she answered, just managing not to grind her teeth in impatience. The note that was still tucked into the elastic waist of her underpants felt like a hot poker against her flesh.

JACK'S SKIN WAS STILL CRAWLING as he walked quickly along the jungle path. Hoping his disgust didn't show on his face, he kept his eyes trained downward.

Reynard had really gotten into a tour of his private playrooms, showing off various setups and equipment. As

Jack had followed his host, it was all he could do to keep from making scathing comments about the man's kinky sexual preferences.

Then he'd felt himself cringing when he'd run into Jormo Kardofski down in one of the corridors. Kardofski had been dressed like a Roman emperor and had given Jack a wolfish grin—assuming they'd both come down there for some kind of fantasy role-playing.

Upstairs again, he had managed to praise the facilities. At the same time, he'd put Reynard off for tonight by acting coy and saying that he needed more time to think about his options. He hoped he'd come across as a man who was interested in trying something new, but who had to work himself up to the good stuff.

Unfortunately, he was now caught in a dilemma that made his stomach churn. The guy he was playing, Jack Craig, wouldn't keep stalling forever. He'd welcome the opportunity for something different—particularly when it meant combining pleasure with business.

On the other hand, there was Maddy.

Oh Lord, Maddy.

They'd come here with the understanding that they'd do whatever it took to free Dawn. But no way was he going to ask her to submit to the kinds of games Reynard had in mind. He shoved his hands into his pockets, balled them into fists.

He had rounded a bend in the path when he almost tripped over one of the gardeners, clad in the usual green overalls. The man was squatting on the blacktop, weeding a section of flower bed.

"Sorry if I'm in the way, sir."

"No problem."

"I'm at your service, sir."

Jack paused and gave the man a hard look. "At my service for what?" he asked.

"Anything at all."

"Like what?"

The man shrugged. "You tell me. I'll be around if you need me."

"Thanks," Jack answered, then turned away. What the hell was that all about, he wondered. Was the guy trying to trap him into something? Or was he running some kind of scam behind Reynard's back?

Either way, Jack was sure he wasn't going to take him up on the offer.

FIFTY MINUTES AFTER SITTING down to get her hair coiffed, Maddy was finally out of the spa. As she took the path back to the villa, she kept her senses tuned to the foliage around her.

She thought she detected movement beyond the edge of her vision, but she wasn't quite sure. So she stopped, pretended that she'd been attacked by an insect as she batted at the air around her head and uttered little distressed sounds.

She made it look like the damn thing had gotten under her shirt, then lifted up the hem and reached for the note. It was in her palm by the time she had calmed down and started walking again. With her thumb, she unfolded the paper and looked down into her cupped hand, scanning the words as she moved along the path.

The note said, "The girl is in the Dark Tower."

As she read the message, her heart began to beat faster. God, now what? The only person she'd talked to about "the girl" was Juanita. So she must have written the note. Unless someone else had heard them and was setting a trap. But even if the note had come from Juanita, it could still be designed to incriminate her and Jack!

JACK ARRIVED at the villa and strode through the rooms. Two serving carts loaded with food stood in the dining area, but Maddy wasn't there, and she wasn't on the patio.

He choked back a wave of panic. She was at the spa. Reynard hadn't scooped her up.

Impatiently, he waited for her to reappear, wondering what the hell he was going to do now. Should he tell her about Reynard's proposition and have her insides twisting as badly as his? Or should he keep this morning's meeting to himself and feel like a rat for not giving her all the facts?

Once, long ago, he'd given an agent a piece of very bad news, and she'd gone off the deep end. She hadn't been able to handle the information—and her subsequent behavior had gotten her killed.

He didn't think Maddy was going to crack under the strain. Hell, she'd been superb all the way through this nerve-wracking assignment. Yet the memory of that long-ago mission in Albania still had the power to turn his skin cold.

His mind flashed back to the narrow, one-lane road, winding along the crest of the mountains. Lisa hunched over the wheel, her face stark white as she fled the danger in the little village behind them.

He'd tried to get her to sit tight. She'd vetoed the idea and made a run for the car. And he'd had no choice but to go with her.

The mountain roads were dangerous under any circumstances. But there'd been no place to escape as the hulking Russian-made car had come toward them, speeding up as it plowed into their smaller vehicle.

He never knew if his door had come open, or if he'd managed to pull the handle. But somehow he'd been thrown free of the car as it started down the mountain side. Lisa had ended up trapped inside as the car hit the bottom of the ravine and burst into flames.

The horror of it closed his throat, stopped the breath in his lungs.

With a terrible effort, he pulled himself out of the past. This was another time. Another place. But the terror and the danger were all too real. He didn't know that his hands were pressed over his eyes until he felt the pressure of his palms against his eyeballs.

A knock at the door made his body jerk. Deliberately he relaxed his muscles, tried to clear his mind of the old feelings of guilt.

After waiting several more seconds, he walked to the door and looked through the spy hole. He saw a man dressed in blue coveralls standing on the threshold, looking down.

When Jack heard a scraping noise, he jerked the door open.

The man looked startled. Quickly he pulled back the hand that had been inserting a key in the lock.

"Can I help you?" Jack asked evenly as he read the man's name tag. It said, "Isley."

The man struggled to wipe the look of surprise off his face. "Oh, I thought nobody was here," he said.

"And you were coming in to do what?" Jack asked pointedly as he looked at the carry bag in Isley's other hand.

"Make some repairs."

"To what?"

He hesitated for a moment, then asked, "Didn't you complain about the stopper in one of the sinks? The basin's not holding water?"

"No," Jack answered calmly. "You must have the wrong villa."

"Oh, yeah. Sorry," Isley answered, backing up.

Jack gave him points for sticking with his story. He

turned and marched down the path like he really had made a mistake—and was going to correct it now.

Probably Isley had been from security—not from repairs. And probably Reynard had requested that the listening or viewing devices be reinstalled.

So did that mean they were presently not wired for sound here? Or was Reynard adding more equipment?

He didn't know. And there was no way he could find out without coming across as hostile. Smashing the TV cameras he'd found when they arrived had been as much to make a point as anything else. Now his mission had changed. He'd established himself as a tough guy, and he was trying to act more cooperative.

Making a rapid decision, he started down the path after Isley, moving quickly and quietly. The man was standing just around the bend, his shoulders hunched, talking into a cell phone.

Jack faded behind the trunk of a palm tree, straining his ears as he tried to pick up the conversation.

"Yeah. I didn't know he was home," Isley was saying.

Someone on the other end of the line was evidently speaking because the "maintenance man" paused.

"Okay. Right. I hear you. I'll do the installation while they're at the party tonight."

As Isley slipped the phone back into his pocket, Jack blended back into the jungle.

Quietly he retraced his steps, thinking his assumption had been confirmed—although he couldn't be one hundred percent certain. Isley *could* be talking about a bathroom sink, but that would be a pretty big stretch.

He returned to the front entrance and stood staring at the lush tropical foliage and bright flowers, wondering if the bushes were wired for sound. So Reynard was increasing the surveillance here. Did that mean there were presently no bugs in the house? Maybe, but he'd better not make that assumption.

HE WAS STILL STANDING in the doorway when Maddy came around a curve in the path, walking quickly.

He saw at once that she was trying to control the expression on her face. But as he took in the tension splashed across her features, he knew what he had to do.

8

MADDY WAS BURSTING to tell Jack about the note. But the warning look in his eyes stopped her cold.

As she stood there staring at him, she took several slow deep breaths. "Did you miss me?" she finally asked.

"Of course," he answered casually, leading her inside and into the dining room. "I found a marvelous lunch waiting for us. Isn't that nice?" He laughed. "Well, maybe not so nice. If we're not careful, we're both going to put on weight while we're here."

She stared at the two buffet carts as though the salads, fruit and main dishes had materialized from outer space. Her throat was too clogged to swallow, but Jack acted like the meal was the only thing on his mind as he sauntered over to the closest cart, picked up a slice of pineapple, and began to eat.

"Come on. This stuff is great."

After a few seconds' hesitation, she followed his example, piling a plate with shrimp salad, smoked salmon and marinated vegetables.

"It's too nice a day to stay inside," he commented, as he opened the sliding glass door.

"You're always right, sweetie," she purred.

He shot her a look that hovered between annoyance and amusement. Then, with a shrug, he picked up his plate and stepped outside.

She followed him onto the patio and joined him at the

wrought-iron table—where they both worked at looking hungry. At least she knew it was an effort for her.

As they ate, she watched Jack from under lowered lashes. He was acting like nothing was wrong—at least on the surface. But the message written on his face wasn't "nothing." He was worried about something, although she could hardly expect him to level with her here, where hidden microphones might pick up their every word.

And he confirmed that line of speculation with his next words. "Right after I got back, a repairman showed up with a bag of tools. He said there was a complaint from this villa about the stopper in one of the sinks not working. Did you turn in a complaint, honey bunch?"

"No," she answered quickly.

"Neither did I. I guess he made a mistake. No harm done this time. But he did have a key to the front door, and when I didn't answer his knock right away, he started to come in. I'd hate for him to have walked in on us in the bedroom or something."

He held her gaze for a long moment.

"That would certainly have been embarrassing," she answered. She understood Jack's words had nothing to do with his real message here. The guy had come to the villa with a story about the sink—but he'd been on another mission entirely. Probably to work on the surveillance equipment.

She tried to ease her clenched muscles. Jack was reminding her to be careful. Maybe he'd taken her outside because he thought there was less chance of being video-taped—which meant they still had to watch what they said.

So maybe those were the negative vibes she'd sensed when she'd first come back here—his frustration with their inability to speak frankly.

She clung to that explanation as she leaned back in her

chair, considering how to clue him in to her own morning's activities. Maybe there was a way to talk—and act on the message she'd read a few minutes ago.

After working her way through some of the food on her plate, she slid him a seductive smile from her side of the glass-topped table. "You know, I was having this fantasy while I was lying there with my eyes closed, getting a facial treatment back at the spa. I was thinking, wow, it would be fun to make love with Jack outside in this tropical paradise." She lifted one shoulder. "What do you think? Shall we go for it?"

He waited a beat. Then his face broke into a lecherous grin as he pushed his own plate back and climbed to his feet.

"Yeah. Come here and let me show you how much I missed you, baby."

Taking the suggestion, she stood, moved toward him, swaying slightly on unsteady legs as she reached into her pocket and pulled out the note and cupped it in her palm. Her shakiness wasn't an act, exactly. She was feeling jittery. About the note. About Jack. About their relationship.

Did they have a *real* relationship? she wondered. What would happen when they got back to the outside world? Would Jack Connors make sure he stayed as far away from Maddy Guthrie as possible?

She knew there was no point in dwelling on those thoughts. She and Jack had a job to do. And they'd better make it look good.

When she was within reach, he slipped his arm around her shoulder, ran his fingers up and down her back as he pulled her close.

It was so easy to let her body melt against his. She knew his words and the gestures were for the cameras that might be watching and for the microphones that might be planted out here. But as always when Jack took her in his arms, she couldn't prevent herself from reacting to him.

In her hypersensitive state, his touch was instantly erotic. And when he began to hum a slow tune, the melting process accelerated. Eyes closed, she swayed against him as he twirled her slowly around in an impromptu dance step.

Still, she'd had enough practice by now to keep her mind on business—at least if she concentrated hard. She brought her lips to his ear, murmuring nonsense as she shifted her hand in his grip, pressing her palm against his. She knew at once that he'd felt the folded piece of paper wedged between his heated flesh and hers.

"What's this?" he asked, keeping his voice light and playful as he danced her slowly around the patio bordered by lush foliage and bright flowers. A tropical paradise, she thought—where you never know which plants had thorns. So you had to be wary of them all.

Putting that image out of her mind, she purred. "I read you so well. I know you love it when I make sexy suggestions."

"Yeah." He kept up the swaying motion, bent to skim his lips against the top of her hair. "You smell so good, baby. Good enough to eat."

The words sent a little quiver through her. "So are you going to take me up on my offer of a picnic?"

"Um-hum." He continued to move her around the patio as if it were a dance floor.

"Where should we go?" she purred.

"Down one of the paths we haven't taken. Maybe we'll find a nice private spot where we can have some fun. A little cabana or something—for the convenience of guests."

She made a mock pouty face. "I want to do it outside,

where we've got the blue sky overhead. And the swaying palms. That sounds so romantic.''

''Hmm. Maybe we should take a blanket.''

As though sex were the only thing on his mind, he strode back into the bedroom and reappeared a few moments later with the light blanket that was folded on the top shelf of one of the closets.

''Won't we get it dirty?'' she asked.

He laughed. ''Better than getting your pretty little butt dirty, honey. You did say you wanted to look up at the sky, didn't you?''

''Yes.''

He slung the blanket over one arm and took her hand on the opposite side—the paper between their palms again. It had gotten damp from the contact, and she wondered if the words would still be readable.

''SIR, THIS IS HAMILTON.''

''Go ahead,'' Reynard invited.

''You asked to be informed if Jack Craig and his girlfriend left their villa.''

''And?'' Reynard snapped.

''They're on the move.''

''Keep them in sight. I want to know where they go and what they do.''

Tension buzzed through his body. Deliberately he ordered his muscles to relax. Craig's background had checked out. On paper he was exactly what he seemed to be—a powerful crime boss who wanted to open up more avenues for illegal profits.

But Oliver had stopped believing that the information he'd gathered on the man told the whole story, because Jack Craig wasn't behaving like the ruthless criminal he was supposed to be: a man bent on achieving his own goals at any cost.

Don Fowler was pushing the theory that Craig was an impostor. He'd never heard of the man, he said. And that automatically made him suspect.

But then Fowler had his own ax to grind. He wanted Craig out of the way—at all costs.

And Craig had passed a little test on his way back from the main house. One of the security operatives had stopped him, pretending to be selling his services. Craig had declined the offer, which might only prove that he was smart—smart enough to know it might be a trap.

Oliver leaned back in his comfortable chair and stroked his chin. Of course, there was one interesting explanation for Jack Craig's odd behavior regarding their business dealings: He really was in love with Maddy Griffin. Or at least besotted with the woman. And he was letting his feelings for her overrule his better judgment.

It was a plausible theory. But there was another one just as reasonable. Jack Craig and Maddy Griffin were here to accomplish some hidden purpose.

Well, Oliver had the resources to find out which was true. And if he discovered that Craig was a spy or an operative, then he was going to have the man executed. Probably he'd have his fiancée executed, too. But not before he did all the things he'd been wanting to do with her.

As THEY STARTED down the path, Maddy caught a flash of movement. Two of the gardeners were checking them out.

She looked away from the men as though they were simply part of the scenery, beneath her notice, really.

They came to a branch in the path they hadn't tried before, heading toward the interior of the island. As Jack led her down the new trail, he transferred the piece of paper from her palm to his. Then he brought his hand up to casually scratch his chest through the knit fabric of his shirt. She watched him look down to read the words she'd already seen:

"The girl is in the Dark Tower."

He slipped his hand into the pocket of his slacks, taking the paper along with it, then gave her a questioning look.

They'd been speaking words and phrases with hidden meanings for so long that she didn't miss a beat. "You like my hair? They do a good job at the spa, don't they?"

"Um-hum."

"And the facial was really neat. I was lying there with my eyes closed, and goop all over my face when it happened—that inspiration that we come out here and have some fun."

"Um-hum," he answered again, and she was pretty sure that he'd followed the gist of her carefully crafted remarks.

He was silent for several seconds. Then he said, "You know, this island might be a paradise, but there are too darn many people around. What do you think the chances are of finding some privacy?"

"I don't know. Maybe this is our lucky trail—since we haven't tried it before."

"Exactly what I was thinking. Let's find a spot where we can be alone."

She nodded, sure they were in agreement to concentrate their search in one of the more isolated sections of Reynard's kingdom.

They'd both studied the aerial maps of the island. And she remembered a building off by itself that might be the Dark Tower mentioned in the note. Jack was definitely heading in that direction.

But they certainly couldn't march right up to the place. They had to make this look good. Like the other night when they'd searched Reynard's house.

Jack was undoubtedly thinking the same thing, she decided as he pulled her close, shifting the blanket so that it was behind her body.

Then his mouth lowered to hers, rubbed back and forth so seductively that she had to grab his shoulders to stay on her feet.

Her eyes drifted closed as his mouth moved expertly over hers.

"That's nice," she breathed, business completely fleeing her mind.

He brought her back to earth with the barely audible question she'd been half-expecting earlier. "Who gave you the note?"

Tipping her head to the side, she spoke softly. "My eyes were closed from that facial thing. I couldn't see."

"Um-hum." He nibbled at her lips, and she was lost again, struggling to keep her mind on business.

Maybe he was having the same problem. "Let's not get carried away right here," he muttered. Breaking away from her, he took her hand and moved farther down the path, his hip bumping seductively against hers as they strolled deeper into the interior, the manicured greenery of the inhabited areas giving way to wilder jungle. The vegetation on either side of them was thick, and she was glad of the path.

A bird screeched overhead, and a rustling of movement in the branches of a nearby tree had her glancing quickly up to see if the guard were following them with some kind of James Bond mechanical spy satellite. But it was only a trio of monkeys swinging through the trees.

She was just breathing a little easier when the foliage near ground level shifted, and she saw a flash of a man's leg in camouflage attire.

Well, Reynard wasn't using spy satellites. But he

wasn't leaving them alone either. They were still being followed by one of the damn guards.

Curse the man!

"We've got company again," she announced, not bothering to lower her voice. What did it matter if the guy knew that they'd spotted him?"

"Yeah. I'm not going to make love to you in front of an audience," Jack grated, then led her several yards farther on. When he came to a tree with gracefully bending frondlike branches, he ducked under the canopy of greenery and pulled her close again.

The thick, feathery leaves gave them some privacy. Not enough to make love, she decided, if they cared about spectators. But enough so they could get close enough to talk again.

He braced his back against the tree trunk, spread his legs in a vee, and brought her body in line with his. Lowering his mouth to her jawline, he began stringing a row of tiny kisses along her flesh, as though satisfying his sexual appetite was the only thing on his mind. But his words were anything but erotic.

"The note could be a trap."

"I thought of that. But it could have been given to me by Juanita or someone else who feels sorry for Dawn. The question is—does she want to help us, or is she trying to score brownie points with Reynard?"

"You're sure it's a woman?"

"Who else would be in the spa?"

"A maintenance man?" he asked innocently.

She nodded, thinking that the same guy who had been to their villa could have been wiring the spa for sound, too. Or checking the equipment, since the place was probably already wired up.

Jack transferred his attention from her jaw to the column of her throat, and the hazy thought flitted through her brain that the neck was as erotically sensitive an area as you could find.

She closed her eyes and arched for him, giving him better access, her thighs turning to jelly as he aroused her.

She forgot about guards and microphones. Now there was only Jack, touching her, kissing her, stirring her senses.

She couldn't hold back a small moan as his fingers lightly skimmed the outlines of her nipples that must be clearly visible through the knit fabric of her designer T-shirt.

She could hear Jack's breath rushing in and out of his lungs—hear her own labored breathing. And she wondered if he was planning to lift her up and fit her body to his. She could kick off her shorts and panties. And she wouldn't even have to take off his pants. Just open them in the front and free his penis. As the thought took her, she remembered how that part of him had felt in her hand last night. So hard. So hot. So blatantly male. No wonder the term penis envy had been invented by guys. They'd think of the male organ in those terms.

Her terms were different. She didn't want one dangling between her legs or standing out like a flagpole off her body when she was aroused. She wanted this one inside her, filling her, rubbing against her hot, sensitized female flesh.

That was the only thought in her mind as she cupped her hand over the bulge behind his fly, stroking and pressing.

She felt his whole body tighten. Blindly, her fingers found his belt buckle, began to slip leather through metal.

"Don't," he growled, bringing her back to reality, even though it was perfectly obvious that he wanted her as much as she wanted him.

"Don't," he repeated. "I'm not going to put on a sex

show for the guards. Let's find a better place to make love.''

Her lids blinked open, and she stared at him. His green eyes were dark and dilated, yet she could almost watch the struggle going on in their depths. The struggle between desire and business.

Her hands dropped away from his buckle. Then, finding her own voice, she answered, ''Right.''

They both stood in the screen of protective greenery, fighting the needs and desires that seemed to leap and crackle between them like heat lightning every time they let their guard down.

''Come on,'' he finally said, picking up the blanket she hadn't realized he'd dropped and leading her back through the branches.

It felt strange to walk when her knees were weak and every step made the crotch of her shorts rub uncomfortably against her aroused sex. She tugged the fabric down, trying to ease the pressure, and saw Jack catch the movement. She gave him a little shrug, her only consolation being that he was obviously in as bad shape as she was. If her shorts were rubbing her the wrong way, what must the fabric of his slacks feel like pressing against his erection? Another good reason why she wouldn't want to be a man, she thought.

The insanity of their predicament hit them at the same time.

''Hot and bothered in paradise,'' he muttered, then laughed.

Her own laugh helped break some of the tension.

His fingers tightened on hers as he led her farther down the path, both of them scanning the underbrush as they pretended to look for a place where they might be alone.

Only now Maddy couldn't stop herself from wondering

if they were still pretending. If they found a suitable spot, would they take advantage of it?

She abandoned that thought when they came around a curve. Ahead was a break in the trees, and she could see a stone building about fifty yards farther on. Surprisingly close, she thought. Yet the jungle foliage had hidden it from view.

The walls were dark and forbidding, and one feature was the prominent tower jutting from a far corner like a phallic symbol.

A high stone wall enclosed the structure. And the windows she could see above it were barred. As they came closer, she saw that the entrance to the compound was blocked by an iron gate.

She craned her neck upward, her gaze sweeping the window. Did she see a flash of movement behind one of the curtains, she wondered. Or was that just her imagination working overtime?

"Ooo, this place looks neat," she murmured. "Like something out of an adventure movie."

"Yeah. It doesn't look like anyone's around. That wall should block out prying eyes. Let's see if we can find some privacy in the courtyard," Jack suggested.

He and Maddy quickened their pace and reached the gate. This time he didn't try the lock, but headed for a smaller door in the wall. Before they reached it, two guards materialized from the interior. Both had faces as harsh and unyielding as the stone walls behind them. Both had taken their machine guns off their shoulders and held them pointed downward.

Maddy felt the hairs on her arms stir. This place might look like a fantasy movie location, but the guards meant business. If they decided to shoot her and Jack, nobody would know about it. The two of them would simply disappear into unmarked graves in the jungle. And none of the other guests would protest for fear that they'd jeopardize their own safety.

On the other hand, she was sure that one guest—Don Fowler—would be ecstatic because he'd know that his chief rival had been eliminated.

Thinking of the drug dealer made a terrifying thought leap into her mind. Suppose it was Fowler who had sent these guys, decked out like Reynard's troops. Swallowing, she told herself that was nonsense. Fowler didn't have a private army here. She was just reacting to the men and the guns and the isolated setting.

Beside her, Jack cleared his throat. "Is there some problem?" he asked in a voice so smooth that you could spread it on a dinner roll.

"Sorry, sir, this is a restricted area," one of the guards replied, his tone more deferential than she might have expected, given the machine guns.

Jack eyed the weapons. "We didn't mean to trespass. Is that Reynard's prison compound?"

"It's off-limits, sir," the guard repeated without giving away any information.

Jack shifted the blanket draped over his arm. "Yeah, all right. We were just looking for a nice romantic spot."

"Not here."

"Okay. Sure. Come on, baby, let's go back to our villa." He loosened her death grip on his fingers, then slipped his arm around her shoulder, pulling her against his side.

Glad of the support, she exhaled a small breath. When he turned her in the opposite direction, she went willingly.

Still, she couldn't stop her mind from picturing a hail of bullets or her body from bracing for the impact. And it wasn't until they'd rounded a curve in the trail that she felt herself relax.

The guards and their machine guns had had a temporarily dampening effect on her ardor, she realized.

Jack slid her a sidewise look as they headed toward their villa, and she suspected his thoughts were paralleling hers.

"So much for a private clearing in the jungle," he growled.

"This place does have its frustrations."

"Yeah, that reminds me. I forgot to tell you. We've got another reception tonight at the main house."

She closed her eyes for a moment, then forced them open as she gave him a tight nod.

"I'm going to cool off with a little solitary walk. Why don't you rest up? Then we can get ready for the evening."

She might have objected, but she knew that time alone to cool off wasn't such a bad idea.

MADDY KEPT HER ARMS slightly bent and her hands lightly at her sides, ignoring the impulse to fold them protectively across her chest. She'd already worn her most modest dress to the party last night, if you could use the term for any of her evening wear. But she couldn't show up in the same thing two nights in a row—not with this crowd where all the guys were competing to show how much they'd spent on their ladies' outfits. So this evening, she was forced to choose one of her other dresses. This one was a clingy black number that was longer than her thigh-skimmer of the night before. But it would have been impossible to walk in the narrow skirt without side slits. And the slits ran up both sides, showing flashes of her legs from ankle to upper thigh with every step she took. The bodice was even more disturbing, with a neckline that plummeted almost to her navel, barely covering the sides of her breasts on its way down.

And the strands of gold beads that went with the outfit only accentuated her feeling of undress.

Lucky Jack, she thought. The tuxedo didn't leave any of his important parts hanging out.

She cut him a look as they strolled up the path to the main house. He might appear to be relaxed, but she'd come to recognize the small signs of tension that he exhibited. There was the set of his shoulders. The tightness around his jaw. Even the hands thrust into his pockets. With anyone else, that might be a relaxed gesture. But not with Jack. It meant he was reminding himself not to slug anyone.

Of course, she could put the tension down to sexual frustration. She was feeling a pretty heavy dose of that herself—after all the kisses and caresses they'd exchanged that afternoon. But there had been nothing they could do about it. Nothing but move carefully around each other as they got ready for another stimulating evening in the panther's den.

Yet she was very sure sexual frustration wasn't the only thing that had set Jack on edge. Their failure to locate Dawn had to be a major factor in his mood. And there was something else, too. Something he wasn't telling her. Something dark and dangerous. She needed to know what it was, and why he had chosen to keep quiet.

So what was his motivation? Was he trying to protect her? Or had he come to some kind of agreement with Reynard, the terms of which he wasn't prepared to share with her?

She stopped thinking about Jack as she spotted Reynard near the door. He'd been looking out into the darkness as though impatient. And now his face broke into a smile of welcome as she and her escort stepped forward.

"My dear." He greeted her first, reaching out to clasp her shoulders.

The gesture was so much more bold than any he had used before, that she was instantly on guard.

Still, he drew back quickly, flooding her with relief. When he looked to his right, a woman who had been talking to Arnold Ving and Cynthia politely detached herself and glided toward them.

Maddy had a moment to register Ving's disappointment. Then her attention was switched to the woman as she tried to see her the way a man would. She was tall and slender, but with curves in all the right places. Her dress wasn't quite as low cut as Maddy's. But it gave a tantalizing view of breasts that rode high and proud without benefit of a bra. And her skirt was short enough to show off her tanned legs. In fact, her skin looked tanned all over—making Maddy wonder if she sunbathed in the nude. Probably the guys were wondering the same thing.

The woman's face was drop-dead beautiful. She could have been a movie star, Maddy thought. Only she was apparently living here on Orchid Island, at Oliver Reynard's beck and call. Maddy hoped she was well paid for her services.

She came up to Reynard, linked her arm with his and gave him a quick kiss on the cheek.

"Calista, I'd like you to meet Jack and Maddy. Jack, Maddy, this is Calista, one of my favorite companions."

She smiled at them, a secret smile, her eyes roaming over their bodies—her interest in Maddy as frankly sexual as her interest in Jack.

She held out her slender hand to him first. He would have been rude to refuse the gesture. As his flesh touched hers, Maddy saw the woman sweep her thumb sensually along her palm, her long nail grazing his flesh before breaking the contact.

Jack gave her a small nod, even as Calista reached toward Maddy. Again there was no polite way to refuse the gesture, and again the thumb swept over flesh, offering an unmistakable and disturbing sexual invitation. Even more disturbing was the way Reynard was watching the exchange—with obvious enjoyment and keen interest—as though he was eager to see more.

Maddy pulled her hand back, cutting off the impulse to wipe her palm against her skirt. Despite Calista's beauty, or perhaps because of it, the woman gave her the creeps.

And Reynard's next words didn't help. "I'm hoping we can all become better friends," he said in an oily voice designed to convey the offer of intimate activities.

Over my dead body, Maddy thought, then considered the phrasing. What if her life depended on getting to know this woman better? What if Dawn's life depended on it?

She dredged up a smile. "If that's what Jack wants."

"Very good, my dear." Reynard's gaze dropped to her cleavage as he spoke. "I like a woman who understands where her priorities lie."

You wish, Maddy thought as they chatted for a few more minutes. Relief washed over her when Reynard went off to talk to some of his other guests, taking Calista with him.

But she was on edge most of the evening, especially when Reynard called Jack over for a private conversation, and Calista came gliding back to make small talk.

"How are you enjoying your stay here on Orchid Island?" she asked.

"Oh, very much."

"We try to give our guests an experience that would be impossible on the mainland."

"We?"

"Yes. Oliver and I."

Maddy hadn't known he was part of a couple. Was it true, she wondered, or was Calista overstating her role here?

"The place is so luxurious," she gushed.

"Yes. The facilities are beautifully maintained. And you can indulge your every whim." She paused and smiled. "There's no need to worry about all the old rules you learned back home."

"Such as what?"

"I mean, you can satisfy any taste you like here."

"I thought that might be true for the men. Not the women," Maddy answered.

"Some of the women. The bold ones get to let their hair down."

"I don't need to let my hair down with anyone else, if that's what you're implying. I have everything I need in Jack."

"How do you know if you don't give yourself a chance to find out?"

"I'm comfortable with what we have."

"You do your best to please him?"

"Of course."

"What if he wanted to see you making love with another woman? Would you please him that way?"

Maddy swallowed around the sudden tightness in her throat. To her vast relief, Jack rejoined them before she was forced to come up with an answer.

Still, she felt her face grow hot, even though she hadn't been the one to initiate the conversation. Calista looked perfectly at ease.

"I think we should be getting back," Jack said, slinging an arm around her shoulder.

"Yes," she answered, sliding her hand up and down his arm.

Outside, she took a deep breath of the night air. "Calista was making some surprising suggestions," she whispered.

"Don't let that worry you."

Which meant what, Maddy silently wondered. She was just about to ask him that question, when a raucous voice from above her head made her jump.

"Go for it!"

Looking up, she saw it was one of the parrots making a suggestive comment.

Jack managed a chuckle. "Never alone."

"Um-hum."

They passed from the portion of the path that was brightly illuminated into the area that was lighted only by the small bulbs that lined the edges.

After leading Maddy a few yards into this dimmer area, Jack stopped to pull her close and nuzzle his lips against her cheek, sliding them slowly toward her ear. In a barely audible voice, he whispered, "When we get back, I'm going out to investigate that prison."

"I'm coming with you!" she said, then realized her mistake. She'd spoken aloud when they were supposed to be having a very private conversation. She went very still, waiting for armed guards to descend on them and demand to know where he was going.

"One hot session in the shower is enough for me," Jack said, instantly covering for her.

"Yes," she breathed, grateful and at the same time angry with herself. What was wrong with her? She'd made a bad slip. Probably because Reynard and Calista had set her nerves on edge.

She felt a tremor go through her and knew he had felt it too. His hands slid across her back, then up and down her arms, stroking and soothing. Her head drifted to his shoulder, and they stood there on the path. She hoped they looked like lovers stopping to dally for a while, before getting to the main event.

"You're doing great," he murmured in her ear.

"No," she answered, remembering to keep the comment to a whisper. Before she could stop herself, she added, "I didn't know how claustrophobic this place would be."

He didn't say, "I told you so." He simply stroked her as he began to whisper again, "This is what we're going to do."

Maddy listened to Jack's instructions, thinking once more that he was a brilliant strategist when it came to undercover work.

The thought made her giggle.

"Um?"

"Nerves," she mouthed.

"Yeah."

9

WHEN THEY'D STEPPED into the villa, Jack loosened the formal bow tie that now felt like a noose around his neck. Crossing to the bar, he poured them each a drink. Bourbon for himself. White wine for Maddy. He didn't know about her, but after the hours they'd just spent at Reynard's mansion, he needed something to wash away the taste of the man.

Still he kept his voice light as he clinked his glass against Maddy's. "Well, here's to a memorable evening, now that we're finally alone."

He smiled as she made her eyes round, following the scenario he'd outlined in hushed tones on the path while he'd been pretending his mind was on other things.

Her voice was all innocence as she said, "I thought we couldn't do anything here. Not with all the cameras and the microphones. I mean how do we know they're really gone?"

After downing another swallow of bourbon, he answered, "I thought of a way around it. We can make love in the dark—very, very quietly."

As he spoke, he reached to stroke his finger suggestively down the front of her dress, skimming the sides of her breasts as he traced the line of the deep V that plunged toward her navel.

He was pleased to hear her words slur as she said, "Oh Jack, you're so clever."

"Um," he answered, hoping anybody who was listening wasn't expecting brilliant dialogue.

It was easy for him to slide his finger farther under the fabric, for that one invading digit to skim over the tender flesh of her breast, then tease the very edges of her nipple.

"Oh!" Her fingers clamped on his arm, and he didn't know if she were trying to still his hand or simply reacting helplessly to the intimate touch.

All he knew about himself was that he couldn't stop. Not yet.

Lord, it was getting worse. At least for him. All he had to do was touch her with one finger and his whole body was on fire. He bent his head, nibbling along the tender line of her jaw, then finding the column of her throat. He loved the soft flesh there. There and everywhere else on her body.

"Jack, don't," she murmured. "Don't make me hot until we're ready for bed."

He blinked, reminding himself that this was supposed to be for show. Swiftly he lifted his head and pulled his hand away, as if he'd come into contact with a hot stove.

For several seconds, he stood there, breathing hard, trying to remember what he'd intended to say. Then he cleared his throat as he recalled his lines. "But I like a little visual stimulation. So here's the deal. Go in the bathroom and put on one of your sexy gowns. I'll be in the bedroom waiting for you."

She took a quick sip of her wine, then set the glass on the bar. After she'd hurried into the other room, he followed more slowly, as though he were savoring the anticipation. But he was in time to see her take an ecru gown out of the drawer. It was the one he'd hoped she'd wear. The one with the fitted bodice edged with lace. The one he knew would cup her breasts so beautifully.

She followed directions, disappearing into the bathroom, and he pulled back the spread, then piled two pillows along the headboard.

While she was gone, he kicked off his shoes, then unbuttoned his shirt and slipped it over the back of the desk chair.

Like a man anticipating an evening of hot sex, he turned off all the lights but the one on the nearest bedside table, then lay down on the bed and stacked his hands behind his head.

When he heard the bathroom door click, his whole body went instantly hard with anticipation. Making love to her now might be out of the question, but he hadn't been kidding about craving the visual stimulation. As Maddy stepped into the bedroom, backlit by the light streaming in back of her, his breath caught.

He'd anticipated how beautiful, how sexy she'd look. But his imagination never seemed to do her justice.

And it didn't help that she looked hot and hungry—as hot and hungry as he felt.

"Come here, baby."

She took a shaky step toward him, then another. Her eyes as intense on him as his were on her.

She stopped beside the bed, and he swung his legs over the edge, planting them on the floor as he drew her between his knees. Her body swayed in his arms, swayed closer, so that her scent enveloped him and her torso filled his vision. He could see her breasts through the translucent fabric of the gown. Indecently translucent, he thought, with the few brain cells that were still functioning. The rounded shape and the nipples were showcased rather than hidden.

He should leave. Right now before he forgot the evening's mission. But he couldn't do it yet, not when she looked so sweetly tempting.

Knowing he was playing with fire, he bent to rub his

face against her breasts, turning his head this way and that, his lips grazing one taut nipple and then the other.

A breathy exclamation escaped her lips as he closed his mouth around her, suckling through the silky fabric.

Her hands came up to cradle his head, her fingers restless as they tunneled through his thick hair.

He couldn't stop his hands from sliding up and down her flanks, the silky fabric teasing his fingertips. She was naked under the gown. He'd seen that immediately, seen the tempting blond shadow at the top of her legs.

Now he slipped his hands under the hem, and slid them upward, his fingers playing over her hips, over the rounded swell of her bottom.

She made a soft, pleading sound that almost drove the last shreds of coherence from his mind. He wanted her. Now. With a driving need he could barely control. And when her fingers dug into his shoulders, the only thought in his head was that if he wrapped his arms around her and fell back onto the bed, she'd tumble right on top of him.

The anticipation of her body coming down on him sent a spasm of heat through him. And he knew he was on the edge of losing control. He had to quit now or forget about the mission he'd set for himself tonight.

"We'd better turn out the lights," he said, hearing the raspy quality of his own voice as he reached for the lamp. When he snapped the switch, the light lowered considerably. But there was still enough illumination from the bathroom to see Maddy's shadowy form. She hadn't moved from the spot where she'd been standing.

He rose and caught her in his arms, pulling her tightly against him, absorbing the familiar feel of her slender curves. Then he turned and laid her gently on the bed. As she lay there gazing up at him, he bent to give her a quick, sharp kiss.

Her arms raised and slid around his neck as though she could hold him there. But they both had work to do, so he gently loosened her grip, then stood up, backing away because he knew that if he didn't put distance between them, he would reach for her again.

"Hold that thought," he growled. Striding across the room, he turned off the bathroom light. The room was dark now. As dark as it needed to be.

In the blackness, he crossed to the bureau and got out some dark slacks and a dark knit shirt—expensive but casual sports clothes that would double as stealthwear. Mindful that the room might well be wired for sound, he quietly changed. Instead of the white running shoes and socks he'd worn during the day, he opted for black.

From the bed, Maddy made a low sexy sound like a woman who was being stroked and petted. It was what he'd asked her to do—to make anybody listening believe that the two of them were lying there together—getting into something hot and heavy.

Unfortunately, it sounded so real that he felt his chest constrict. He stood for a moment with his hands squeezed into fists. Then he forced himself to turn away and move to the sliding glass door.

As he pulled the drapes aside, Maddy moaned, almost sending him striding back to the bed.

If he didn't know the truth, he'd think she was a woman having a very rewarding time with her lover. And he wanted to *be* that lover. For a moment he stood with his cock painfully swollen and his teeth clenched. Then he very deliberately unlocked the door and stepped onto the patio, hoping that Reynard hadn't turned his leopard loose to patrol the grounds.

He was thinking that if he were caught now, he'd have no way to explain what he was doing. He couldn't say he was cooling off with a nighttime stroll. Because as far as the listeners were concerned, he was still back there with Maddy.

Of course, there *was* one other explanation. Maddy could be back there having a good time by herself. Would she be willing to follow that script? Her guy had said he was going for a walk, and she'd taken advantage of his absence to engage in a little self-pleasuring.

The idea made him squeeze his eyes shut for a moment. He didn't like someone thinking that he couldn't take care of all Maddy's sexual needs. But if he had to play out that script to save her life, he'd do it, and hope she'd take her cue from him.

He pulled his mind away from that scenario, then sucked in several deep breaths and let them out slowly, willing his blood to cool down.

It didn't help that the atmosphere outside was warm and muggy, much less comfortable than the bedroom where he'd just left Maddy.

Again, his thoughts went back to her. For long moments, he couldn't stop himself from picturing her in that sexy gown, lying on the bed, her head thrown back, a contented purring sound rising in her throat.

He hoped the sound effects were going to drive the damn guards who were listening crazy.

He willed away the image, then used one of his old mental exercises to center himself. When he felt more in control, he opened his eyes and probed the darkness, thankful that there was enough moonlight to illuminate the grounds around the villa, because using a light was out of the question.

An insect buzzed around his head, and he swatted it away. But at least he wasn't going to come back with too many bites. He'd learned from his research that Orchid Island had a spraying program that kept the bug population in check.

He stayed where he was on the patio for several minutes, listening to the sounds of the night. The rustlings in the underbrush. The occasional call of an animal.

He hadn't thought he was a praying man. But he'd asked for divine help more than once since this assignment had begun. He said a silent prayer now. For Maddy and Dawn, because if he screwed this up, they were both in deep trouble.

With that thought in mind, he stepped into the foliage. Soon well-tended greenery gave way to denser jungle as he moved in the direction that he and Maddy had taken that afternoon, staying off the path to avoid patrols.

He wished there were some way to know the guards' schedule. But that detail hadn't been available. So all he could do was keep out of sight and hope for the best. More than once he got slapped in the face by fronds and branches. And several times he stepped onto uneven ground and almost lost his footing.

When he came to a place where a tangle of vines blocked his path, he swore under his breath, wishing he had a knife. But bringing a weapon of any kind to the island had been out of the question. So he moved carefully around the obstacle, then took a sighting on the stars to get his bearing.

He had just emerged from a tangle of underbrush and corrected his course again when he saw it—a dark shape looming against the skyline.

With silent thanks, he glided forward, then went stock-still when he heard footsteps hitting a solid surface.

Two uniformed men moved rapidly by along the path—only a few yards from where he stood frozen beside a tree trunk.

So how long did he have before the next patrol—ten minutes? Twenty?

He counted slowly to one hundred, then took a deep

breath and stepped from the screen of foliage. He was across the path in three seconds—and heading for the tower.

A light was shining in the high window that he'd seen earlier. The courtyard was also illuminated.

When he got close enough to make out details, he saw that the entrance to the courtyard was guarded as it had been that afternoon. Earlier there had been two men on duty—both out of sight initially. Tonight there was only one, right at the entrance.

Was that standard operating procedure? Did Reynard change the drill at night, or were there two men on duty—one out here and one somewhere inside the grounds?

He stared at the large stones that made up the wall. They were put together in rough fashion—rough enough to find convenient hand and footholds. Which meant that he might be able to gain the inner courtyard without going through the front entrance.

Dangerous, he thought. But suppose it was the only way to get into the tower?

He was about to circle the wall and look for a place to climb over when a new development stopped him cold. A small figure stepped out of the darkness.

The sentry straightened, then brought his weapon to firing position.

"Miguel, don't shoot. It's me, Juanita," a woman's voice called out. "I came to bring food."

The man lowered his machine gun, then eased it back onto his shoulder. "For me? Or for her?"

"Both."

For me or for her? So there was a woman being held here. Dawn? Or somebody else?

"You're late. I thought nobody was coming."

"I had other work to do."

Miguel moved forward and lifted a covered basket out

of the woman's hands. "You're not supposed to be bring-ing me anything," he said gruffly.

"I like you, Miguel."

"We could both get in trouble if the captain finds out that I'm eating on duty."

"Who's going to turn us in? The patrol won't be back for twenty minutes."

He laughed. "Right."

Twenty minutes. Well, that was another piece of prime information.

From the shadows of the trees, Jack watched Miguel inspect the contents of the basket. Reaching inside, he took out a piece of chicken and began to gnaw on it.

"Can I go up? Do you want to escort me?"

"I should go with you," he said around a mouth full of food. After several seconds' hesitation, he added, "But the key's in the usual place. Go on."

The usual place. So the key to the cell or cells was within easy reach. Good.

When Jack saw the woman quickly cross the lighted courtyard and enter a door, he made a rapid circuit of the wall, looking for a good place to climb over.

When he was halfway around the circle, a grating sound drifted to him from above.

The noise came again. From the cell near the top of the tower?

He shouldn't be able to hear anything. He was down on the ground. And the cell was far above his head. Yet he suddenly remembered a time when he'd experienced exactly the same phenomenon. He'd been on vacation, visiting Tikal, a ruined Mayan city in Guatemala, that had been completely buried for hundreds of years in the jun-gle. The archeological team that had excavated some of the buildings had only uncovered the front portion of many temples—leaving huge dirt- and plant-covered hills in the back. He'd climbed one such hill, pulling himself up using roots and vines, but his female companion had been afraid to risk it. So she'd remained on the ground—and when he'd moved around to the front of the two-hundred-foot-high temple, they'd been able to talk to each other easily, without shouting.

Something similar must be happening now, he thought as he strained his ears.

"Juanita!" a female voice exclaimed. "Thank God you're back."

"I can't stay long."

"Please. I'm so scared." The last part came out as a sob.

"I know. But the woman you told me about is here."

"Maddy! Thank God."

"I told her where you are. You must wait."

"I...I think I'll go crazy if I have to stay here any longer. I was so stupid. So stupid to run away."

"It wasn't your fault."

"Yes, it was!"

There were whispered words of comfort. Then the woman said, "I must go."

"Please. Don't leave me."

"The guard will be suspicious. I gave him part of your dinner, but he gets restless."

"Okay. Yes. Thank you so much. My father will be very grateful."

Jack stood there in frozen silence. That had to be Dawn up there—and the woman who had given Maddy the note this afternoon. Juanita.

Quietly he faded back into the jungle foliage. He'd just picked up some important information. But he wasn't sure how to interpret what he'd learned.

He'd easily overheard a strategic conversation. So was that just a lucky break for him, because he'd been in just the right spot? Or had someone arranged for him to hear Juanita talking to Dawn?

There were just too many damn factors.

Like…maybe the guard had heard the women talking, too. And he was going to make a report.

He wanted desperately to discuss what he'd just found out with Maddy. Maybe she knew something more about Juanita. Was the woman a spy? Was she telling Dawn the truth? Or was she setting a trap?

He'd like Maddy's insights. But he knew he wasn't going to exchange information with her any time soon. Not when that maintenance man—Isley—had probably been back at the villa setting up more spy equipment.

Well, he might as well stick around for a while and see if there was anything else to find out. Again, Jack moved around the building, until he was back where he'd started—at the guard post. The man had finished his chicken. After carefully wiping his fingers on a piece of cloth, he wrapped up the bones.

Through the doorway, Jack saw Juanita step out the door at the base of the tower and cross the inner courtyard once more.

The man thrust the packet of chicken bones at her. "Take these away."

"Of course. I wouldn't want to get you in trouble."

"You were up there a long time."

"I feel sorry for the poor girl. And—she tells me things."

"Like what?"

"Her father is rich. Maybe he will reward—"

Her words broke off abruptly. Quickly she thrust the hand with the packet of chicken bones into the pocket of her skirt. Moments later, Jack realized what had caused the abrupt change in behavior.

Two armed guards were coming rapidly up the path—heading straight for the tower.

The sentry at the door snapped to attention as the two men on patrol came abreast of the doorway.

"What's going on?" one of the newcomers asked.

"You're early," Miguel said.

"We're doubling the shifts."

From the jungle Jack silently cursed.

"So you thought we wouldn't be here now," the man on patrol said. "What were you up to?"

"Juanita was delivering food to the prisoner, the way she does every night," the man in the doorway answered.

"Well, I don't see any basket of food," one of the men on patrol answered.

"I've already taken it up," the woman replied.

"Then why are you still hanging around?"

"Miguel and I were just passing the time."

"That's against the rules."

"We weren't doing any harm."

"What if somebody tried to help the prisoner escape?"

Juanita laughed. "Who would be stupid enough to do that?"

"I don't know. But we have our orders to be watchful. You could be in big trouble," he added.

"I hope not," she said, moving forward.

Jack watched as she reached out a hand and touched the front of the man's shirt.

His arm shot out, and he pulled her closer.

When he lowered his head to her mouth, she didn't resist. In fact, she twined her arms around his neck and pressed her body against his.

The man's hands slid down her back to cup her bottom and pull her more tightly against himself.

Probably not part of his official duties, Jack thought.

He'd bet that Reynard would like to know about this little incident.

Maybe it would make a good bargaining chip. On the other hand, then Jack would have to explain what he was doing out here by the tower.

"That's very persuasive," the guard was saying, his voice thick with arousal.

Probably not just his voice, Jack thought.

"But not quite persuasive enough. You've left me wanting a lot more."

"Then we'll have to do something about that." Juanita looked from him to the three other men. "But not here," she added quickly. "We could all get in trouble for this."

"I'll be off duty in two hours."

"You could come to my room."

"Where is it?"

"You go in the entrance to the servants' complex. Turn to the right. My door is the fifth one down. The number is 22."

"Twenty-two," he repeated.

"Yes. I'll be waiting for you," she answered, making her voice husky and seductive. Like she was really looking forward to having sex with a man who'd threatened her. Without waiting for further comment, she turned and hurried away into the darkness.

Jack heard the men talking in low voices, heard sharp laughter. The one who had kissed her probably thought he was getting away with murder. He didn't know that Juanita had her own agenda. And the scene Jack had witnessed made it appear that the woman was desperate to stay out of trouble. For Dawn's sake, he hoped.

IN THE DARKNESS, Maddy glanced at the illuminated green numbers on the clock face. Jack had been gone for almost two hours, and she was worried.

What if Reynard's men had discovered him out there in the darkness and taken him into custody? What if he was being questioned now?

She wanted to pull on her clothing and rush out into the night. But that wasn't an option. Her job was to stay here and convince anyone listening that Jack was here too.

A small sound escaped from her lips, something between a moan and a sob. She clapped her hand over her mouth, then took it away, her face twisting in the darkness.

That's what she was supposed to be doing, wasn't she? Making noises.

"Oh, Jack," she murmured. "That's so good. Don't stop." She punctuated the request with a series of breathy pants—thinking that this was a damn strange way to conduct a secret mission.

Yet at the same time she knew that Jack's life might depend on her midnight performance. She hoped that if somebody was listening they'd decided that Jack was a hell of a good lover.

Actually, he *was* a hell of a good lover, she thought, her body heating as she remembered that first time. And then in the shower.

He was sensual and focused and as concerned about her pleasure as he was his own.

For a few moments she allowed herself to remember the feel of his hands and mouth on her body.

This time when a little sound of pleasure escaped her lips, it was genuine.

"Jack," she said his name aloud again. "Jack."

Just thinking about him had her whole body on fire, and before she could stop herself, she brought her hands to her chest and cupped her breasts.

She could feel her hardened nipples though the silky

fabric of the gown. Restlessly, she stroked her fingers over them, making her blood heat even more.

She thought of Jack touching her. Thought of Jack sliding his hand down her body and caressing the slick flesh of her sex.

Her own hand slid downward, but she stopped when she reached her hip bone.

She was only making things worse. She couldn't let herself dissolve in a pool of sensual pleasure. She had to keep her mind alert.

Ruthlessly, she struggled to quench the flames that thoughts of Jack and her own hands had ignited. She needed to calm herself down, and she knew how to do it. She could think about this afternoon, when she'd known that Jack was hiding something from her.

The remembered scene had the desired effect. And now her mind went spinning off in another direction. What if Jack had lied about where he was going this evening? What if he had a secret meeting with Reynard or somebody who worked for the man.

No! She silently screamed.

Impossible.

Yet the evil thought lodged like a knife blade in her skull.

Tomorrow, she knew, she had to bring it out into the open somehow. She had to know where she stood in this operation. But lying here getting upset wasn't going to do her a damn bit of good.

Eyes closed, she made her mind blank, concentrating on breathing slowly and deeply in a pattern that she hoped would relax her brain and body.

For a short time, it seemed to work. She even drifted into a peaceful sleep.

JACK WAITED until the patrol had passed, waited until the sentry was once more standing beside the archway. Then he took his bearings by the North Star again and began retracing his steps to the villa.

Because he knew the route, he could move faster through the jungle. Although he had to keep stopping and checking his position by the stars, he reached the villa in forty-five minutes.

From the protection of the foliage, he studied the back door. Everything looked okay, but he couldn't be absolutely sure until he got inside.

Under the protection of the greenery, he used a stick to scrape the bottom of his shoes, then stepped forward and wiped them on the grass beyond the patio.

A NIGHTMARE GRABBED Maddy by the throat. Her mind knew at once that it was a dream, that it couldn't be real, because reality had shifted. She hadn't come to Orchid Island to rescue Dawn. Dawn was safe at home, and Maddy was the woman locked in the Dark Tower, her hands wrapped around the bars of a small window as she peered out into the blackness of the jungle night.

She was listening for something. Waiting.

Then, from her high vantage point, she saw a man moving through the foliage, making his stealthy way toward the tower. She couldn't see his face, not from up in the tower. But she knew it was Jack—coming to save her.

Then, to her horror, she saw a group of men heading toward him.

Reynard and his soldiers.

She pressed her face against the bars and screamed a warning. "Jack, watch out. They know you're there."

He stopped dead in his tracks, but it was already too late. They were on him, beating at him with their fists and with the butts of their weapons, and she was helpless to do more than watch the horror unfold.

Then somebody yanked her roughly away from the window. She kicked at him. Clawed, because she knew it was Reynard. She might have gotten away. She had almost struggled free—until more hands clamped onto her body, and she screamed again because it was Calista. Touching her, whispering that she had her now.

Horror rose inside her, and she put forth a mighty effort, yanking herself free of the woman and yanking herself free of the dream.

Her body drenched in sweat, she lay among the tangled sheets, listening to the sound of her own heart beating—until another noise told her that she was still in danger—real danger.

JACK CROSSED the remaining distance to the concrete pad. It was darker closer to the house where the wall cast a shadow, and he cursed as he bumped into one of the patio chairs.

Anxious to get inside, he pulled open the sliding glass door and stepped across the threshold. As he did, an arm slipped around his neck and took him in a stranglehold.

10

JACK TRIED TO DRAW in a breath. The arm tightened, and he staggered forward, the assailant on his back weighing him down.

Lord, the guards had come here to investigate, found Maddy alone, and taken her into custody.

Now they were after him.

The thought was canceled immediately. The person reaching across his back to clamp his windpipe wasn't heavy. Then he registered the twin pressures against his shoulders.

Breasts.

It was Maddy. She'd heard him outside, thought he was someone from Reynard's goon squad, and gone on the attack.

In his mind, he screamed out his own name. *Jack. It's Jack. Stop it; you're choking me.*

But no sound made it past the stranglehold around his windpipe.

Lord, the woman was determined. She was weaponless, but she'd come after a man she undoubtedly thought was armed. Too bad he was the victim.

He had little time to dwell on her bravery. Not when she was cutting off his breath. In the darkness he could see nothing. Hear nothing besides the roaring in his own ears. The one thing he knew for sure was that he had to break her stranglehold quickly, before he lost consciousness.

And he had to do it without hurting Maddy.

He reared back, taking her by surprise. He felt her hold loosen just a little. Leaning forward, he flipped her over his head and onto the rug.

He had time for a quick, grateful gulp of air before she grabbed his leg and toppled him.

She was on him again, like a woman fighting for her life—a woman bent on doing serious damage to the man who had invaded her bedroom.

He grunted when she slammed her fist into his chin. The blow was surprisingly solid, but didn't slow his own reactions. This time he was ready for her. His hands came up, grabbing her wrists, keeping her from strangling him again.

Once more he flipped her over and off his body—this time onto her back. Before she could slither from his grasp, he came down on top of her, his hands manacling her wrists as he held them against the carpet.

''Don't,'' he growled when she tried to get her knee into position to do serious damage to his manhood.

At the sound of his voice, she went very still, then sucked in a shaky draft of air.

''Surprise,'' he hissed in the darkness, easing his hold on her.

When she didn't try to fight him again, he rolled to his side, taking her with him.

They both lay there on the rug, breathing hard.

''I'm sorry,'' she murmured. ''I didn't know....''

Right. She hadn't known it was him. She must have been on overdrive, he thought, waiting for the worst. When she'd heard an invader in the room, she'd defended her turf.

In his mind, he tried to reverse their positions. If that had happened to him, he'd want to explain his thinking to the person he'd just attacked. Unfortunately, explanations could be fatal, under the circumstances.

Before she could say anything else, he moved his hand to her mouth, keeping it there for several seconds. She gave a little nod, and he eased up on the pressure.

This time when she spoke, she brought her lips to his ear, then said in a barely audible whisper, "Jack, I'm sorry. I…I was trying to make myself relax, and I fell asleep. I had a dream…."

"Bad?"

"Yes," she murmured, and he knew she was thinking about how to phrase her response. "This island makes me feel…nervous. I guess I fell asleep for a while and dreamed that Reynard and his men had captured you…they…" She broke off abruptly and started again. "When I woke up, I heard a noise, and I thought…I thought…"

He nodded his head in the darkness, his forehead pressed against her cheek.

"I'm here," was all he could say. He wanted to tell her that it had taken longer than he'd expected to get to the tower. He wanted to relate what had happened when he did. And he wanted to tell her that he knew she was in danger from Reynard—but he wasn't going to let anything happen to her.

He thought about dragging her out into the star-filled night, where presumably they would be able to talk. But he'd already pushed his luck pretty far this evening. Which made going outside again a bad idea.

What was he going to tell the guards if they got caught? That they'd wanted to have sex outside in the darkness— after they'd presumably been enjoying each other in bed for hours.

Not likely.

"Jack?" she murmured, probably sensing the tension coursing through him.

There was nothing he could tell her about the night's activities—not now. But at the same time, he wanted to ease her mind.

He raised up. "At your service, baby," he said, feeling her warm breath against his lips. He wanted to see her then, wanted her to see the reassurance in his eyes. But the room was too dark for eye contact, so he simply lowered his mouth to hers. He meant it to be a quick kiss, just a way to connect with her as best he could. But the moment his lips touched down on hers, he knew he was kidding himself.

He felt as if he were drowning, with no one to save him except the woman in his arms.

Perhaps she was feeling the same thing, because she made a hungry sound, and slid her arms around his neck. Her lips never leaving his, she deepened the kiss.

He wanted to tell her to stop. He wanted to tell her they shouldn't be doing this. That he had no right to take any more from her than he'd already taken. But the words stayed locked in his throat because he didn't have the strength to utter them.

He'd wanted her all day. No, he'd wanted her again almost as soon as they'd stepped out of the shower. And the roles they'd been acting while they were together hadn't helped. Not when every touch, every taste of her had fueled his blind, selfish need.

Now he felt his heart slamming against the inside of his chest as he gathered her to him.

He was lost in the woman taste of her, the feel of her mouth on his. He forgot about the trip to the tower. For a moment out of time he forgot about why they'd come to Orchid Island and why they were in the worst fix of his life.

There was only the reality of the warm, pliant woman in his arms. Swamping his senses, threatening to drive every coherent thought from his mind.

Some part of him was waiting for her to pull away. This was wrong—for her. He was no good for her. Not on any long-term basis. He was a man who couldn't afford commitments. But in the short term, he simply couldn't turn her loose. Not when she was making small whimpering sounds in her throat, begging him to deepen the kiss.

When her hands slid to his hips, and she pulled herself to him, rocking her body against the rigid flesh behind his fly, he thought he would go out of his mind if he didn't have her now. Here. On the rug.

Somehow the realization of where they were brought back a measure of sanity.

"Not here," he said. "Not on the damn floor."

He eased away from her and lay on his back, his breath coming in great gasps.

"Jack?" she questioned, and he could hear her breath, fast and uneven.

When she rolled toward him, he put his hands on her shoulders. "I'm trying to remember I'm a civilized man."

"What's that supposed to mean?"

He turned his head toward her. In the darkened bedroom he could see her profile but not the expression on her face.

"It means we're getting back into bed," he answered, his head clearing enough to remember that someone might be listening to this conversation.

Damn! He wanted privacy. He wanted the lights on so he could see Maddy, see the arousal he knew was painted on her face. And he wanted to watch that arousal build and grow.

But he wanted privacy more. Because he was damned

if he was going to stand for anyone watching them make love.

He stood, reached for her hand, and helped her to her feet. When she swayed toward him, he put his palm up again, preventing her body from touching his—preventing either one of them from reaching flash point too quickly.

She made a small sound of protest. He only led her to the bed, then looked down at the sheets. There was enough light for him to see that she'd twisted them into a tangled mess while he'd been gone. Well, she hadn't been lying about her anxiety.

He bent to smooth out the bottom sheet, then folded back the top one, along with the light spread.

"Lie down," he murmured.

She slid onto the bed, moving across the mattress and holding out her arms to him.

Standing beside the bed, he gazed down at her, feeling overwhelmed by emotions that pierced him to his very center.

He wanted her with a physical need that bordered on madness. But that was only a small part of what he felt for her. He wanted things he had never wanted before. Things he was afraid to put into words. Things that frightened him.

The need for self-preservation made him cut off his thoughts as he kicked his feet out of his shoes, then tugged at his socks before pulling his shirt over his head. When he got to his slacks, he hesitated. He was already rock-hard, and hot enough to go off like a firecracker.

And if he eased into her now, climax was only a few lightning strokes away.

But he had never been a selfish lover. Not even the first time with her. Or during the frantic scene in the shower. He wanted more than a release of the tension that had been building inside him all day.

He wanted to arouse her slowly, to enjoy every moment of her pleasure before he took anything for himself. But if he were naked beside her on the bed, he knew it might be impossible not to indulge his own greed for her, impossible not to plunge inside her and slake his own raging desire.

So he kept his briefs on, then stretched out beside her. Her hand slid down his back, came to the narrow band of knit fabric and stopped. When she raised her head, he knew she was staring at him in the darkness.

''Not yet,'' was all he said, as his own hand reached to stroke the soft fabric of her gown while he remembered how sexy the ecru silk had looked against her creamy skin. Remembered the tantalizing details he had glimpsed through the translucent fabric—the shadows of her nipples and the curly blond hair at the juncture of her legs.

He stroked her from shoulder to hip, enjoying the feel of his hand sliding over the silky fabric, and the feel of her body stirring under his touch. Then he stroked upward again, his goal the ecru lace at her bodice. He stopped to play with the raised texture of it before he slipped one finger underneath, just at the edge of the V.

Delicately he stroked the inner curve of one breast, then the other, gratified when he heard her breath catch and then quicken for him.

Every movement was slow and deliberate as he stroked inward toward one nipple, almost touching it before withdrawing.

She made a frustrated sound and strained toward him in the darkness, silently begging for a more satisfying touch. But he wasn't about to give her what they both wanted. Not yet. Not until he'd built her arousal to the same molten level of heat he was feeling.

She moved restlessly under his touch. Then she grabbed at his hand and tried to drag it where she wanted it. He resisted, then caught her wrists in his hand and pulled them above her head.

Maybe he would take off her gown, he suddenly decided. And use it to his advantage.

His fingers tugged at the sheer skirt, dragging it up and over her head. But he kept her arms tangled in the thin fabric, using it like a rope to bind her wrists and loop them around one of the bars of the brass headboard.

When he was finished, she was naked, her arms raised above her head. The silky gown was a fragile restraint. He knew she could have gotten free if she'd wanted to. But she stayed where she was, her face turned toward him.

He brought his lips to her ear. "Are you okay?"

"Yes."

He nodded in the darkness. He had never wanted to tie a woman up like this before. And he knew that in his mind he was binding her to him—even if he understood that he had no right to do it.

His eyes traveled over her body. He could see her smooth skin against the sheets. But he couldn't make out much more.

Again, he longed for the light. He wanted to see the look in her eyes now. It took a great deal of restraint to keep from reaching for the lamp beside the bed. But he kept it off, because the idea of anyone watching them set his teeth on edge.

He knelt beside her, gently stroking below her breasts and down over the curve of her hip, just a light, teasing touch as he let his own fantasy build. He had her in his power now. He could do anything he wanted to her. And he knew exactly what that was.

When she called his name, her voice soft and pleading, he turned his face upward, seeing the outline of her jaw. He leaned to kiss her there, stringing a line of tiny kisses that moved downward to the slender column of her throat.

He spent considerable time there—first with little nibbling kisses that grew steadily more openmouthed before he moved lower to her collarbone.

He bound himself to his own set of rules, using only his mouth and his face to caress her. Slowly and deliberately, he worked his way downward, teasing the tops of her breasts, then made tiny forays to her erect nipples.

He could feel her chest rising and falling as she gasped for air. He could feel heat coming off her in waves that seared his own flesh. When he raised his head, he saw that her hands were wrapped around the brass bars of the headboard, and she was holding on for dear life.

Her breasts were not large. But they were so very responsive. Gratifyingly responsive, he thought as he bent to her again—sucking one nipple into his mouth, drawing a pleading gasp from her as he used his tongue and teeth to advantage. Then, temporarily abandoning his rules, he used one hand on the other nipple, gently squeezing and twisting in ways he knew would push her higher.

Her body arched and writhed under his mouth and hand, and he savored the sound of her voice as she called out for mercy. He had never wanted a woman more in his life. Desperate for her, he pressed his swollen cock against her thigh.

But at the same time, he had never been more bent on giving pleasure, and the briefs he'd prudently kept on stayed on.

With a shaky breath he inched his lower body away from hers. He ached to see her clearly now. He wanted to see all the fine details of her arousal. Her erect nipples. The flush that he knew must be spread across her skin. The hazy erotic look in her eyes.

But he must do with other senses, touch and hearing—and taste.

Taste! Yes, taste, he thought, as he licked delicately at

the crowns and indentations of her ribs, then moved toward the center of her body to flick his tongue into her navel.

He felt her stomach muscles quiver, felt his own mirror the response.

Reaching up, he snagged one of the pillows at the top of the bed, then lifted her hips with his other hand so he could slide it under her.

As he raised her middle off the mattress, she called out his name again, her voice low and throaty and questioning.

"Right here," he answered as he opened her thighs and moved between them.

She made a small sound that might have been a protest—or an invitation.

He didn't know which. And he didn't care. He knew what he wanted. To kiss her. Feast on her essence.

Gently he parted the folds of her sex with his fingers, feeling his own body quicken as he discovered the extent of her arousal. She was soft and swollen and slick with moisture.

With a tortured sound deep in his throat, he bent to her then, finding her with his mouth, sipping her sweetness with his lips and tongue.

She tasted of heat and honey and feminine desire. And as he began to explore her with his mouth she moved urgently against him.

When he grasped her hips, stilling her with a kind of gentle savagery, she whimpered in protest.

But tonight he wanted the control. Wanted the power and the satisfaction of bringing her to climax.

She belonged to him, he thought in some deep recess of his mind. And he belonged to her in a way that went beyond the mere joining of bodies.

There was no way to express his emotions in words. Instead he used his mouth on her body.

He kissed her, caressed her with long lazy strokes that wrung panting little cries from her. Experimenting with the pace and the pressure and the angle of his mouth, he found out what she liked best.

She pressed against him, her breath coming in gasps. Her body twisting in excitement. And when he felt the first tremors of her climax against his mouth, he felt something fierce and tender clench inside his own chest.

She cried out his name as he pushed her up and over the top. And he drank in her orgasm, awed by the sensations transmitted from the core of her to his lips.

He drew out her satisfaction, waiting until the tremors subsided. Then, half mad with his own need, he tore off his briefs and plunged his aching shaft into her.

His body shuddered with the force of their joining, shuddered with the tumult of his emotions.

Sex had always been a form of pleasure. Physical pleasure. Tonight physical pleasure was only a tiny part of what he felt.

Some dark, hidden core inside him shattered as he began to move. He was seized by emotions he could never articulate. Yet he felt them to the depths of his soul.

He felt her moving under him, her hips wildly bucking. Her arms came around his shoulders, and he realized that she had freed her hands from their bonds.

Then she was moving in concert with him, her breath rushing in and out of her lungs with his.

Her fingers worked their way up and down his back, her nails digging into his flesh.

And then he was shuddering with the force of his release, his head thrown back as ecstasy washed over him.

He felt her body convulse under him, felt her grip him

more tightly, heard her moans of pleasure as she followed where he had led her again.

He collapsed on top of her, too spent to move. When his brain could function again, he tried to shift to his side, but she held him where he was. "Stay inside me," she murmured.

He wanted that, too, wanted to stay connected with her as long as he could. Shifting his arms around her hips, he rolled to his side, still joined to her.

She nestled her head against his shoulder, and he stroked his lips against the top of her head.

"We should sleep. It's been a long night," he murmured.

"Yes," she answered, and for the first time that night, he was glad that they had to be careful of what they said. He didn't want to get into a discussion about what he was feeling, because the last thing in the world he wanted was to share his emotions with Maddy. They were too new. Too raw. And too dangerous.

OLIVER READ the security reports as he sipped his coffee with cream and ate his perfectly-prepared eggs Benedict. Too bad he couldn't have reinstalled camera equipment in Agapanthus Villa. But if Jack Craig had found it, the man would have considered it an open act of hostility. And he wasn't ready to confront Jack Craig yet. Not without more information. Which he expected to arrive from the States soon.

Craig had been an aggravation and a challenge.

Still, it was amusing to spar with him. Because there was no way he could win. Not on Orchid Island. Where Oliver Reynard controlled every variable.

While Jack and Maddy had been at the evening's reception, his electronics experts had made sure all the audio bugs in the place were in perfect working order.

Too bad they hadn't picked up anything besides a few gasped sentences and the sounds of wild, enthusiastic lovemaking. Including what sounded like some pretty rough sex in the middle of the night.

Still, the information was useful. It meant that they'd stayed put after they'd retired for the night.

From the sound of things, Jack Craig must be a sexual athlete. But he had his inhibitions. He really did like his privacy. During the first part of their private party, he'd remained silent, and Maddy had done all the talking.

The woman was certainly hot, and he knew how to make her even hotter. Thinking about his plans for later in the day, Oliver felt a surge of carnal anticipation flow through his veins.

MADDY WOKE SLOWLY, dreamily as she remembered how Jack had made love to her the night before. He had still been inside her when she'd fallen asleep, exhausted by the night's activities—all of them.

Rolling to her side, she reached to clasp him in her arms the way she had in the darkness. But he was gone, and when she smoothed her hand over the sheets, she found them cool.

So he'd been up for a while. And he hadn't bothered to wake her. Or kiss her. Or anything else.

Unaccountably, a deep throbbing sense of loss settled over her. She rolled to her back, staring at the ceiling, feeling tears gather at the backs of her eyes.

It was worse than after the last time he'd made love to her. Then she'd almost expected him to leave her in the morning. This was different because she'd thought something important had changed between them.

She knew the empty ache inside herself was irrational. But she couldn't shut it off.

Don't do this to yourself, she ordered sternly. *You knew what you were getting into when you begged to come along on this assignment. Nothing's changed. So don't invest too much in what happened last night when Jack made love to you. It didn't mean the same thing to him as it did to you. Probably he had a bad time out there in the jungle, and he was letting off some steam.*

But it hadn't felt like that. It had felt like a man showing a woman how much he cared.

She clenched and unclenched the hands that lay at her sides, but she couldn't stop the memories from flooding back. Jack had used her body like a painter bent on bringing a masterpiece to life. His tongue and lips had been his creative tool. Until he'd finally allowed himself to let that other full, rigid tool plunge into her.

When she'd freed her hands from their bonds, it was because she'd been overwhelmed by the need to touch him, hold him. Clasp him to her breast and show him what she was feeling—because talk had been forbidden, and there was no way to tell him he had transported her to paradise.

She ached to tell him that now. Yet he'd taken himself from their bed before she'd even awakened.

She pressed her palms against the outsides of her thighs, as though holding her own body could hold back the pain in her heart.

But as she lay there caught by her own misery, shame washed over her. What was wrong with her? She was doing it again—focusing on Jack when making love with him was beside the point.

He'd come here to help her find Dawn. They had a job to do, and the sooner they could free Stan Winston's daughter and get the heck off the island, the better for all of them.

If they got back to New York—no, when they got back to New York—they'd have time to sort out their personal relationship. And until then, she'd better keep her focus where it belonged.

The mental dressing-down was exactly what she needed. Swinging her legs over the side of the bed, she stood. She was naked, the way Jack had left her.

Too damn bad if there were cameras here.

Defiantly, she lifted one hand, holding up her middle finger in a rude salute. Then she got out underwear and marched into the bathroom, carefully closing the door behind herself.

A hot shower helped put her in a better frame of mind. While she was still under the warm spray, she grabbed Jack's razor and shaved her legs. Then, wrapped in a large fluffy towel, she returned to the bedroom and selected a pair of lemon-yellow shorts and a matching knit shirt with tiny butterflies embroidered over the front. Then she slipped her feet into comfortable but stylish sandals. By the time she strolled into the living room, she had control of her emotions and control of her features.

Jack was seated at the table, reading that morning's *New York Times,* which Reynard had doubtless imported at great expense from the States.

"Did you sleep well?" he asked, folding the paper and setting it aside as he gave her what looked like a satisfied masculine smile.

She wanted to wipe it off his face. Then she checked herself. Whatever had happened between them in the night, they were back to playing their parts this morning. The man who had spent so much of the night pleasuring his lady surely had a right to that smug look.

She took a deep breath, then forced herself to purr, "I slept very well after all that lovemaking."

Her gaze caught and held his for a long moment. Then he looked down into his coffee cup.

So much for meaningful eye contact, she thought, as

she crossed to the serving cart and poured herself some of the strong brew, then added half-and-half.

"So what's on the agenda today?" she asked.

"One of the guys asked me to play golf."

"Are you going?"

He gave her a direct look. "Of course. Why don't you relax around here? Then we'll get back together at lunch."

Maddy wanted to scream. She didn't want Jack going off. She wanted him with her—wanted him to tell her what had happened last night while he'd been outside. But Jack Craig's mistress—or his fiancée—or whatever she was wouldn't raise a protest.

He stood, crossed the rug and gave her a peck on the cheek. "You be a good girl while I'm gone."

"Oh, I will."

"Stay here so you don't get that pretty skin sunburned."

Stay inside? Was that a warning?

As soon as he left, it was difficult not to start pacing the room. But she was pretty sure Maddy Griffin would be perfectly at ease doing nothing much. So she went through the video library next to the television set, popped in a soap opera tape, and treated herself to two boring hours.

By the time Jack came back, she felt as if half of her brain had rotted away.

He regaled her with stories of his exploits on the golf course while they ate the lunch that had been delivered on another rolling cart.

Then he stood and stretched.

"What do you think about a walk on the beach?"

"Cool."

The enthusiastic exclamation brought a sardonic lift to his lips.

She ignored him and thought about the hidden context of the conversation—such as it was.

The beach, where the waves would be pounding the shore. They'd headed there before to talk. But a guard had stopped them. Maybe this time they'd have better luck.

Jack reached for her hand as they stepped onto the path. His fingers felt cold, and she slid him a questioning look. But he said nothing as they passed one of the damn gardeners who seemed to be all over the place.

Gardeners. Guards. There was probably no difference, except that the guards' weapons were showing. Or maybe the gardeners only carried communications equipment—to summon men with guns.

No one stopped them as they topped the rise that led down to the ocean. She kept hold of Jack's hand as they negotiated the sandy slope, then stood looking out at the turquoise water—watching the foam-tipped waves roll in and crash against the sand, feeling the wind ripple against her skin.

Jack stood still as a statue, looking out to sea.

"You wanted to talk?" she finally said.

"Yeah."

Lord, there were so many things bubbling inside her. She wanted to ask him what his passionate lovemaking last night had meant. But their personal relationship was way down the priority list. What she needed was to find out about Dawn.

When he said no more, she asked, "Was Dawn in the tower?"

"Yes."

"Thank God."

"That woman you told me about—Juanita—showed up to bring her dinner. It looks like they're friends. I could hear them talking, and Juanita told her that you're here."

"She's on our side?" Maddy breathed.

"She offered to sleep with one of the guards, when he got suspicious."

"Do you have a timetable for getting Dawn out of here?"

"Maddy, there's stuff I need to tell you."

She raised her questioning gaze to his. "Like what?"

"Like you're in danger."

11

MADDY'S WHOLE BODY TENSED. She was in danger? From what?

Her questioning gaze searched Jack's face, but before he could say any more, a shadow blocked the sun. They both turned to find one of the security men standing at the top of the rise.

She felt her chest tighten. How long had he been there? Had he heard any of their conversation? Because if he had, they were in big trouble.

Fight or flight, her brain screamed.

Then the man spoke. "Mr. Reynard sent me to ask you to join him this afternoon."

For what? A tea party?

"We'd be delighted," Jack answered. Really, it was the only answer he could give—unless the two of them were planning to dive into the ocean and swim for the mainland.

Jack kept his hand firmly on hers as they climbed the dune. When she felt her fingers going numb, she eased up her death grip on him.

The guard didn't speak again as they followed him up the path toward the mansion house. When they passed one of the outdoor pools, she saw several of the other male and female guests relaxing around tables and on chaise longues. So they'd finally gotten friendly with each other. Maybe they'd had an orgy the night before. Everybody looked up with interest as Maddy and Jack followed the guard inside.

Something about those looks made her feel like she was strolling toward her own funeral. Trying to ignore the speculative stares, she focused on the guard's back.

They proceeded through the familiar French doors, then across the reception area and down the hall where they'd first explored the private rooms. But the man took a sharp left into another part of the house. They stepped through more double doors onto a beautifully landscaped, enclosed patio. Bougainvillea festooned one stucco wall, and small palm trees in pots cast patches of shade over the ceramic tile floor. Other pots held flowering plants. And water cascaded down a small waterfall into a pond where lilies bloomed and koi swam.

Chaise longues and comfortable cushioned chairs were scattered around the area. The only thing that marred the peaceful scene were the occupants of the patio—Oliver Reynard and Calista.

"Oh, there you are," Reynard said as he saw them step into the sunshine.

His voice sent a shiver down Maddy's spine.

"Jack, I wanted to show you my dock area, since we're discussing transshipment of goods."

"Right," Jack answered, his voice hearty.

"I'm sure the women will be bored, so they can relax and chat while they wait for us."

"Oh, I think the dock area would be fascinating," Maddy said quickly as she cast a glance at Calista. The woman looked like she wanted to eat her for lunch.

Reynard shook his head. "Another time, my dear. Jack and I will be talking business."

She might have protested, but she knew better than to make waves. "Oh well, a business discussion," she murmured. "I don't have much of a head for business."

"We won't be too long. I'm sure you ladies will enjoy getting to know each other better."

Yeah, sure, Maddy thought. But she kept the observation to herself.

Reynard clapped Jack on the shoulder. "Let's go."

He cast her a look that she couldn't read, then followed their host through the door.

Maddy wandered over to the pond, watching the fish dart in and out of the foliage.

"Want to feed them?" Calista asked.

"Um, sure."

The woman brought over a slice of bread from the covered basket on the table. As soon as the fish saw it, they congregated near the edge of the pond. Calista tore off a piece and tossed it into the water. The fish fought for the morsel.

"Your turn," Reynard's mistress said, tearing off another piece and holding it out. There was no way to avoid brushing her fingers as Maddy took the bread. Quickly she drew her hand back and tossed the food to the fish.

"Can I offer you something to drink? Or to eat?"

"No thanks, I just finished lunch."

"Well, I do want a cool drink. And I'd feel strange unless you joined me."

Maddy nodded. "Okay then."

"What would you like?"

"Um, iced tea."

"Excellent. We have a wonderful tropical blend here that Oliver keeps for special guests. And I'll have a rum punch."

Rum punch. Alcohol was the last thing Maddy wanted.

Calista crossed to a wrought-iron table with a pattern of blooming irises worked into the surface. Picking up a small bell, she rang it twice. A man in a waiter's uniform appeared instantly as though he'd been standing right inside the door waiting for Calista's summons.

"Bennet, we'd both like a drink. And a bowl of cut fruit, I think. Some of that wonderful watermelon, pineapple and raspberry combination we had at lunch. Bring Ms. Griffin a glass of iced tea, and I'll have rum punch."

"Very good," the man said and turned to leave.

Calista pulled out a chair and sat down. Maddy did the same.

"So how was your night—after you left us?" Reynard's mistress murmured.

"Fine."

Calista gave her a little smirk, as if they were sharing a private joke. Had she been listening to what the microphones had picked up, Maddy wondered.

The drinks arrived on a silver tray, along with the bowl of requested fruit. Fast, she thought. Was there a service kitchen inside?

"When do you think the guys will be back?" Maddy asked as she stirred liquid sugar into her tea.

"They shouldn't be too long."

Maddy took a sip of her drink. It tasted strange. "What kind of tea is this?" she asked.

"Our special blend."

Cautiously Maddy tried another sip, then set the glass down and stabbed a toothpick into a melon ball, which she set on her plate.

Calista was watching her intently. For a few minutes, they made idle conversation, but the other woman seemed about to snap in two.

"What's wrong?" Maddy asked.

"Oliver will be annoyed if I haven't done a good job of entertaining you. Please, don't tell him you don't like the tea."

"Oh, I won't," Maddy agreed, taking several more

swallows. What she really wanted to do was pour the damn stuff into one of the flower pots. If this was the best he could do, he'd better get a better blend.

Calista seemed to relax.

"You really should have taken my advice in the first place," she said.

"About what?"

"About enjoying what the island has to offer."

"I am."

Calista gave a small laugh. "I don't think so. But I can assure you, you will."

"What's that supposed to mean?" Maddy demanded, a little frisson of alarm zinging through her.

Calista shrugged. "You're about to find out."

Maddy's throat was suddenly dry as sand. Reaching for the glass of tea, she took another gulp. When she set the glass back down, it thunked onto the table, rocking back and forth in her unsteady grasp. She struggled to hold it upright, sure that some of the liquid was going to spill. It might have, if the glass had been fuller.

Her head was foggy; her heart was pounding. "I'm not feeling well," she said carefully. "I think I'll go back to the villa." To her own ears, the words sounded slurred.

Cold prickles of worry bit at her. Something was wrong. Very wrong. Had Calista poisoned her tea? Was that what this was all about?

The prickles escalated to a stab of real fear. She wasn't thinking very clearly now. But the overwhelming thought in her mind was that she had to get back to the villa and throw this stuff up.

A GATE DECORATED with spouting dolphins barred the entrance to the wharf area. As Reynard approached, two armed guards snapped to attention. They looked a lot more polished than the jerks last night at the Dark Tower, Jack thought.

"At ease," the Master of Orchid Island said.

The two men changed position, but they relaxed only marginally.

Pulling a key from his pocket, Reynard opened the gate. He stepped aside, and Jack walked in first.

They proceeded down a ramp to a very long, very wide wooden dock where several boats were moored: six high-speed patrol cruisers and several pleasure craft. The largest was a big mother of a yacht that looked like it could have been built for European royalty. He could see a wide expanse of polished teak deck and an interior salon as big as a ballroom.

"So what do you think?" Reynard asked.

Assuming that Reynard was asking for comments on the docks, not his little fleet, he answered, "This is certainly adequate for my transshipping."

"The water's very deep here. We can bring in craft as large as a small cruise ship."

"I don't need that much cargo space. Two kilos of coke is about my limit."

"No problem."

"So do we have a deal?" Jack asked.

"I like your proposal best, but I'd like a little bigger cut."

"I'm already offering you top dollar for your services," Jack shot back.

Reynard chuckled. "Well, it's nice to have a bidding war between you and Don."

"What would swing the deal for you?"

"I think you know," Reynard answered.

Jack studied the wolfish look on the man's face, and all at once, despite the hot sun beating down from above, he felt his skin go cold.

"I think I'd like to go back now," he said, working hard to keep his voice even.

Reynard glanced at his watch. "What's the rush? The ladies will be there whenever we return—waiting eagerly."

The silky way Reynard murmured the last comment did nothing to ease Jack's disquiet. Turning, he walked rapidly back toward the gate without waiting to see if Reynard was following.

"I THINK I need to go back to the villa and lie down," Maddy whispered, wondering if she'd already said that. It sounded familiar, but she wasn't exactly sure if she'd spoken the words aloud or only formed them in her mind.

Calista was watching her with a kind of excitement that made Maddy's breath catch.

"You can lie down over there." She pointed to one of the chaises.

"No. Home," Maddy insisted, hearing the note of desperation in her own voice. Her body felt alternately cold and hot now, as if some little demon inside her were playing with the thermostat. Clenching her teeth, she gripped the arms of the chair and tried to stand. She made it to her feet, then almost fell back, but Reynard's mistress moved quicky to her side, steadying her. She hated the feel of those long, red-nailed fingers on her flesh, but she didn't have the energy to push Calista away. Or the energy to keep insisting that she needed to leave. All she could do was allow herself to be led across the patio, where she sat down heavily on the chaise.

"Let me make you comfortable," Calista said.

"Really, I'll be okay in a minute," she answered in a breathless voice.

Ignoring her, Calista knelt beside her and lifted first one of her legs and then the other onto the cushion. Next she unbuckled her sandals, slipping them off, giving each foot a little caress. This time, the touch of the woman's fingers on her skin sent a tiny current up Maddy's leg. A disturbing little current.

She tried to focus on the face hovering above hers, but now the features looked blurry.

Maddy's whole body felt heavy, and at the same time her head felt like it was filled with nothing more than heated air. The cushion under her was making her body prickle. Sending currents of heat along her nerve endings and through her system. Heat she tried not to acknowledge.

Squeezing her eyes shut, she struggled for control. But she felt as if she had climbed onto a roller coaster that was plunging down a steep incline—and she had no say about what would happen next.

"What's wrong with me?" she whispered.

"I've just given you something to help you enjoy yourself."

"No."

"You're feeling turned on, aren't you? Don't fight it."

Maddy squeezed her eyes more tightly closed. That was exactly what she felt, and she tried to will it away. "No," she denied.

"You're lying."

A hand reached out to stroke her cheek, a hand that slid across her jaw, down the column of her neck and over the tops of her breasts in a much too intimate caress.

"Don't," she moaned.

"It feels good. Admit it."

"No."

Calista smiled at her. "You can lie to yourself. But you can't lie to me. I've taken this drug. I know very well what it does. You're on fire now, aren't you."

Maddy moaned. It was true. She was hot and shaky and

aroused. And the sensations kept building. "Don't touch me like that," she pleaded.

"Just relax. You're going to have a very good time. Most women would kill for the drug I've given you. It's like when a man takes Viagra. Only better. You'll see. You'll come and come. And each orgasm will be better than the last."

"Let me go."

"It's too late for that. You're going to need to come soon. Your body is demanding it already, isn't it?"

She wanted to scream her denial, but she knew it was true. Her nipples felt painfully tight. And an insistent throbbing pounded through her sex. She had never felt anything like this before. Not this wild, blinding need for sexual release.

Calista had given her something that had done it. Something in the iced tea. Lord, she never should have drunk the strange-tasting stuff. But it had been impossible to refuse.

She felt the woman hovering over her, stroking her hair.

"They'll be back soon. But I want to tell you something first. All the things that I said to you last night, those were things he told me to say. He likes to see me come on to women. And he likes to watch me make love with them. He'll watch us together in a while. But you can close your eyes and pretend it's Jack doing stuff to you, if it helps."

"Let me go."

"No. I can't. Oliver wants this, and I do what he wants. He'll love the way you look now, with your nipples poking against your shirt," she whispered. "I know he'll like it even better when we get that shirt off of you. Did you know there are some women who can come just from breast stimulation—when they're really hot. We'll find out if you're one of them. Or you can touch yourself while

I stroke your breasts. Making yourself come the first time has its advantages. Then I'll be able to see what you like. And I can do it for you later.''

Maddy whimpered in fear and frustration and tried to struggle. But she didn't have the strength, didn't even know what she wanted any more. Volcanic pressure was building inside her. Pressure that must find release—one way or the other.

But God, not like this. Not like this!

She tried to push herself up, tried to escape. But Calista shoved her roughly back onto the chaise—just as an icy voice cut through the fog in her brain. ''What the hell is going on?''

It was Jack. Jack had come back. She croaked his name like a prayer of thanksgiving.

He repeated his question.

She heard someone else speaking. Calista. ''I just gave her something to…you know…help her relax.''

''Relax. Is that what you call it?'' Jack snapped.

Reynard was speaking now. ''You didn't have my permission to give her anything,'' he said, emphasizing every word as if he were talking to a stupid child.

Calista said something Maddy couldn't catch.

Then Jack was beside her, his palm against her cheek. ''You're going to be okay,'' he murmured.

She stared up at him, ashamed and confused. ''I feel…'' Her voice trailed off. She didn't want to tell him she felt like her blood was on fire. Not in front of these other two people.

Calista and Reynard were talking again. Reynard sounded angry. But she knew he was lying. He'd told Calista to do this—hadn't he? Or had that been the lie? Calista sounded like a little girl who'd been naughty—but she knew her father wasn't really going to punish her.

Jack's voice cut through the conversation again, and

she focused on him like a drowning swimmer clamping desperate hands around a lifeline. "Okay, I'm taking her out of here now. And you'd better tell me where the two of us can have some real privacy. I mean a room with no damn recording equipment!"

The other voices were just a dim buzz in the background. But when Jack spoke, she heard him clearly. "She and I are going to be alone for as long as she needs me. And if anybody barges in, I'm going to kill them, got that?"

She didn't hear the answer. She only felt Jack slip one arm under her shoulders, the other under her hips. Lifting her gently, he stood and cradled her against his body.

She turned toward him, helpless to keep from pressing her aching breasts against his chest. God, it felt good. So good. But she needed more.

"It's okay, baby. You're going to be all right," he rasped, then turned and strode from the patio.

She kept her eyes squeezed shut and her face against his shoulder, trying to block out everything besides him as he carried her out of the sunshine and into the building.

Once she heard him curse. And once he snarled, "Get out of my way."

She didn't know how long she was in his arms, but some time later he set her down on a wide bed.

The room around her was shadowy, and she knew the light was dim. She also knew her vision was fuzzy.

But that didn't matter. Nothing mattered but what she needed from Jack. Desperately. Now.

She reached for him, tried to pull him on top of her. But he loosened her clutching fingers.

"Let me lock the door."

"Please," she moaned.

Seconds later, he was with her on the bed, telling her

he was sorry, telling her that he never should have left her alone with Calista.

"Just…just…" Beyond desperation now, she grabbed his hand, pressed it to the throbbing place between her legs, rocking frantically against the pressure of his palm while she stroked her own breasts through her T-shirt and bra, finding her nipples, pulling and twisting at them.

She came then, in wave after wave of sensation that jolted through her like a freight train that had jumped the rails.

For long moments she could only ride the pounding rush of feeling. Then the shock wave finally subsided, and she pressed her face against Jack's shirt and started to sob.

"I…I…don't want you to see me like this," she gasped between sobs.

"It's okay. You're okay," he murmured, stroking her back and shoulders.

"No…I'm not okay…I need more…" she sobbed out. "I can feel it. Inside me. It's starting to build up again. Oh God, Jack, I don't want this."

"It's all right. I'll take care of you."

"And I'll never be able to look you in the eye again," she answered, keeping her face buried because she couldn't bear to look at him now.

"That's crazy talk. You didn't do this," he said, his voice fierce. "It's not your fault."

"I'm a mess."

"Shhhh," he soothed, kissing her cheek. Lifting her face so he could kiss her wet eyelids as well.

She clung to him because there was nothing else she could do now—because she needed him more than she could imagine needing any man.

"It's okay. Baby, I'll take care of you," he crooned.

"I need…"

"Anything. Just tell me."

She pushed herself up, pulled her shirt over her head, then yanked up her bra without bothering to take it off. "Your hands on me. Oh God, I need your hands on me. Right now."

He lay down beside her, gathered her to him, his hands stroking her swollen breasts, caressing her aching nipples. She arched into the caress, then rolled on top of him and found that he was hard. With a sob she pressed her sex to the rigid shaft, then began to move her hips, stroking her throbbing center against his erection, rubbing frantically to produce the friction she needed while he continued to play with her breasts.

The orgasm took her on a gasp, sending her spinning out of control and into some alternate universe where the only thing that mattered was release.

When it was over, his hands soothed over her back, then snapped the catch on her bra and removed it.

"Better?" he asked urgently as he lowered her to the bed.

Lord, the poor man probably wanted to escape. She lay back, breathing hard, staring up at him. She was wearing only her shorts and panties, but they felt too tight for her heated skin. The physical sensation against her flesh was intolerable. Reaching for the elastic waistband of her shorts, she pulled them off along with her panties so that she was lying naked on the bed. She wanted to hide, to disappear. She didn't want to be the person this was happening to.

But there was no choice. No choice at all. And the only thing she thanked God for was that Jack was with her. Because the idea of being like this with Calista and Reynard made her almost physically ill.

"She gave me something that made me this way. Something in my tea."

"I know, baby. I'm so sorry."

"Why are you sorry? You didn't do anything."

"Except leave you in her clutches," he growled.

She rolled her head against his shoulder. "Hold me."

"Anything. Just tell me what you need."

"I'm okay now. Sort of okay. I know it's going to sink its teeth into me again. I can feel it. Crouching like his panther. Ready to spring at me."

His lips stroked against her hair, slid to her mouth.

"Jack, take off your clothes. Maybe this will seem more normal if you're naked too."

"Okay." He stood, tugged his shirt over his head. Then unzipped his fly. His slacks and briefs came off together, leaving him naked and aroused, his penis jutting toward her.

"This is making you hot," she murmured.

"I'm sorry. I can't help it."

"Don't apologize. I'd rather you be hot too." The observation ended with a giggle that she knew could easily escalate to peals of hysteria. She struggled to contain the laughter, then stopped worrying about it as another wave of heat started building.

"It's going to hit me again," she said in a shaky voice. "Please, come back. Please."

"I'm right here. For as long as you need me."

"I feel so naked," she said, and that struck her again as funny. She was still laughing as Jack pulled down the covers, eased them under her, then pulled the sheet up again so that it covered her body.

Slipping into bed beside her, he held her gently in his arms, giving soft kisses on her cheeks, her neck, the tops of her breasts.

"Gentle isn't going to do it," she gasped, dragging his hand to the juncture of her legs and pressing against him. She sighed as two of his fingers slipped into the hot, wet folds of her pulsing sex.

The need built quickly—taking her by storm.

She anchored her hands to his shoulders, feeling his powerful muscles flex. Eyes closed, she clenched her legs around his fingers, rocking again, wringing everything she could from the friction he was providing.

What he was doing felt exquisite. When he angled his hand to give her maximum internal and external stimulation, she cried out with the pleasure of it. Her body contracted, then exploded, sending more orgasmic shock waves through her system.

He stayed with her until the end, feeding the sensations with his knowing caresses.

When it was over, she flopped back against the pillows, breathing hard.

"Better?"

"For now."

JACK ROLLED TO HIS SIDE, looking down at Maddy. He was so damn angry that he could barely keep from pulling his clothes on, striding down the hall and wringing the neck of the skinny bitch who had done this.

Maddy licked her lips, and he instantly tuned in to the tiny movement.

"Are you thirsty?"

She gave a small nod.

"I'll get you some water."

"You don't have to do anything...I mean...anything else. I can do it."

She pushed herself up, looking suddenly flushed.

"Let me," he insisted, wanting to do as much for her as he could, and at the same time needing some breathing space.

"Will you be okay by yourself?"

"Yes."

Taking her at her word, he swung his legs over the side

of the bed and strode toward another door, which he assumed would lead to a bathroom. It did.

He stood in front of the long counter with its double sinks, trying to control the tumult of emotions raging inside him.

Deliberately, he turned on the water, letting it run cold while he focused on breathing steadily in and out. When he'd come back and found her lying on the chaise longue, looking like someone had dosed her up with a combination of uppers and downers, a bolt of panic had shot through him.

Jesus!

Coping with the scared, aroused look on her face had been bad enough. Then he'd focused on the bitch leaning over her, and a red haze had dropped over his vision. He'd known that he had to get her out of there—or beat somebody to a pulp. Calista or Reynard. Or both of them.

And at the same time, he'd known that beating Reynard up wasn't going to do Maddy any good. Looking back on that supercharged few minutes, he realized that he could have gotten them both killed by his heavy-handed tactics. But he hadn't been thinking about that at the time. He'd only been thinking about getting her out of there—to somewhere private and safe. Where he could give her what she so obviously needed.

And now here they were in this room—in the main house of all damn places. If Reynard wanted to, he could break down the door. But so far, so good.

Maybe Reynard knew he had gone too far. Maybe he was afraid he'd killed the deal.

Still, any way you looked at it, they were in trouble. You didn't defy a man like Reynard and not pay the consequences.

But he'd worry about consequences later. Right now he

had to take care of Maddy. Because he was pretty sure she wasn't over the effects of that drug.

He filled a tumbler with water. Then schooled his features into calmer lines as he came back to the bedroom.

Maddy had propped herself up against a couple of pillows. Reaching for the glass, she took several huge gulps.

"More?"

"No. Thanks," she answered politely, handing him back the glass. He set it down on the nightstand, then glanced around for the first time. They were in a large, sumptuous bedroom, furnished with priceless antiques. It was not unlike the room where they'd first made love, he thought, noting the irony.

When he saw that he'd set down the wet glass on a very expensive table, he shrugged.

Maddy followed his gaze. "You're going to make a ring," she murmured.

"Too damn bad." He peered at her, trying to assess her condition. Never mind his own arousal. That was just a side issue. "Are you...okay?"

"Sort of." She swallowed. "It's...um...still there. I can feel it. Waiting for me. But the edge is off. Well, not the edge. I guess what I mean is that I'm feeling more like I've got some control. Like I can use it—instead of being used by it." She tipped her face toward his. "Do you understand what I mean?"

"Yeah. Maybe. I'd just like to know what the hell she gave you."

Maddy slid back down to a prone position, watching him intently, and he realized he was standing there with his cock jutting out like a telephone pole.

He glanced down, then up again in time to see a silly grin spread across her face. She giggled. "If you think about it, you realize guys look funny when they're hot."

"Thanks."

"I was thinking about that yesterday," she went on garrulously. "On our walk. I wouldn't want something thick and hard sticking out in front of me every time I got turned on."

"Um-hum."

"It's so big. So nice and hard. I think it would feel very very good inside me."

The suggestion was like a jolt of electricity that went right to his cock.

"Don't!" he muttered.

"Okay. No more talking," she murmured. Sliding across the bed, she reached out and took his penis in her hand.

"Don't," he said again. This time the order ended in a gasp.

"Why not?"

"I don't have any right to get off on this," he grated. No damn right. Not when he had gotten her into this mess.

"I don't want to be the one having all the fun," she purred.

"I didn't bring you here to have fun," he managed to protest. But it was hard to stay focused on that thought as the maddening hand began to stroke him, sliding the skin up and down his erection in a way that sent his blood pounding.

"Lord, you taste good," she murmured, nibbling the words against his hot, distended flesh. His breath caught, then he stopped breathing altogether as she worked her way along his shaft, then up to the sensitive tip where she licked a circle around his head with her tongue, licked a bead of liquid from the tip.

He could only stand there in an agony of pulsing pleasure, his hands rigid at his sides as she took him as fully as she could into her mouth, lapping and sucking as though someone had given her a particularly delicious lollipop while one hand reached under his cock to lift and fondle his balls.

He could barely catch his breath. And he certainly couldn't move, not when she was driving him rapidly toward climax.

She drew back, wringing a moan of protest from him. The last hour had been almost more than he could endure.

Then her words penetrated his brain.

"Jack, I want you inside me. I need you inside me."

The request released him. Coming down to the bed, he took her in his arms and pressed her body against his.

"I was hoping I could persuade you to participate." She giggled again.

He'd never plunged into a woman without making sure she was ready for him. But Maddy didn't give him the choice. She took him in hand again, dragging him to her. And he was helpless to do anything besides follow her lead.

Any doubts about her readiness vanished as she began to move frantically, matching him thrust for thrust, setting a pounding rhythm that sent her into a shattering climax. He managed to hold himself back, keeping up the rhythm, bringing her to another orgasm that had her gasping his name, digging her fingernails into his buttocks.

He came then, giving himself over to the pleasure of pouring himself into her.

Afterwards, he held her tenderly, kissed her. Then watched her eyes flutter closed. Almost at once he sensed the change in her breathing and knew she was sleeping.

He gave a shuddering sigh. On the beach, she'd asked if he had a timetable for getting off the island. He hadn't given her an answer then. Now he knew that it had to be tonight. Because the danger was escalating. For both of them.

But was Maddy in any shape to help him? Let alone get off the island under her own power.

It all depended on the aftereffects of the damn drug—which he didn't know because he'd never encountered anything like this before. Too bad he was learning about it the hard way.

Maddy lay next to him, breathing quietly at last. He held her gently in his arms. But just as he was beginning to think they were home free, her eyes snapped open, and she looked wildly around the room, obviously on the verge of panic.

"Jack," she moaned, her hands clutching her shoulders.

"I'm here, baby. I'm here."

"I need you again."

The breathy words made him instantly hard. Instantly ready to give her anything she asked. And more.

12

A COUPLE OF HOURS LATER, when Jack got up to make a quick trip to the bathroom, Maddy stirred beside him on the bed.

"Jack?"

"It's okay. I'll be right back," he told her.

When he slipped back into bed, she clung to him.

"How are you?" he asked, nibbling at her ear.

"Better. I think it's…uh…run its course."

"Good."

She raised her head and looked at him. "Jack, thank you. Thank you for rescuing me from Calista. Thank you for…for…" Her voice faltered.

"You don't have to say anything. It wasn't exactly hardship work."

He saw her swallow. "You don't know what it was like. Being out of control like that."

"I wouldn't have liked having it happen to me." He scrubbed his hand over his face. "Maddy, I knew Calista wanted you. Yesterday when Reynard had me up here, he proposed that the four of us get together, that he and I watch you and Calista make love."

He felt her shudder, then shake her head. "It wasn't quite like that. She doesn't really like being with women. She does it because he wants her to."

"That hardly makes it better."

"He's controlling her. The way he controls everything else around here."

"Yeah," he answered, thinking he wasn't going to minimize his role in all this. But he needed to judge what he could say, because despite what Reynard had told him when he'd brought Maddy here, he didn't entirely trust this room to be free of bugs.

He drew in a breath and let it out. "Any way you slice it, I knew you were in danger. First I kept it from you because I was afraid you'd freak out. And I'd convinced myself that Reynard wouldn't try anything without my permission. Then I knew I had to come clean with you. That's what I meant down on the beach when I started talking."

She nodded, but the look in her eyes didn't make him feel any better.

"You don't have to apologize. This isn't exactly like Albania," she murmured.

"What?"

At his sharp question, she looked confused, as if she wasn't quite sure what she'd said—and why she'd said it.

"You know about Albania?" he asked, his throat so constricted that he could barely speak.

She lay very still, and he waited with his heart hammering against his ribs to find out if he'd heard her right.

When she gave a little nod, he struggled to contain the sick feeling threatening to force its way up his throat. Jesus! All this time—she'd known. And she hadn't said a damn thing.

"I—I don't seem to have much self-control right now," she stammered, obviously sorry that she'd mentioned the delicate subject. "A thought pops into my head, and I blurt it out...."

He cut her off with a fierce look, then struggled to contain his roiling emotions.

"We have to talk," he mouthed, knowing now more than ever that they couldn't risk a frank conversation in the bedroom. Which was good, because he needed a few minutes with his own thoughts.

"Do you think you can stand up?" he said aloud. "I want to find out how you are on your feet. And I'm sure a shower would feel good about now."

"Yes. Okay," she agreed.

He moved aside, and she slid to the edge of the bed. When she stood, he could see her legs weren't quite steady.

"I'm fine," she muttered when she caught his look of concern.

Still he slung his arm around her, holding her close as they made their slow way to the bathroom.

She leaned against the wall while he opened the glass door and turned on the shower. Now that the water was running, they could start talking. But he postponed the inevitable while he adjusted the temperature.

Finally, there was nothing left to do besides step under the pounding spray. When he held out his hand to her, she followed him inside.

He breathed out a small sigh as she turned to face him and laid her head against his shoulder. So she wasn't condemning him without hearing what he had to say. That was good. For a long moment he stood there sliding his hands up and down her water-slick arms and across her back.

Neither of them spoke, and he knew he was the one who had to break the silence.

"You know my partner was killed when we were on an assignment in Albania? *How* do you know?"

Apparently she'd decided that the time for ducking inconvenient questions was over. "One of my security men had heard about it. He warned me not to come here with you."

"But you did it anyway."

"Yes." She swallowed. "Can you tell me what happened?"

He did, in a flat, dead voice. "Someone had ratted on us. Men in town were looking for us. But we had a place to hide out, and I thought we'd be safer under cover. Lisa wanted to make a run for it—and we had to stick together. They have these one-lane roads running along the tops of the mountains. We came around a curve, and there was a big car, smack in front of us. It sped up as it plowed into us. I have to assume that the bad guys knew we were trying to make a getaway, and sent someone to stop us. Our car went into a ravine. Somehow I got out. Either I pulled the door handle, or the door flew open on its own. Lisa wasn't so lucky."

"That doesn't sound like your fault."

"I should have kept her calm, made her wait it out!"

"Could you have?"

"I don't know! I've asked myself that question a million times."

Her hands tightened on his arms, then caressed his back in a gesture that might have been erotic. Now it was comforting.

"I think you've got nothing to feel guilty about," she murmured.

"Easy for you to say."

"Jack, I know what kind of man you are. If I didn't know before today, I'd know now."

He swore under his breath. "I'm no saint."

"But you're a good man. You know what the hell you're doing. You're calm in the face of a crisis. And you go out of your way to do your job."

He focused on the last part. Was that what she thought? That he'd been doing a job for the past few hours? He wanted to tell her it had been a hell of a lot more than a job, but thought better of it. Maybe after what had just happened to her, she needed to believe there was nothing personal between them. And if that was what it took to get her off Orchid Island safely, then that was the way he was going to play it.

"How are you feeling now?" he asked.

She stepped away from him, flexed her legs and arms. "Better. Not a hundred percent. But I'm coming back."

He watched her calmly evaluating her physical and mental condition. "Do you think you can be ready to leave tonight? Because I don't think that staying around much longer is a good idea."

"I agree. And if I have to be ready tonight, I will be," she answered, her voice all business.

Lord, she'd just been down for the count, but she was coming out of her corner swinging.

Then her next words made him blink. "I'm not going to let you down, like Lisa did."

"She didn't—"

"Okay. I guess I shouldn't have said it. We're not going to focus on what happened back then. We're going to concentrate on getting out of here."

The tone of her voice told him that she was definitely on the mend.

"Right," he muttered.

"Then tell me what you have planned."

Jack leaned close, brought his mouth next to her ear, and told her what he'd been thinking about while she was sleeping.

OLIVER HAD BEEN PRIMED to enjoy Maddy Griffin's out-of-control arousal. After Jack spirited her away, he'd called in two of his favorite young women to help Calista satisfy him. Their attentions had taken away the physical discomfort, but his mood hadn't improved.

Jack Craig had gotten the better of him. He could have

had the man executed on the spot, of course. But he was still trying to figure out who the bastard was. And he wanted the satisfaction of confronting him about his background—before the execution.

He was getting ready to step into the hot tub off his private rooms when the red phone rang in his bedroom. The line that hooked directly into his security center.

Striding naked across the thick carpeting, he snatched up the receiver, thinking that it had better be important.

"What is it?" he snapped.

"Your operative from Winston Industries has just arrived by private plane. We're holding him here."

"What? What the hell is going on? He's supposed to be keeping tabs on things inside their operation."

"Yes. But he says that he's been under observation. He used an excuse to get away. And he says that it's urgent that he talk to you."

"All right. Give me fifteen minutes. I'll meet him down there."

He replaced the receiver in its cradle, thinking that his Winston operative was no good to him here. And if he didn't have a good story to tell, he might be the one who was executed tonight.

"LOCK THE DOOR behind me. And don't let anyone else in," Jack said as he reached for the knob.

He saw Maddy's face pale and knew that despite her calm exterior, she didn't much like the idea of being left alone now. But they'd both agreed during their strategy session in the shower that having her lie low for as long as she could was their best alternative. Maddy had told him Calista had bragged about taking the drug. Probably she'd followed a session like Maddy's with a nice long rest. Which made Maddy's staying in the room entirely in character.

As he stepped into the hall, he found one of the household staff stationed about twenty feet away.

Like the gardeners, he thought. Undoubtedly part of the security force but wearing a different uniform.

"I was told to inform Mr. Reynard when you came out," the man said in response to Jack's inquiring look.

"Well, Ms. Griffin still isn't feeling very well," he answered. "I'm just getting some of her things from our villa. Some fresh clothing. Her makeup case. You know how women are. They always want to look their best. So you can tell Mr. Reynard we won't be available for socializing any time soon." He paused for a moment. "But I would like a cart of food brought up. Something light. Sandwiches and fruit. And some coffee. Just leave it outside the door, and I'll bring it in when I come back."

"Very good, sir."

Jack walked briskly back toward Agapanthus Villa, as though his only mission was to make his sweetie feel more comfortable.

Once inside, he slowed his pace, giving the impression that he was thinking about the items that Maddy had presumably requested. He found her hairbrush on the counter in the bathroom and stuck it in the makeup case. He got out underwear and pretended to consider what he thought would look good on her. He found a dark-colored knit outfit and put it in a small suitcase—along with a change of clothing for himself, which also, surprise, turned out to be black.

But he left almost everything else in place, as though they'd be back to the villa as soon as Maddy felt up to it.

As he retraced his steps, he stopped briefly and looked down the path that he knew led to the workers' quarters—where Juanita lived. He wanted to contact her now, but he decided that it would be a bad idea. So he let it go for the time being.

MADDY WAS PACING back and forth across the room, from the Oriental rug to the hardwood floor and back again. Then a knock on the door made her go stock-still. She lowered the eight-inch-long metal statue she held in her hand so it was hidden beside her leg. Then she walked to the door and called out, "Who is it?"

"Jack."

"Thank God," she breathed as she unsnapped the lock.

As Jack walked into the room, she carefully placed the statue on a table. He didn't comment, only set down the makeup case and small suitcase he was carrying before taking her into his arms.

She didn't want to show any weakness now, but it was impossible not to cling to him for several moments. His hands ran up and down her back, and he turned his head, skimming his lips over her cheek and the tender line of her hair.

"We'll be out of this hellhole in a couple of hours," he said.

She hoped it was true. She knew they were taking risks. But not getting out now was even more of a risk.

All she said was "I'll pull my weight."

"I know you will," he answered, and she took some comfort in the confident tone.

He opened the door again and wheeled in a cart with food. She managed to get down half a sandwich, but the bowl of fruit was beyond her. Not when Calista had served fruit to her along with that drugged iced tea.

"Probably we should relax for a while," Jack said, after he'd wolfed down a couple of sandwiches.

She nodded, thinking that he was making the suggestion because she was the one who needed rest, but she didn't voice the observation. He had enough to worry about without her voicing her insecurities.

Dutifully, she lay down on the bed and closed her eyes. She felt the mattress shift, felt Jack lie down beside her. Reaching out his hand, he covered hers. They lay like that for a long time. Maybe she even drifted off to sleep. Lord knows, she needed it.

Some time later, her eyes snapped open. Jack had dismantled one of the Venetian blinds and was laying out the cord on the end of the bed.

She glanced at her watch. It was one in the morning. The time when Reynard would be least expecting trouble. No. She canceled that optimistic assessment. Reynard was probably attuned for trouble at any time. But the small hours of the morning offered the most chance of a successful escape.

After finishing with the cord, Jack picked up the makeup kit and emptied out the contents. Stan Winston's diamonds were inside, and he stuffed them into his pocket. Then he began tearing out the flowered fabric lining of the case. First he removed the packing material, which was actually a long rope, made of a strong but lightweight synthetic. Then he removed a sheathed knife which he handed to Maddy. When he uncovered the transmitter, he gave her a satisfied grin. A cocky grin.

The process of sending a message was automatic. The transmitter was simply a communications device designed to send a spurt—a quick burst of information—on a specific frequency.

Out in the ocean, a small cabin cruiser was waiting to pick them up. The message would alert the agents on the boat to proceed to a small cove on the west side of the island, a pickup point that they'd agreed on before leaving New York.

If there had been a change in plans, it would have been

possible for Jack to reset the device and code in new information. But that wasn't necessary. The cove was within a reasonable distance of the Dark Tower. All they had to do was get Dawn out of there, and get to their taxi service.

"Are we ready?" Jack asked.

"Yes."

He pressed the button, sending the signal. Setting the final act of this play into motion.

The rescue team would arrive at the cove in two hours. If Jack, Maddy and Dawn weren't there, it was too risky for the team to wait around. The next pickup time would be twenty-four hours later.

When they'd first worked out the strategy, it had made perfect sense. Now she realized how many things could go wrong before the rendezvous. They had to avoid the guards, rescue Dawn, and get her to the cove. That was just from their end.

With Reynard's tight security, they also had to worry about one of his patrols intercepting the rescue team.

She tried not to focus on the negatives as she stood up and started pulling on the clothing Jack had brought. Before putting on the pants, she strapped the sheathed knife to her right ankle.

Two hours, she mused. Not a long time.

Jack pulled off his shirt, then wound the rope from the makeup case around his waist before changing his own clothing.

Then they both efficiently cleaned up the room, stowing everything they'd dumped on the bed into a pillowcase, which they set beside the door.

"Ready?" Jack asked.

"Yes."

As they'd arranged, Maddy lay down on the rug, sprawled out her arms and closed her eyes.

Jack opened the door and stepped into the hall.

"Come here quick. Something's happened to Ms. Griffin," he called out frantically to the guard he'd told her was watching the exit.

Through slitted eyes, she watched the man run into the room, then stop inside when he saw her on the floor.

"She fainted," Jack told him, his voice filled with alarm. "I can't wake her up. I know it's the damn drug."

When the man bent over her, Jack hit him with the statue that she'd been carrying earlier.

She rolled away, then reached for the Venetian blind rope, which she'd shoved under the edge of the bedspread. Within minutes the guard was tied and gagged with a towel.

Jack gave a satisfied grunt as he found a handgun strapped to the man's leg. He stuffed it in his belt and kept searching. After removing anything that could be of use, including a portable phone, he dumped the man on the other side of the bed.

She waited while he snatched up the pillowcase full of evidence, then followed him out of the room and down the hall. They encountered no other guards and exited the building, walking at a normal pace down the trail. Once they were out of sight of the building, they stepped off the path and moved through the underbrush.

Jack paused to toss the pillowcase into a clump of thorn bushes, then turned toward her. She was breathing harder than she might have liked.

"You okay?" he whispered.

"Yes," she assured him, then let him lead the way through the foliage.

Jack paused to let her rest several times, and she didn't waste her breath objecting. They were standing under a clump of schefflera trees when she heard a sound that made her blood run cold. It was the howl of a wild animal. A big cat, as best she could tell.

Unconsciously, she moved closer to Jack and whispered, "Is that Reynard's panther, do you think?"

He shrugged.

"Would he let it loose?"

"I hope not. Not tonight of all nights."

She shivered, glad that they at least had a gun.

After a few moments, they moved off again. By the time they reached the wall around the tower, she had a stitch in her side, but she did her best to ignore it as they stood in the shadow of the branches, watching the sentry at the entrance to the courtyard.

Jack had told her in the shower about how the man had responded to Juanita. She hoped that she would get the same favorable reception as they waited for the patrol to pass.

There was no way of knowing when they'd arrived in the cycle. It took twelve minutes for two guards to come strolling down the path. Jack had said they'd stopped to pass the time of day with the man at the entrance. Tonight they only nodded and walked rapidly past.

Perhaps they'd been given a lecture on discipline, she thought. Or maybe two other men were on duty. Men who weren't as friendly with the sentry.

She stood in the shadows, breathing in and out, making sure she was in good enough shape to play the role she'd been assigned.

Then she walked forward, waving and calling out softly to the guard so that he wouldn't shoot her before she had a chance to do her thing.

"Stop where you are," he ordered when she'd gotten within thirty feet of him.

At least his machine gun stayed on his shoulder, she

noted as she came toward him at an angle, turning his attention to his right. "Please, I want to talk to you."

"About what?"

"Juanita sent me with a message for you."

"What do you know about Juanita?"

She moved her hips sensually, seductively. "I know she's your friend. She sent me to warn you. There's going to be trouble tonight."

"Oh yeah?"

She kept the man's focus on her swaying body so that Jack could circle around behind him. As Jack closed in on him, she played with the neckline of her shirt, rubbing her hand just inside the collar and downward toward her breasts, watching with satisfaction as his gaze followed the movement. He looked like his whole field of vision had contracted to that view of her shirtfront.

A smile flickered on her lips as she caught and held his gaze—until Jack brought the butt of the gun down on the back of his head.

Together, they pulled him inside the wall, where he was out of sight, and relieved him of his machine gun, also his clothing. Jack quickly changed into the military uniform, which was a bit too short. But they couldn't do anything about that. Working quickly, Maddy gagged the man with Jack's shirt and tied his hands and feet.

When they were finished, Jack pulled the cap down low over his face and stood at the guardpost with the gun slung over his shoulder while Maddy hurried across the courtyard and into the building.

She had a bad moment when she couldn't find the key. Then she spotted it on a peg on the far wall. After lifting the ring free, she hurried up the winding stone steps. At the top she stepped onto a small landing, where she found a stout metal door with only a small barred window in the center.

Inserting the key into the lock, she pushed on the door.

It creaked open, giving into a small stone cell, with a narrow cot and a dim bulb dangling from the ceiling. In the far corner, she found Dawn cowering near the stone floor. She was dressed in clothing that must have come with her from New York. Jeans and a T-shirt. Her face was pale, and her long dark hair looked as if it hadn't been washed since she'd arrived on the island.

When she focused on Maddy's face, she gasped.

"Oh, Maddy. It's really you."

"Yes."

"Juanita told me you were here. But I was afraid to believe her." As she spoke, she crossed the small room and threw her arms around Maddy's neck, a small sob escaping from her lips. "I'm so sorry. I was such a jerk. I never should have put that stuff in your drink and run away."

Maddy gave her a tight hug, then released her. "I know you want to talk. But we'll have to do that later. Right now, we have to get the heck out of here."

"Oh God, yes. I thought I'd never get away. I thought he was going to kill me."

Maddy's fingers tightened around the girl's arm as she remembered her own recent experiences. If Reynard had done anything sexual to Dawn, she was going to enjoy shooting the man. "Did he…do anything to you?" she asked softly.

"No. I mean he didn't molest me or anything. He just locked me up here."

Maddy nodded as she turned and ushered the teenager out of the cell. Together they descended the stone steps.

When they reached the bottom, Jack turned to face them, and Dawn cringed away from the man in the guard's uniform.

Maddy was quick to reassure her. "It's okay. This is

Jack Connors. He came here with me—and he's going to help me get you off the island.''

Dawn nodded.

"Pleased to meet you, Dawn," he said. "We'll get out of here as soon as I put the guard and my clothing where nobody will find them."

The girl nodded again.

Jack picked up the man and carried him into the tower. He was still inside when Maddy stepped through the doorway of the courtyard—and came face-to-face with a snarling panther padding out of the darkness.

13

EVEN AS PANIC BUBBLED in Maddy's chest, she thrust
Dawn protectively behind her back.

A small electric shock seemed to ripple over her skin
as she realized Jack wasn't here.

He wasn't in back of her. He'd carried the guard into
the building. So he was out of sight. Could he get a shot
at the animal without hitting her and Dawn?

The panther snarled, lifted a paw and slashed at her
with its unsheathed claws.

The needle-sharp tips penetrated the fabric of her shirt,
grazing her skin. She managed to hold back a scream, but
she knew from the animal's eyes that it heard her indrawn
breath.

Ducking, she pulled out the knife that Jack had taken
away from the guard. If she held it pointed upward, the
cat might come down on it when it sprang.

But the animal never got a chance to make its move.
A sharp command stopped it in its tracks. The command
was accompanied by a yank of the chain attached to the
collar around its neck.

Only then did she realize that the panther wasn't running around on its own. It was on its leash. And Oliver
Reynard was holding the other end. As he'd done the
night of the party, he secured the handhold to a post.

"Stay," he ordered the beast. The panther obeyed.
Lowering itself to the ground, it made a low, growling

sound, keeping its eyes on Maddy. But at least she knew it wasn't going to rip her to shreds.

The gun in Reynard's other hand was an entirely different problem. Two armed guards stood beside him, their machine guns also pointed at her.

"Drop the knife," he said to Maddy.

She dropped it, hearing Dawn make a sobbing sound behind her. "It's okay," she soothed, reaching to sling an arm around the girl's side and gather her close.

One of the guards came forward and scooped up her knife. Then the Master of Orchid Island stepped forward into the light that shone down from the wall, and Maddy could see the look of triumph in his eyes. He was riding on a power trip. Did that make him more dangerous, she wondered. Or could she use his mood to her advantage?

"Don't try anything cute," he said.

"I won't. I know when I'm beaten."

"Very astute of you."

Beside her, she could sense Dawn shaking. "Steady," she murmured.

Reynard was looking around the courtyard. "Where's your partner, Jack Connors? That's his real name, I believe?"

Praying that Dawn wouldn't give him away, she said quickly, "He's arranging transportation."

"Where?"

"He didn't share that information with me. He's in charge of this operation. I'm just working for him."

Reynard snorted. "You're lying. You're the security chief at Winston Industries. You brought him in to help you get Stan Winston's daughter back. Winston thought she'd vanished into thin air. Then you showed up less than a week after I snatched her."

Maddy shrugged.

"I'll get all the information I want out of you. Maybe

I'll give you another dose of that drug you just enjoyed—
tie you down, and let you writhe around until you tell me
what I want to know.''

Maddy struggled to keep her face calm while her mind
screamed *God, no! Not that nightmare again.* And with
her in Reynard's clutches. The idea made her shudder
inwardly, but she managed not to reveal the reaction.

"Let's hold that in reserve." Another voice joined the
conversation. A man stepped out of the jungle, and
Maddy's mouth fell open. It was Ted Burnes, the guy
who'd come to her that night with the warning about Jack.

Maddy stared at him in confusion. He worked for her.
What was he doing with Reynard? Somehow she didn't
think he'd come to rescue her.

He took in the look on her face and shrugged. "Sorry,
sweetheart. I'm on the other team."

"But you helped me get out of the mansion," the girl
insisted. "You were my friend."

Maddy struggled to take in that piece of information.
"Ted?" she questioned.

He kept his gaze focused on her. "Yeah, I helped Dawn
get away from you. I gave her the Mickey she slipped
into your drink." He laughed. "You seem to have bad
luck with beverages lately. Maybe you'd better start hav
ing your food tested."

"You bastard. You were in on this all along. Why
would you turn on Stan? He's been good to you."

"Well, I do want your job. I've wanted it for a long
time. And you know I want your body, too, of course.
Now it looks like Oliver and I get to enjoy you here on
the island. Then I'll go back to Winston Industries with
the sad news that you failed in your mission. You won't
be coming back. Which leaves me in the perfect position
to feed Oliver information about what's going on at Winston Industries.''

She could only stare at him, trying to take in his words.

"It's just business, Maddy. And lust—for you and for power. I want to be at the top of the Winston food chain."

"You didn't earn that position," she spat at him.

"Maybe not by your standards. But I think I've done some pretty good work lately."

Reynard cut into the conversation. "Yes, Ted's been quite a valuable asset. Too bad he couldn't get a message to me earlier. I've been trying to dig up information on Connors. But no harm done. Ted's here now. And you and Mr. Ex-CIA agent won't get away. I've got you as a hostage. And from what I've seen of his behavior, he's not going to abandon you."

"Jack will cut his losses," she said, trying to play for time.

"I'd make you a small wager on that. But you don't have anything to bargain with besides your body. And I'm going to get that anyway."

She saw his gaze shift in back of her. "Where the hell have you been?" he asked sharply. "You're supposed to be guarding this place."

She knew the only man standing behind her was Jack. But he was dressed in a guard's uniform—apparently with his face hidden by his cap.

She imagined him with his head bowed, looking contrite. She also imagined the machine gun slung over his shoulder, and her whole body tensed as she waited to find out what he was going to do—although she thought she knew.

"Connors hit me over the head," he said in English— with a pretty good Island accent.

"You'll be disciplined for letting him get close enough to you for that."

"Yes, sir," Jack answered meekly.

She could hear him moving slowly forward, and she

got ready to react, praying that Reynard didn't figure out who he was. If that happened, the show was over.

Every muscle in her body tensed for action.

Then Jack shouted, "Maddy, down."

Pulling Dawn with her, she hit the stone pavement of the courtyard, covering the girl's body with her own as machine gun bullets sprayed over their heads.

Taken completely by surprise, the guards never had a chance to fire their weapons. They went down like bowling pins, along with Ted, Reynard and the big cat that had been his pet.

The hail of bullets ceased, leaving an eerie silence around them in the jungle.

Maddy sat up. Beside her, Dawn had started crying. "Oh God, oh God," she repeated between sobs.

"It's over," Maddy murmured, pulling the girl's head against her shoulder so she couldn't see the carnage and soothing her hands over Dawn's back. "It's all over," she repeated. "We're getting out of here."

Jack came down to her, his hands urgent as he ran them over her arms, her head. "Are you all right?"

"Yes."

"You did that perfectly."

She gave a strangled laugh. "I guess I had to."

"Yeah."

He stood again and looked in all directions, his gaze probing the darkness. "If we're lucky, nobody heard that burst of fire."

"Or if they did, they assumed it was Reynard's men shooting."

"Right," Jack agreed, walking to the bodies, where he checked for signs of life. Then he turned back to her, and their eyes met.

When he shook his head, she nodded. They were all dead. But her heart was still pounding in her chest, and

she knew she wasn't going to feel safe until they got off
Orchid Island.

"Do you think his people will be angry? Or glad he's
gone?" she murmured.

"Let's hope it's the latter."

Just then a voice called from the jungle, "Do me a
favor and don't start shooting again. It's me, Alex. Glad
I was behind a tree, by the way. I wasn't exactly expecting
a fusillade of bullets coming in this direction."

Jack's head jerked up. "Alex Shane?"

"Yeah."

A tall, dark-haired man stepped into view, walked forward and clasped Jack's hand.

"Nice to see you, buddy. Sorry you were in the line of
fire."

"I didn't know you were in back of the women with a
gun. I was thinking I'd wait for you to show up, then
we'd get Maddy and Dawn out of trouble. When another
guard came out of the tower, I figured the odds had gotten
a little worse—until I found out it was you."

Jack nodded, then turned back to Maddy and Dawn.
"This is Alex Shane, formerly of the Howard County,
Maryland, P.D. He works for Randolph Security now.
Cam Randolph and I have a working agreement to share
information and personnel. He grew up on the Eastern
Shore of Maryland, so he knows his way around boats.
He's here to get us out of this place."

"Hank Daniels is acting captain at the moment."

"Good. So how did you know where to find us?"

"Hank and I have had plenty of time to study your
notes and the maps of the island. And we have some more
current information—courtesy of Mr. Burnes."

"What?" Maddy asked.

"The reason he wasn't able to get in touch with Reynard is that he's been restricted in his movements—by

some Randolph and Connors men who are at Winston Industries right now.''

He inclined his head toward Jack. ''Too bad we couldn't get a message to you. After you left for the island, we found Burnes's fingerprints on the packet from the knockout drops Dawn used. So we searched his apartment and found a hidden stash of messages to and from Reynard. When he broke out of our security net and headed down here, we knew we had to make our move. So if you hadn't called us, we would have come anyway.''

Jack's jawline tightened as he heard the explanation. Maddy felt her own anger rise.

All along Ted had been playing her for a fool—which must be why he'd told her about Albania. He'd *wanted* her to mistrust Jack so they'd have trouble working together. The bastard. She glanced over at his body with narrowed eyes.

''I'd suggest we get out of here,'' Alex said.

''Yeah,'' Jack agreed.

Maddy helped Dawn to her feet.

''The boat's in the cove?''

Alex nodded.

As he took a step in the direction of the jungle, Dawn grabbed his arm. ''Please, we can't go without Juanita. She helped me. She told Maddy I was here. You can't leave her. She's from New York. She used to work at my father's house. Then she came back to Orchid Island because her family's from here.''

''So that's why she helped you,'' Maddy said.

Dawn nodded. ''When I was little, we used to be friends. Please. Can we take her with us?''

''Stopping for her means extra risk for us,'' Jack answered.

''I'm sorry,'' Dawn murmured. ''But I know how much she hates it here.''

"Okay," Jack answered. "But you're going to the boat."

"Thank you," she breathed.

Maddy led Dawn inside the wall while the men dragged the bodies into the jungle.

Alex came back and put his hand on Dawn's arm. "Come on."

"Let me stay with Maddy."

"I'll meet you at the boat," Maddy said. "Go with him. Jack and I will be right there."

Alex took Jack aside for a moment; then he and the girl started for the cove. Jack and Maddy headed toward the servants' quarters. When they were several yards into the underbrush, he turned and pulled her into his arms, holding her tightly.

"When I saw that cat go for you, I almost lost it," he whispered.

"Thank you for keeping your cool. And thank you for taking Reynard down," she answered.

"It didn't look like we had much choice."

Maddy nodded against his shoulder. All she wanted to do was hole up with him somewhere safe and find out where the two of them stood now. But they weren't out of danger yet.

"I'm so proud of you," he murmured. "I didn't know how well you'd be able to function after what Reynard did to you this afternoon. But it seems you're in fighting shape!"

"Well, I'm not quite up to par."

He laughed softly. "Par enough to think about taking on a panther with a knife."

She couldn't hold back a little grin. "It was a desperation measure."

She liked his light teasing tone. Liked his praise. But

there wasn't time for an extended personal discussion now, and they both knew it.

She felt him slowly, reluctantly ease away.

"We'd better go," he whispered, then stopped. Reaching into the waistband of his uniform, he withdrew the pistol he'd taken away from the man outside their room and handed it to Maddy. "I think you could have used this earlier."

"Yes. Thanks," she said, back to business as she tucked it into her own waistband.

"By the way," she asked, as they started moving again, "what did Alex tell you a few minutes ago?"

"That he's planning to blow up the security office—if he has the time."

Maddy laughed. "Good thinking. Do we have an ETE?"

"Estimated time of explosion? As soon as he can manage it. So we'd better get in and out of Juanita's place as soon as we can."

Jack was excellent at navigating the darkened jungle, and it took only about fifteen minutes to reach the servants' compound.

From under a clump of palm trees, they studied the scene. It looked peaceful enough, but Maddy had learned that looks could be deceiving here.

"I could go in alone, but I'd probably frighten her," Jack said.

"No, she'll be more likely to trust me." She turned toward him. "You know which house?"

"Yes. But I'm staying with you. Just look relaxed. Like we're two lovers out for a stroll."

"Sure," she answered, feeling the thickness in her throat.

Jack gave her a quick glance, but said nothing. After pulling his uniform cap low over his eyes, he took her hand. Together they stepped from behind the palm trees. At this time of night, there were few people out and about. Casually they crossed the stretch of greenery that bordered the compound, then ambled down the dirt road lined with low, whitewashed buildings. Maddy cast him a sidelong glance. He still had the machine gun slung over his shoulder, and she wondered if he'd be carrying it off duty.

Maybe, she decided, as they stepped toward the door of one of the small houses.

Maddy let him take the lead.

He knocked softly on the door. Then knocked again.

"Who is it?" a woman's voice called out.

"Friends," she answered.

Seconds stretched. Then the door opened a crack.

Maddy heard Juanita's indrawn breath.

"Let us in," Jack said. "We can't talk out here."

Without giving the woman a chance to answer, he pushed his way inside. Maddy followed and stepped into a sparsely furnished room that served as a combination living room and bedroom. Juanita, dressed in a frayed robe over a white cotton gown, was backing toward a small kitchen area, her eyes filled with terror.

Then she focused on Maddy. "Everybody's talking about you. About what Calista did to you."

"Well, they're probably lying. She gave me something...bad. But Jack rescued me. Reynard didn't get a chance to do anything to me."

The woman stared at them, taking in their words. Then she heaved a sigh. "That makes it worse. You can't be here. Reynard will kill us all," she hissed.

"Not likely," Jack informed her quickly. "Reynard is dead."

"Are you lying to me?"

"No," Maddy answered. "Thanks to the information you gave us, we went to the Dark Tower to rescue Dawn.

Reynard came after us, and Jack shot him—and that damn panther of his."

The woman's features were still tense, as though she couldn't grasp what she was hearing.

"I was there last night, watching, when you brought Dawn food," Jack said. "She's on her way to the boat that will take us off the island. She asked us to come get you. If you want to leave with us, we'll take you. But you have to hurry. There's going to be an explosion at the guard station any minute now."

Juanita looked stunned. Then her features firmed. "Yes. All right," she agreed. "Just let me get dressed."

She rummaged in a dresser, then stepped into a small bathroom and closed the door.

Moments later, she emerged, wearing a T-shirt, knit pants and scuffed sneakers.

"Do you want to take anything?" Maddy asked.

She snorted. "There's nothing here worth anything. Even the money I've saved is only good on the island."

"I'm sure Stan Winston will reward you for your good deeds," Jack said.

"I didn't do it for money. I did it for Dawn. She's a sweet girl."

"Yes. Come on."

Jack opened the door. As they stepped outside, the loud blast of a siren sounded, shattering the quiet of the night.

JACK SWORE.

Up and down the street, doors were opening.

Maddy stood by the small house, her chest suddenly so constricted that she could hardly breathe.

Jack bent to Juanita. "What does the alarm mean?"

"We're under attack. I mean, we've had drills before, never the real thing. But I didn't hear any explosion."

"Someone must have figured out that we're breaking out of here."

She looked at his uniform. "Guards are supposed to report to their command posts. The rest of the men and the women are to go to the closest safe area."

"Well, we're sticking together." He moved behind them and lowered the machine gun. "Come on. You're both my prisoners."

He started marching them up the street against the tide of people moving farther into the compound. Only men were hurrying in their direction. One of them grabbed Juanita's arm, halting them.

"Where are you going with those females?" he demanded of Jack.

"I have orders to bring them to the main house."

The man peered more closely at Jack. "Hey, you're the guy from Agapanthus Villa. I was supposed to bug your place."

Him! Maddy groaned. Him of all people.

"Yeah. I thought that's why you were there. Only you were wearing a different uniform," Jack answered, keeping his tone easy, despite the fact that the guy was bringing his gun into firing position.

The man's whole attention was on Jack, which was why Maddy was able to pull her own weapon and shoot him in his gun arm. He screamed as Jack wrenched the Uzi away from him, and some of the people in the street turned to see what was going on.

"There's a bomb in the compound. Run to the shelter in the big house," Jack shouted.

Panic ensued, and Isley stumbled away, holding his arm. But Jack, Maddy and Juanita stuck together, making for the shadows under the trees as the rest of the people fled in a wave toward the mansion.

They moved as quickly as possible through the underbrush, then broke out onto the beach and followed the coastline around to the cove.

In back of them, an explosion shook the ground, the sound wave rolling over them.

Juanita stopped and looked back.

"That was the guardhouse," Jack guessed. "Just keep moving."

They rounded a promontory and came to an area where the waves were smaller. Scanning the water, Maddy spotted a cabin cruiser anchored about a hundred yards from shore.

Alex Shane ran down the beach toward them. "Come on," he urged. "It looks like the place is turning into riot city. I wonder what's going to happen to Reynard's other guests."

"I guess it's every man for himself," Jack answered.

Alex had pulled a panga up onto the beach. He pushed it into the water again, holding it while Dawn climbed aboard, soaking her pants legs in the process. Maddy followed her. Then he and Alex maneuvered the craft farther into the water.

After the two men climbed in, Alex started the motor, and they headed for the cabin cruiser, where Hank Daniels helped them aboard.

Minutes later they were aboard and speeding away from the island under the power of two giant engines.

Maddy took a quick trip around the boat. It was small, with cramped lower cabins that hugged the narrow companionway. There was no room for doors. Curtains gave a small bit of privacy. And the only furniture in each cabin was a set of upper and lower bunks against the bulkhead.

Maddy led Dawn down the ladder-like steps to one of the cabins. They sat on the lower bunk while the girl poured out her confession of the mistake she'd made by escaping from the mansion—and her fears that her father would skin her alive once he had her back.

Maddy kept reassuring her that it wasn't going to happen—that Stan Winston loved her, and he'd be so thankful that she was home again that he wasn't going to think about punishment.

After she and Dawn had been together for over an hour, Jack came down and knocked on the wall beside the entrance to the cabin.

"Come in," Maddy called.

Jack pulled aside the curtain. But there was no room for him to stand in the cabin with the two of them inside. So he stayed in the hall, his eyes meeting Maddy's. She sensed that he wanted to speak to her in private. But she knew that wasn't going to be possible yet. Not when Dawn needed her.

He turned to the young woman. "How are you?"

"Scared."

"It's all over," Jack reassured her. "You can relax now. You probably want to take a shower and have a decent meal."

"The island part is over," she answered. "But not the part about facing Daddy."

"Trust me—he'll be so happy to see you, he won't even raise his voice," Jack said, then continued with his own version of Maddy's soothing words. She wished he had soothing words for *her*. But she knew that would have to wait until later. Much later.

She lowered her gaze so that her own emotions wouldn't show on her face. They'd been partners on Orchid Island. They'd gotten close. Closer than she'd ever expected. And he'd helped her through the worst experience of her life. But she didn't know what any of it meant to him. And she didn't know if she was capable of asking.

MADDY BLINKED BACK TEARS as she watched the reunion of Stan Winston and his daughter at JFK airport.

The girl had been afraid that her father would punish her. Instead he hugged her tightly, telling her he was sorry for restricting her life so much. But after he'd lost her mother, he'd been terrified that he'd lose his daughter too.

His arm slung around Dawn, he turned to Maddy and Jack as they stood beside the black stretch limo that was taking them all into the city.

"There's no way I can adequately thank you for bringing my daughter home. You risked your lives to save her."

"I was just correcting my mistake," Maddy murmured as she followed Dawn into the car.

"Oh Lord," the young woman interjected. "Is that what you think? Maddy, it was all my fault. Mine and…" She stopped, her lip quivering. "Well, Ted Burnes put the idea into my head. I never would have done it if he hadn't helped me."

"Ted?" the senior Winston asked.

"Yeah," Jack growled, filling him in on the man who had really been working for Oliver Reynard.

The industrialist looked stunned, until Maddy put her hand on his arm. "He fooled us all. I had no idea he was moonlighting on Reynard's payroll."

Maddy kept the talk on business as they drove back to the Winston building in Manhattan.

But when they reached the plush suite where they'd first started planning their attack on Orchid Island, Stan Winston changed the subject.

Looking from Jack to Maddy and back again, he said, "I know money is a cold way to express my appreciation, but I've transferred a million dollars to each of your accounts."

She felt her jaw drop open. "S-sir…" she stammered.

"I can't accept that kind of money. Not when I was just doing my job."

Beside her Jack was making a similar protest.

Winston snorted. "Your job? Maddy, you could have backed out of this so fast it would have left my head spinning. And Jack, you came in on the assignment even though you knew the odds were against getting out of there alive. So don't refuse my reward for a job well done. And, Maddy, don't turn down my offer of some time off. You deserve that, too. If you want a couple of months, don't hesitate to ask for them. I know you've been through an ordeal. Jack phoned me from the boat while you were with Dawn."

Her eyes shot to Jack. What had he told Winston, exactly? She was inwardly cringing when he caught her eye. "Not the part you're worried about," he mouthed.

She felt a surge of relief. If there was something she wasn't going to put in her official report—it was the drug Calista had ordered slipped into her iced tea. Would Jack agree to leave that out? She'd beg him if she had to.

They talked for several more minutes, but Maddy could see that Winston was anxious to take his daughter home.

"You two go on," she urged. "I'll write up an official report and have it on your desk by the end of the week."

"You're supposed to be on vacation," Winston told her.

"I need to get this on paper while it's fresh." What she didn't say was that she wanted to put down the details, then banish them from her mind.

The industrialist inclined his head toward Jack. "She can write the report. Then I'm counting on you to make her relax."

"Yes, sir," Jack answered smartly.

Moments later he and Maddy were alone in the living room of the guest suite.

She saw him swallow and slide his palms against the sides of his pants. And she realized he was nervous.

About what? Brushing her off now that the assignment was finished?

"Jack, you don't owe me anything," she said quickly. "Well, except, I'd like you to keep some stuff confidential. Like the...uh...incident with Calista and the iced tea."

He kept his gaze squarely on her. "If I'd moved the timetable up, it wouldn't have happened."

She came to him, reached up to grasp his shoulders. "Jack, don't blame yourself for something that's not your fault."

"Like you've been doing, you mean?"

She sighed in exasperation. "Okay. I won't if you won't."

She was still holding his shoulders. To her surprise, he slipped his arms around her and pulled her close.

"Jack?"

"Maddy, just let me say what I need to say. Okay?"

She felt her chest tighten painfully, sure that this was it. He was going to let her down gently. But he was still going to brush her off. Somehow, she managed to say, "Okay."

As she felt him drag in a breath and let it out quickly, her own tension doubled.

"That stunt I pulled when we began this assignment. I'd apologize for forcing you into bed, but making love to you that first time was mind-blowing. And each time has only made me want you more." He stopped, ran a hand through his hair. "I'm not saying what I mean. It's not just incredible sex I want from you. I want a whole lot more than that. But I've always known that you were married to your job. So I kept our relationship strictly professional. For all the good that's doing me now.

Maddy, I don't think I can get along without you. I want you in my life, any way I can have you.''

Her mouth was so dry she could barely get the next words out. "You mean an affair?"

"If that's all you can give me. I mean, I know how important your career is to you."

She nodded. "Dad taught me to be the best. I wanted to live up to the standard he set. But I realized when I was with you that there are other goals in life. Like building something important with the man I love. I mean you—if *I'm* not being clear."

His green eyes blazed with astonishment. "You love me?" he asked in a halting voice.

"Jack, I wanted you for years. Then that first time we made love, I realized what I felt for you wasn't just lust. I mean, it was that, too. But a whole lot more."

"Thank God," he whispered, lowering his lips to hers for a long, drugging kiss. Then he whispered, "Maddy, I love you so much. If I asked you to marry me, what would you say?"

"I'd say yes," she answered.

"Thank God," he said again. Then he brought his mouth down to hers once more. And when he finally lifted his head, they were both breathing hard. As his hands began to move over her body, she responded as she had to him every time. Strongly. Deeply. Incredibly.

"It was hell being on that boat with you—being so close and not having any privacy," he growled.

"Oh yes."

"If I'd tried to talk to you then, everybody would have heard us. Or if we'd tried to make love."

"But we're alone now. Like we were that first time. When you were such an arrogant bastard," she added for good measure.

He grinned at her. "Yeah, I was, wasn't I?"

"It turned me on," she murmured.

"I kind of figured that out," he said, a cocky grin spreading across his face.

"Watch it, or you're going to get a punch in the gut."

"How about letting me make amends for my arrogance?" Taking her hand, he led her into the bedroom. With soft kisses and warm endearments, he began to undress her. And while he removed her clothing, she did the same for him.

Bodies brushing. Hands touching. Hearts melting.

This time it was so different from all the others, she marveled.

This time as they aroused each other, they were sealing a commitment. No more uncertainty. Only the wonder of knowing that this man loved her, and she loved him.

He had brought her pleasure before, pleasure beyond imagining. But now as his hands and lips moved over her body, she felt something more. A deep abiding certainty that she belonged with him. Belonged with him in every way that a man and woman could bring meaning to their lives together.

There was no need to prove anything. No need to hurry. Instead there was a long, slow loving that ended with a soul-shattering climax.

She called out his name—and heard his words of love as he poured himself into her.

Emotionally and physically spent, she slept then.

Some time later, she woke to find him lying on his side, looking down at her.

"How long have you been awake?" she asked, reaching to stroke his cheek.

"A while." He moved his lips against her forehead. "I was lying here wondering, what would you think of a job change?"

She lifted her head and looked at him inquiringly. "To what?"

"To a partnership in Connors Security."

"I...I'd love it," she answered immediately. Then just as quickly had a second thought. "But I'd feel like a rat leaving Stan Winston in the lurch."

Apparently he'd been working out a plan, because he answered at once. "We don't have to. When you're ready to make the move, we could offer to take over security for him—on a contract basis. He already knows we're a great team."

She grinned. "Yes."

"And, uh, you could work part-time, if you want to. After our vacation—which is going to be our honeymoon."

"Are you rushing me into marriage?"

"Yes. Before you come to your senses."

"There's no danger of that." She snuggled against him. "Your offer of part-time employment. Is that while we're raising the kids?"

"I was thinking that would be a good plan."

She angled her head, giving him a serious look. "Dad was so wound up with his job, he didn't have much time for me and Mom when I was growing up. So I'd...want..." She stopped, swallowed. "I'd want us both to make family as important as career." She giggled. "And then there's my poor cat waiting for me at home. Can you make room in your life for a cat, too?"

"Yeah. Any cat of yours is a cat of mine." Then his face turned serious. "I think giving family top priority is a good plan. I admired your father enormously. But I knew he had one serious defect. He didn't know how to enjoy life."

"But we do," she said, sliding her hand down his body, feeling his response.

He grinned at her. "Yeah, and with the bonus Stan Winston gave us, we're not going to need to pour on the heat at work to make ends meet."

She giggled. "I think there are more rewarding ways to pour on the heat."

"Yeah," he agreed, pulling her against him, and began to show her all over again how much he loved her.

Blaze™

What is your secret fantasy?

Is it to have your own love slave, to be seduced by a stranger, or to experience total sexual freedom?

Enjoy all of these and more in Blaze's newest miniseries

Heat up your nights with...

#17 EROTIC INVITATION *by Carly Phillips*
Available December 2001

#21 ACTING ON IMPULSE *by Vicki Lewis Thompson*
Available January 2002

#25 ENSLAVED *by Susan Kearney*
Available February 2002

#29 JUST WATCH ME... *by Julie Elizabeth Leto*
Available March 2002

#33 A WICKED SEDUCTION *by Janelle Denison*
Available April 2002

#37 A STRANGER'S TOUCH *by Tori Carrington*
Available May 2002

Midnight Fantasies—The nights aren't just for sleeping...